THE ORDER OF SEVEN

***

AND THE BOOK OF KNOWLEDGE

To Lynette,

You are simply the best!
I'm glad that we work in, I mean
Teach in the same building. However
the best part is that I call you
friend. Thank you for being you
the welcoming, assisting, just good person
you are!

MR. CHARLES J. SAPORITO

Best,
Charles J. Saporito

ISBN: 1492879584
ISBN 13: 9781492879589

PROLOGUE

The Egyptian sun is setting over the Sahara. The small city of tents was empty for the evenings work. The crew, under the leadership of John Williams, decided that they would be working later than usual. The large, heavy-duty lights are turned on and quickly change the darkening evening back to day. The crew has been working in the Sahara for the last seven months. John is in his tent studying the satellite imagery of the dig site; he is certain that the artifact visible in the pictures is located in the area where they have been digging. John's team estimated that the artifact would be reached in roughly three months. Seven months later, most of the archeologists are beginning to doubt that the artifact actually exists.

Modern technology has improved many aspects of human life and activities. The new breakthroughs in using satellite imagery have uncovered several tombs of prominent Pharaohs. There was no reason to doubt this wondrous technology. In fact, several of the archeologists had worked with satellite imagery in the past John being one of them.

"Seven months of digging...something's got to give," John said to himself out loud. He had been examining the photographs for the last five hours, trying to convince himself that the imagery was not a mistake. This dig was not John's first time using the new technology. However, a more pressing concern was that John knew that if they didn't reach the artifact soon they were going to be shut down by the Egyptian government.

The reason for this was because Egypt had recently passed a depth limit on all excavations. The government was forced to pay millions to a team of archeologists for injuries caused at a dig site. Even though the findings proved that the equipment issued by the Egyptian government had caused the injuries they insisted that the injuries were due to the excavators not following their depth advice. When their argument did not hold up in the World court, they were forced to agree on a settlement. They agreed to settle in order to enact their excavation limits and stricter inspections. John's team was three hundred feet away from reaching that depth limit. Government officials had been notified by the liaison --Egypt's version of the CIA-- assigned to the team by the Egyptian government. As the dig site deepened, the liaisons contacted the government for the possibility of a shutdown.

As John prepared himself for the official government representatives, he heard screaming coming from the mammoth dig site. John ran out of his tent fearing the worst. The last thing he needed was an injury at the depth where they were digging. The government was not keen on archeologists digging in their backyard, let alone a team from the U.S. When John reached the site, he became aware of several of his team members dancing around with the hired Egyptian laborers. As he was climbing down he also noticed the liaisons talking excitedly on their cell phones.

John finally reached the team, and was waved over to a hole that now revealed the top of a building. Elated, John joined the men in their celebration, but felt regretful that he was not able to be there for the initial find. But that feeling quickly faded as the thought of their new find being included in the history books, which would be credited as a dig that he personally led. In the past he had only either been a consultant or a second in command. This time however it was he alone who had led the excavation. The euphoric feeling of being right about something so many doubted even with the images from the satellite felt very rewarding.

The men spent the next two hours carefully digging around the building. Caution was the operative word. They did not want to abruptly disturb the ground, causing a collapse of the land around the structure. As they neared finishing the excavation everyone noticed that the building did not match the era or the construction type of the Ancient Egyptians. Carbon dating on a sample from the roof section dated the structure to be nearly ten thousand years old placing it in an era that came before the Egyptians, Sumerians, and the Babylonians. This information was kept confidential from the Egyptian officials. For safety and security reasons they were informed that the date of construction was at the height of Ancient Egyptian rule and dominance in the world.

John entered the structure first. Once inside, he was amazed that the interior of the structure was soundly intact, which was rare and unheard of for a structure of such age. The building was estimated to be one hundred feet by fifty feet. Small by today's standards but John figured big for back when it was built. There was a series of stone benches in rows. John was puzzled as he neared the back of the building. In the back was a raised section with an altar in the middle. He circled the altar and walked to the back wall, noticing an object on the wall directly behind the altar. As he wiped away the dust, he thought to himself how fortunate he was that the object was intact and fastened to the wall. As he finished wiping the object, John gazed at it and stumbled backwards. He could not believe what he was looking at!

John's attention was drawn away from the object; one of the archeologists had located a chamber underneath the altar. John instructed the man to gently open the front panel. The panel came off, and the man became upset by his clumsy attempt. Inside the cabinet was a large item wrapped in cloth and appearing to be bound in leather. The cloth had helped preserve the square item. The man carefully handed it to John. Once it reached his hands, John carefully began to unwrap it. As he removed the cloth, he looked at it and quickly turned to the object on the wall. The object on the wall matched the center of the item. John quickly ordered pictures to be taken of every nook and cranny of the building. He took the item with him as he exited the structure, and practically ran to his tent. Once inside he grabbed his iPhone and placed a call. John heard only two rings.

"This is a major find." John didn't wait for pleasantries.

"Slow down John, what could you have possibly found that would be any different than the other tombs in Egypt," said the voice on the other end of the line, with a British accent and a laugh.

"This is not a tomb. Our preliminary carbon dating that we conducted places this structure before any of the ancient civilizations," said John. "Any of them!"

"I sense there is more," said the voice on the phone.

"Yes, there is more, much more. I found it."

"Please, John. Be more specific. You found what?"

"The item that never existed," said John.

There is silence from the other end. John waited several seconds before saying anything. He knew the significance of his find. John also knew that action needed to be taken quickly to avoid the tentacles of the Egyptian government.

"Are you still there?" Asked John.

"Yes, I'm sorry but I always thought it was a myth."

"Jonathan Andrews, I think you will need to pull some strings and we'll keep this find to ourselves until we can decipher it," said John.

"Agreed. Thankfully the Egyptian dictator is a greedy man. I'll simply give him the usual payment. But what is it doing in Egypt?" Andrews asked.

" I don't know... I thought the Order traced the book to Medieval Europe," said John.

"They did; but remember we also believed that this book was a myth. Now that we know it's real, this could place everything we hold true and important in jeopardy. Bring the book to Andrews Castle ASAP. We will examine it here," concluded Andrews.

1

PRESENTATION

John Williams had waited five years for this moment, since finding the artifact. He made his way to the stage. He was not happy making his presentation on a Sunday, but particularly this Sunday, the third of July, was even harder for him to handle. The fourth of July is John's favorite holiday and Chicago celebrated the fourth of July with a large fireworks display on the third. John had made each one since moving to Chicago in his youth. John enjoyed reflecting back on the days his parents would bring him and his brother to downtown Chicago and watch the display of assorted fireworks. He managed to stay upbeat merely because of the importance of his presentation. He received loud applause from the audience and an incredibly flattering introduction by the head curator of the Chicago Field Museum.

John loved giving lectures at the museum even more so than at the University of Chicago where he taught Ancient Civilization and Medieval European History. Giving a lecture at the Field Museum signaled the importance of the topic he was discussing this evening. At all of John's presentations, he always insisted on seats being made available to students. However, this night the audience included dignitaries from different countries and prominent religious figures from all sects. Because of this fact, there was a decrease in the number of seats available for students. There were also distinguished historians and an assortment of professors from all fields of education in attendance. Scattered among them were also individuals that were very charitable to the museum.

John had been a Professor of History at the University of Chicago for the last twenty years. Along with his Doctorate in Ancient History, he also held Masters degrees in Anthropology and Economics. The University of Chicago had offered him the History Department Chair position several times, but John had always preferred teaching and conducting field research to sitting in an office and attending fundraisers and faculty functions. He had turned down the position each time it had been offered. As one of the most respected professors in the field of medieval history, John had also been asked to conduct presentations at many of the most prestigious Universities throughout North America and Europe. The only activity that he enjoyed equally to being in the field was lecturing.

Walking to the podium, John knew the importance of the discovery he was about to discuss. At the podium, he thanked the curator for the wonderful introduction. The lights were dimmed as he finished the formalities of thanking the museum and the University. He emphasized the role that technology played in discovering the artifact. The lights were completely turned off as a giant screen came down behind him. The slide show started with a picture of a typical medieval village that John said was located in the northern part of Italy in the Italian Alps. The next few slides are of similar villages, all the same as the one outside of Rome. The villages were located in parts of modern day France, Britain and Italy.

The audience was fully captivated by John's speaking style. The slideshow added depth and visualization for the audience. The first pictures were of the dig site and the people who had worked with him at the site. John talked about the locals that also worked at the site. He thanked them and the Egyptian government for allowing the dig to be conducted. John also included slides on some of Egypt's more prominent and easily recognizable ancient artifacts, the Pyramids of Giza and the Sphinx. They were also Egypt's greatest tourist attractions as well. The sixteenth slide consisted of just one word. SCRUTATORES.

It was believed that the Scrutatores were a group of people that existed at the turn of the first century. It was said that they believed in true magic and another plane of existence. The Scrutatores were rumored to believe in traveling from one plane to another by obtaining the needed materials and conducting the proper ritual.

John continued to describe how the Scrutatores existed merely in legends and folklore. There was never any actual proof of their existence. The next few slides showed how the Scrutatores had been confused with other groups of their time, and John noted how there had never been technology invented that could have led to their beliefs. John felt that it was necessary to discuss the Scrutatores, for some had been insinuating that the artifact he discovered was proof of their existence.

After the Scrutatores' slides came slides of an ancient book: the Book of Knowledge. This was the artifact that John had discovered and was presenting on this night. The slides showed different angles of the brown, leather-covered book. The thickness of the book was quite massive. The book appeared to be a couple of thousand pages, and it was evident that the book was extremely old. Several slides showed the writing in the book and focused in on the language used. John explained that since it was written in old Latin, the book's authenticity could not be argued. He explained that the process of carbon dating had been implemented, and the results of the process placed the book to have been written in the early part of the thirteenth century. John explained that he and a team of experts would examine the book in greater detail at the Field Museum. The University of Chicago organized the team that included John, and gave him the lead in the examination of the ancient book.

The rumors that surrounded the Scrutatores and the book were in large part due to the cover of the book. The symbol was believed to be the symbol of the Scrutatores, a triangle with an emerald sphere in the middle. The sphere entering the triangle was the belief of people traveling to other planes. The book was thought to exist only in ancient lore. It had been alleged that the book contained instructions on how to conduct various spells, but it was also said to describe the procedure on how to enter each plane of existence.

John's lecture changed focus to how the influence of the Scrutatores would have changed many of the perceptions of modern theory and beliefs, if they had indeed existed and had flourished. He emphasized how giving credibility to a group such as the Scrutatores would cause religious followers to become further skeptics in regard to their beliefs on true and proven science.

To some, the discovery of the Book of Knowledge was proof that the Scrutatores existed and it was considered one of the greatest finds of the last century. John believed that when people learned that the book's finding was outside of Europe, and actually in Egypt, it would put to end the rumors of the Scrutatores. Along with being studied, the book was going to be on display at the Chicago Field Museum to the general public. The museum had secured the book due to its connection with John. In exchange for getting the book, the museum promised John that he would be giving all presentations on the book, and be credited for the find.

As John neared the finish of his presentation a cell phone started ringing. Audience members started checking their phones. There were postings upon entering and throughout the auditorium to turn phones to silent or vibrate. Nonetheless, the ringing was loud. As everyone checked and looked around, John reached into his jacket and pulled out the ringing phone. He looked at the display of his iPhone and noticed the number.

"I'm glad to see that all of you followed the request of silencing your phones. I now wish I would have done the same," said John sheepishly, as he fumbled with his phone. It took several rings, but John finally managed to send the call to voicemail. Several audience members laughed at John's inability to end the call. John finished his presentation and invited everyone to join him for the reception on the first level.

John actually hated the reception portion of the evening, but he made an effort to stay longer than his usual amount of time. It's not the mingling that bothered him; it was the questions that came with the territory. He especially hated the questions that came from the novice historians.

The museum had placed the book next to the ancient artifacts section for display on the second floor. However, for the reception they brought the book down to the main level, placed next to the giant blue whale hanging from the ceiling. The book rested inside a thick plastic box casing, opened halfway and on a wooden bookstand from the Victorian age. After finishing his lecture and talking to various audience members, John found himself standing by the book answering questions, mainly regarding the Scrutatores. With so many people wanting his attention, John had managed to forget to check his voicemail on the phone call he had received toward the end of his lecture.

One of the audience members who were extremely interested in the Scrutatores walked up to John and proceeded to ask him his opinion on the authenticity of the book, and it possibly being proof of the Scrutatores. John disliked the type of questions that revolved around the existence of the Scrutatores, but sensed that the man was wealthy and should be humored. John assumed that the man was a large donor and so was careful how he answered his questions. He replied that the supernatural portion of the book was just a rumor. After some small talk, John concluded the conversation by inviting the man to his next presentation on the book.

John turned from the man he finished speaking with, only to come face to face with the museum's head curator, standing directly in front of him. Startled, John stepped back.

"Mr. Williams, allow me to introduce one of the museum's most generous Chicagoans," said the curator.

"Victor, no need to mention how the museum knows me. Allow me to introduce myself; I am William Donavan."

William Donavan was a fifth generation descendent of the architect of the Chicago Water Tower and other historical buildings throughout Chicago. William placed his hand on the book's casing. John acted impressed with the newly acquired information, and he talked to him gamely while William felt up the box. William stretched out his hand toward John. The two men shook hands for a second time. He congratulated John on an excellent presentation.

"Thank you," replied John, "which part of the presentation did you find the most appealing?"

"I must confess," responded William, "the portion on spells and the search for the passageway to another plane of existence was particularly fascinating."

It became apparent to John that this was the portion of the presentation that the majority of the audience members found interesting. After he finished his conversation with Mr. Donavan, John said his goodbyes and headed home.

2

IMPROMPTU MEETING

John exited the building, curious about the phone call that interrupted his presentation. He took out his iPhone and checked his voicemail. He noticed that the call came from England. John accessed his voicemail and listened to the message.

"John, we need to talk."

John's curiosity was enhanced. The call came from a number that was not in his contact list. The voice was familiar, so he assumed it was one of Andrews' assistants.

Andrews had been the head of what was known as the "Stamens" for decades. He was an extremely wealthy individual that had been financing all of John's digs throughout the years. The Stamens were descendants of the Knights Templar. The surviving Templar became the Stamens after the King of France hunted them down. Andrews' wealth came from the Templar fortunes. The Stamens helped out over the last few years in deciphering the book. John decided that he would call Andrews from his apartment.

John arrived at his Bucktown apartment, pleased by how the night went. He looked at his watch and noticed the time was just past eleven thirty. The drive from the Chicago Field Museum to the Bucktown area was a quick one, especially at this time. As he neared his home, he noticed a figure leaning against the black column on the stoop of his doorway.

John parked his ten-year-old Grand Cherokee half a block away from his apartment. He walked at a quick pace; anxious to see whom the person was that was standing on his stoop. How he wished he had never changed the bright white light to the dark red one, he thought to himself. Otherwise, he would have recognized the individual. As it was, he could only make out the silhouette of the person. As he neared, he noticed the man was bald and dressed in a dark suit. When he reached the stoop, he was pleased and relieved to recognize his old friend, Andrews.

"Hey! It's been so long since our last encounter," said John sarcastically, seeing as how he had just spent over five hours with him at the presentation and the reception. But he knew that for Andrews to be waiting for him, something important needed to be discussed.

"I'm wondering why you're here but what I really want to know is how you beat me," laughed John.

"Let's get inside and we'll talk there," responded Andrews in his distinctive British accent. John thought this to be alarming, and his smile left his face. John also figured that he'd mention the phone call once inside. Usually Andrews had a great sense of humor and sometimes found his comments amusing. Seeing his serious demeanor meant that something important was going on that required immediate attention. John unlocked the door and both men entered the small, but quaint apartment.

Upon entering John turned on the lights and was glad that he had the apartment cleaned earlier in the day. Walking in, Andrews noticed three rooms in clear view, the front room followed by a large dining room with a small kitchen in back. In the center room was an opening with a hallway that leads to three bedrooms and a bathroom. Andrews walked over to the large dark oak table in the center of the second room. Andrews had known John since he was a young child.

"I see you had the place cleaned recently." Andrews had immediately known that John had hired someone to clean the apartment for him.

John walked into the kitchen and grabbed two rock glasses and filled them with Jack Daniels and cola. He walked back into the center room, and turned on the ceiling fan before joining Andrews at the table.

"Thanks for the drink," Andrews said, and immediately gulped it down. John also took a drink and waited for Andrews to enlighten him about the unexpected visit.

"John, I'm about to share with you some information that only I and my assistants know about."

John simply nodded.

"There has been an incredible discovery that I honestly have no explanation for. Simply put, it will change our knowledge of our world and the universe," said Andrews in a grave tone.

"What could possibly have been discovered that could change the world?" Asked John.

Andrews stood from his chair and walked behind it. He placed his hands on the top of the frame and looked at John with a deeply concerned expression.

"As you know, the book was discovered a little over five years ago," said Andrews.

"Yeah, I know...I was there."

"Well, my assistants in London have been going through our archives of documents dating back to the first Crusade. We have discovered two important documents. The first document confirmed that the Scrutatores existed, the second document explained and described how they were hunted down by the Order of Seven."

The Order of Seven assisted the Christians during the Crusades. It was also rumored that the Catholic Church used them to perform exorcisms and other undertakings. The only people that knew of the Order were members of the Knights Templar and the Catholic Church.

John pushed back his chair and stood up, half-shouting, "This can't be! The Order of Seven could not have been assigned to assassinate all of the Scrutatores! They performed assassinations only during the Crusades."

"John, there is so much more, please let me finish, then I'll try to answer any questions you may have."

John sat back down. He discounted the rumors that the Scrutatores existed. He believed they were just a legend like King Arthur and the Knights of the Round Table.

"Yes, the Order assisted in the disposal of those who had what was considered 'unfavorable' beliefs back then."

John could not wait for Andrews to finish before he jumped back in.

"Are you saying that the Order was assigned to perform assassinations? The current Order members would have no part in any such request," said John emphatically.

"I am not talking about current members," Andrews said angrily. I'm referring to the original Order members and if it was asked, the Order would. It's been a long-standing agreement when the Order is asked to perform an action, they will. Do you need a reminder on the oath that all the Order members have taken?"

"I'm sorry for that ridiculous comment. It's been a long night. I know the oath and have always performed any task asked of me."

"They did, but please control yourself and allow me to finish. We also discovered records of Scrutatores that had not been rounded up by the Order. The Scrutatores were the counter to the Order. They wanted to change the world in their image. I fear that the Scrutatores have been in existence and are living amongst us, waiting for their time to emerge. Finding the Book of Knowledge may be the sign they have been waiting for."

Andrews' demeanor was calm, but there was a sense of uncertainty in his voice.

"There is a Stamens village in Sicily that had been assigned to keep track of them. They were assigned to keep the information quiet until the moment had come to find them."

John had now become skeptical, questioning his beliefs. Andrews noticed John's obvious frustration. "John, ask what's on your mind. I'm not finished yet, but I feel you need to ask."

Without hesitation John fired away. "Okay, first...how could the Stamens keep track of this information and I not know, considering since I'm a part of the current Order? Did you forget that my father was in the Order and through his bloodline I became my brother's natural replacement."

"John, you're the only Order member in the room. An important document was found two weeks ago. You were preparing for your presentation. Those of us searching needed to be sure, and we found out that the Order may have originated from the Scrutatores. The Order wanted no part of their plans or beliefs and came to the Stamens for refuge. Sir Andrews was the last of the Knights Templar. He documented how the Order came to the Stamens. It was after he fled from France to England that he started the Stamens. That's why he inducted the Order into the Stamens, kept the knowledge about the origin of the Order a secret. The Book of Knowledge mentions that all the Scrutatores can perform spells. It also explains how to perform those spells...and we found that the book is legitimate."

"What?" Said John.

"The spells in the book are real, I know because I caused an object to move from one end of a table to the other."

John was overwhelmed. "So you have the ability to use spells?"

"No, I do not. I followed the described procedures and was able to somewhat accomplish the spell."

"Somewhat? This is confusing," said John

"The spell described what should have happened. I should have been able to levitate the object and keep it suspended for a rather long time. I managed to move the object two feet. Only a person with the ability to conduct a spell with the proper training can actually accomplish the spell. I believe that only a Scrutatore or a member of the Order have those abilities and I also suspect that any offspring of either group might as well," said Andrews.

"This is huge. We need to contact the other Order members," said John.

"The Order members have been notified. My assistants in London are looking through the archives for any information that would aid us in tracking the Scrutatores. I have convened a meeting of the Order," said Andrews.

"Does this mean that the theory about the different planes of existence that they believed in is true?" Asked John.

"That I do not know. But I believe anything is possible now," said Andrews with great concern in his voice. "What I do know is that you and the Order members will have your greatest task. It appears that the things you disregarded as lore may now be viewed as quite real."

The two men took a short break and John poured each of them another drink. The information that Andrews was telling John raised great concern. One thing that John was not concerned about was that he might have misled the audience on the Scrutatores. His concern was that the Scrutatores beliefs might actually be true and that they are not the legend he believed they were.

"Allow me to continue John, I can see that you have mixed feelings about this matter. But there is more. We have two new members in the Order. The first is Emily Stone; she is an anthropologist from the University of Boston. The second is Julia Bernard, she is a Scientist specializing in chemistry and biology from the University of Paris."

"Nice to finally know of new members, as a member myself it's always good to find out months later," said John sarcastically.

"Come now John, there have been many new findings and issues that have kept me busy with the book and the Order. Their mother's sudden deaths were a shock to all of us. Since they are their descendants they're in. Along with being a descendant they also displayed the ability to use magic, plus they had the mark on their forearm exactly like yours. The Order can only have seven active members. This is how it has been for centuries. Remember you came into the Order after the disappearance of your brother and his wife seventeen years ago. Anyway, they were inducted a few weeks ago. I know you should have been there, but James' suggestion that they needed to be inducted sooner rather than later made sense. The ceremony can happen with one Order member present for the induction and James has been a member for about as long as you have."

"Apology accepted," said John, his tone indicating that it was anything but.

Andrews continued, "A month ago we discovered that a silver ring with the Scrutatores symbol was forged in Rome around 1100ad. The importance of the ring is that it is mentioned in a book that is two thousand plus years older than the ring. The ring is referred to as the Ring of Seeker," said Andrews.

John found it hard to believe that the ring was mentioned in the ancient book, but he also knew this could not be a coincidence either. The notion that the writings in the Book of Knowledge could be factual was terrifying for John. He started to wonder what would happen if this book fell into the wrong hands. The devastation the book could cause humanity was mind-boggling. All the beliefs held true by many different religions would be questioned and there would be no way to prove them right or wrong.

"John, there is even more that I have to tell you."

"Really, I have already heard more than I think I can handle right now."

Andrews ignored the comment. "The book has also correctly predicted many of the tragedies and the rise of some of the world's most ruthless rulers," said Andrews.

"Name one," said John.

"You know how Nostradamus misspelled Hitler's name by one letter? Well, the book gives his name, the country he ruled and the people he persecuted without missing a letter," said Andrews.

"You're telling me that a book before the time of Pharaohs gives Hitler by name?"

"Yes, and the use of the atomic bomb. It also gives the name of the country using it and the country it was used against," said Andrews.

"Not possible," said John.

"It does, and I will show you when we return to Andrews Castle. Tonight," said Andrews.

"Excuse me, return to Andrews Castle...tonight?" Said John.

"Yes, you are going tonight. I've already explained to the University that an emergency has emerged and you are needed to return. I made the usual promise that they will be the first to house our next finding and they agreed, as usual. You will work with us for the next month or two, possibly longer," finished Andrews.

"This semester is about to end and I need to prepare my students for their finals," John protested weakly.

"Taken care of. You need to meet with the Order and get started on examining the book as soon as possible," said Andrews.

"The book is at the Field Museum."

"True, the museum has the book but it's a duplicate and no one can tell from the casing that it is a replica. Now, I will meet you at O'Hare at the private hangar. My jet will fly us to Andrews Castle together. So pack quickly, see you there. John, something is happening; I don't know what or when it will happen but I can feel it. The Order will be put to the test and the future of humanity rides in the balance. "

Andrews walked to John and placed his hand on his left shoulder for a brief moment and then walked out the door. John stayed at his table for five minutes. He struggled to take in all that Andrews had told him. Through his head, he kept running the thought of the Order of Seven originating from the Scrutatores, the existence of the Scrutatores, the implications if the book was correct and what of humanity's future. John walked into the kitchen, opened one of the cabinets and took out a bottle of Jack Daniels and poured himself a real stiff drink this time. He took it with him to have while packing a large bag for his trip to London. As he walked into his bedroom he realized that he had forgotten to mention the phone call. John figured that the meeting with Andrews was what Wrightwood or another assistant was referring to.

Before he started packing, he reflected on the Order. He felt excitement and nervousness together. He wondered if he'd be up to the test.

3

AN ANCIENT GROUP

The evening air was cool and exhilarating. Three cars had parked outside an abandoned building on the south side of Chicago. Inside the building, five individuals gathered after the presentation at the Field Museum that each of them had attended. The building was dilapidated and the meeting was being conducted on the first floor of what used to be an old meat packing plant. The five individuals dressed in black cloaks stood outside of the symbol of the Scrutatores that was etched into the floor. Each person was standing outside of the triangle.

Inside the triangle on each point is a lit six-inch candle. In the center of the triangle was an extremely large green sphere. There are no other lights in the building turned on. Each person was staring at the symbol, chanting in Latin. The chanting stopped as the person at the top point raised his hand. The only sound came from the wind howling through the old building. The gathered group waited for the central figure to start speaking. After several minutes, the silence broke.

"Our time is nearing. The discovery of the Book of Knowledge is the sign we have been waiting for. Our ancestors are speaking to us. They will soon be speaking to us through the book." The cloaked figure spoke in a deep male voice.

The members of this small fraternity were facing the person speaking, listening intently to his every word.

"The book in the museum is a replica."

The news caused all the members to gasp in disbelief. "Please everyone, listen. The book on display is a replica, which means that the real book is being kept in a different location. That location is what we need to find out."

One of the females in the group interrupted, "How are we to find the location of the real book?"

"Kantra, the location is obvious," said the central figure.

"Please explain how it is obvious, Lannar," said Kantra.

"The book was discovered by a team of archeologists employed by the Stamens the book is in the museum just not on display." Replied Lannar.

"The Order of Seven, why them?" Asked another man in the group.

"The Order of Seven will try to stop us once they figure out what we're planning and who we are, Macnar. I believe that the book will be here at the Museum. No matter, we will attain it," said Lannar.

The candles were extinguished and an outdoor construction light was turned on. Each person removed their cloaks, underneath each were dressed in formal wear.

"Ulra, will you please cover up our symbol?" Lannar turned to the new person in their group. "Wrightwood, you will need to think of a Scrutatore name for our next meeting. I will call you or Ulra will let you know of the meeting. You should plan on the next meeting being in two weeks. Did everyone hear? Next meeting in two weeks," finished Lannar.

John finished his packing minutes before the taxicab company placed a courtesy call to inform him his cab had arrived. John turned his living room light on, locked the door and headed toward the cab. As he exited his building, across the street some people outside the bar were smoking.

They waved to John and asked, "Where are you off to?"

"Off to London for work!" He shouted.

"I wish I had your job!" One replied. John responded with a chuckle and a wave as he entered the cab. If only they knew.

The ride to the airport was quick. The lack of traffic on the highway at midnight made any drive quick from downtown Chicago. The cab dropped him off at the airport, and as he exited the car, he noticed Andrews and two women, one blond and the other brunette alongside him. John placed his duffle bag's strap on his shoulder and headed toward them. Andrews waved to John, and as John neared, he noticed the two females were much younger than his own age of forty-four.

"You made good time, but you still don't get around as fast as I do," said Andrews with a large smile on his face.

"Hey," said John. It was obvious that he was running out of energy after his long day.

"Let me introduce you to the newest members of the Order. This is Emily Stone and Julia Bernard. They will be assigned to work with you on the Book of Knowledge, and in tracking down the Scrutatores."

Emily extended her hand to John. "Nice to meet you, John. Andrews has spoken highly of you. I've also read many of your publications on Medieval History," she said warmly.

"Nice to meet you," said John, taking her hand.

"Hello Mr. Williams, I'm Julia Bernard. It's a pleasure to meet you," said Julia as she also extended her hand to greet John.

"Nice to meet you as well, Julia, please call me John. I am sorry for both of your losses. I knew your mothers very well. They were each great individuals and excellent at their craft. I'm sure you will continue in their footsteps," said John.

Julia Bernard was a chemistry teacher at the University of Paris. She was a professor at the University for the past two years, and was twenty-eight years of age. She was a very attractive, slim woman with dark black hair. Her intellect matched her beauty. She had very distinctive green eyes that were quite visible through her slim-framed glasses.

She was easily offended when people got lost in her beauty and failed to notice that she had a very sharp and intuitive mind.

Emily Stone was a biology and history professor at the University of Boston. Like Julia, she too was slim and very attractive. She had blond hair and pale white skin. She was twenty-seven years old, and had been a professor at the University of Boston for three years.

"Okay, let's get going before the plane leaves without us," said Andrews.

Their bags in hand, they walked and engaged in small talk. The conversation revolved around John's presentation. John was never any good at accepting compliments, but he thanked them and pointed out that he had five years to prepare for the presentation. The four of them walked to the security check and headed for the plane that would take them to Andrews Castle.

Andrews' phone started ringing as they sat in the waiting area before boarding the plane. Andrews looked at the ID of the caller and jumped to his feet.

"Yes." He started walking around, repeating "I see," over and over. His facial expression was serious, and one of disbelief as well.

"I'm about to board the plane and will be there shortly," Andrews ended the call and paused before addressing his traveling companions.

John, Emily, and Julia were anxious to hear what had obviously upset him. He walked up to them and simply said, "We will discuss this when we land in London, where we can not be heard discussing the details of that call.

"We should pick up our pace," Andrews continued, "We will need to rest on the plane." Even though the news of the phone call was obviously alarming, they were relieved to hear that they would get some rest before landing.

4

FREEDOM

The Fourth of July fireworks at Navy Pier were excellent, as usual. They did not disappoint the extremely large crowd that had gathered to watch them. The crowds came to celebrate their country's independence and were feeling extremely festive. Up and down the pier, people were waving miniature American flags. Pride in one's country was in abundance. Bridgette Williams, Dwayne Bordeaux, Rosa Rodriguez, and David Heinrich were celebrating with the crowd, but what they were really celebrating was the beginning of their own independence. Each of them graduated from high school last month and was finally granted the freedom to be out on their own, without any supervision. All four lived in an orphanage for as long as they could remember. In a few months, they would be starting college at the same school. They had been friends since childhood.

The four were very excited, not just at being out, but tomorrow morning they were to head down to a lake house in Saugatuck, Michigan, that was donated to the orphanage by a wealthy benefactor. They decided last month that a road trip was in order before the heat made its descent on the Midwest, and the start of college came upon them. They wanted to head there after the Fourth of July festivities but Mary, the superintendent over at the orphanage, preferred them to drive during the day. The four headed home.

Summer, the season of fun, and the start of new adventures and a goodbye to the past. Out of the four seasons, summer is where hope always found its way into everyone's life. Another hot summer landed on Chicago, and this summer is reminiscent of many past summers hot, muggy, and extremely humid. They had packed the car the night before in order to be ready to head out early the next morning.

Once their destination was reached, they would enjoy summer and the fun that comes with youth. They would also receive relief from the scorching humidity that had plagued the city for the past three weeks. The road trip was long and cumbersome, but they managed to get to their destination in what was perceived as record time.

Bridgette looked at Dwayne in a condescending manner, "Oh yeah, you sure got us here faster than our old driver, Richards. I think even that senior citizen with his two bad eyes would've had the balls to pass that school bus moving so slow it was almost going backwards."

There was spontaneous laughter from all four as they relived the experience of driving behind the bus for twenty-five minutes.

As they pulled into the blacktop driveway, each of them were anxious to get out of the car and soak in some of the sun beaming down from the clear blue sky. The two-floor, bricked house sat in the middle of a large plot of land; with the exception of the driveway, it was surrounded by grass. In the middle of the backyard was a squared, sandy area with volleyball net. On the far right side of the patio was a large Jacuzzi. The teens were extremely appreciative for the usage of the house, the benefactor who lent the orphanage the use of the house, and their monetary donation, remained anonymous.

The temperature read ninety-five degrees on the thermometer. Rosa and Dwayne were the first to stop laughing as the car came to a final stop next to the house. Rosa glanced at Dwayne, signaling that the water was calling their names.

Rosa looked at Bridgette and quickly blurted out, "Dwayne and I are going to check out the lake."

They each had their bathing suits next to them, and with that Rosa and Dwayne made a beeline to the pier. They ran through the well-groomed lawn, a distance of nearly one hundred feet from the paved driveway, to the pier.

As they reached the lake, Rosa and Dwayne quickly shed their clothes and changed, not caring who saw them, including each other. Since there was never any sexual attraction between them, they didn't think twice about stripping in front of each other. They jumped in, paying no attention to their surroundings or the coldness of the water. They swam from the end of the pier to about twenty-five feet out. Next to the end of the pier were a boating dock with three boats and a pair of jet skis. Everyone's favorite boat was the white speedboat, because the other two boats were pontoons. Those were larger, slower boats that were used more frequently because of their capability of accommodating more people.

Rosa dove deep, fully submerging in the clear water. As she came up she disturbed the ground below her. Dirt and debris nestled at the bottom swirled to the top of the water. Once Rosa came back up from her refreshing dive, Dwayne dove under. While he was down, he dove at Rosa's legs and proceeded to pull her underneath. The two of them wrestled for a short stint underwater and surfaced together. Their combined activity managed to disturb more of the ground and debris nestled on the lake's bottom.

Dwayne was clumsily regaining his balance as he came up from his torpedo attack on Rosa. As he straightened up and stepped to his left in the four and a half feet of water, suddenly he felt a stinging sensation in his right heel. The sting was similar to the tetanus shot he had to get at the beginning of the month for his physical. Rosa heard his squeamish yelp and saw the pain on his face.

"You okay?" asked Rosa. She reached out to Dwayne like a young mother reaching for her child that had fallen for the first time since learning to walk. Dwayne was slightly annoyed by the babying attention Rosa was always giving him. He moved and realized there was something underneath his foot. He grazed his foot over the area.

"There's something down there that I stepped on," he told Rosa. "I'm gonna see if I can get it." He took a deep breath, and dove toward the area he had just been standing on. He felt his way around. He moved aside some rocks and stones and then he came across a rather small item. He brought the item to the surface with him. Both he and Rosa examined it.

"Wow! That ring is huge!" exclaimed Rosa.

Dwayne raised the ring into the air to see its reflection in the sun. The ring was covered with dirt and debris from the lake's floor, but Dwayne removed the dirt by submerging the ring into the lake and rubbing it in the water. He then took a good look at it. Dwayne guessed that the ring was made of silver. He wasn't sure if it was solid silver or not. In high school, Dwayne participated in football, basketball, and baseball. He ate, slept, and talked nothing but sports. He was a starter in each sport, and earned a scholarship to play football at the collegiate level. Dwayne tore his ACL and MCL in the last game of his senior year. With those tears to his knee ligaments, his scholarship was lost along with his dreams of playing a professional sport. His knee was so badly damaged that it took all winter and spring for it to heal and for him to finish physical therapy.

"Rosa, there is no way this ring is a kid's ring," said Dwayne. On the top part of the ring was a plate and engraved into it was two triangles. Inside the center was a green-colored rock. "Check this thing out," he said to Rosa. He handed the ring off to her.

"Oh my god! This thing is creepy looking," said Rosa. It had been a long time since she'd seen Dwayne this excited about anything. The injury to his knee had dampened his spirits and forced him to focus more on his schoolwork.

"I think it's cool," replied Dwayne. "I'm definitely keeping this."

"You would," said Rosa, looking disgusted. Dwayne placed the ring on his left ring finger. The ring was a little loose. They both got out of the water and made their way back to the house.

David and Bridgette decided to unload the car before starting the weekend. David lifted the hatchback of the SUV and started to gather the luggage each person brought with them.

While he and Bridgette were carrying their personal belongings he said to Bridgette, "It's great that Mary let us come up here."

"I know, I was shocked when she agreed," said Bridgette.

"I can't wait to get started, those idiots should be up here helping us so we can start having fun too," complained David.

"Agreed," said Bridgette.

Bridgette and David continued carrying in the luggage, "This was bound to happen, Dwayne and Rosa are not the responsible kind. All they think about is having a good time, and I always have to pick up and organize things for them," said Bridgette.

David looked at Bridgette, confused by the 'organized' statement, being that the four of them just graduated from high school and were really too young to care about anything except having a good time.

"We graduated, and there ya go. I'm sure I'll have to do the same at college too," said Bridgette.

They often referred to the lake house as 'the cabin'. David was always amazed by how one room could be so spacious. On the far west part of the room was a large shelving unit that covered the entire wall. The south part was all glass that faced the lake. The east part was the kitchen that had a long table that sat right in the middle of the dining area. The north portion was where three bedrooms and the one bathroom where located in the house. The second floor consisted of five bedrooms. He looked around in amazement; he wondered if he would ever be able to afford a spacious property with a beautiful house nestled in a lake town community.

After hauling all their items from the SUV, David sat down in the family room while Bridgette whipped up a dinner that consisted of the submarine sandwiches that they had brought with them from Bari Delicatessen. Bridgette brought the sandwiches into the family room on paper plates. Dwayne and Rosa returned from the water and grabbed their sandwiches and joined Bridgette and David in the family room. As they finished, Bridgette inquired if they would like to play a board game.

"Something interesting, I didn't drive 7 hours to play Chutes and Ladders," teased David.

Bridgette gave a grinning look at Dwayne, because the ride up was usually six hours.

"There are games along the right side of the shelves, why don't you go and pick one out David, so that we don't bore you by picking Sorry or Clue," said Dwayne

David walked over to the section where the board games where. He looked up and down for several minutes when he spotted a game at the bottom of the shelf. It was in a white box. He slid the game out carefully, so not to drop the games on top of it.

"Come on David, hurry up," Rosa yelled.

Outside the night had turned pitch black. All that was noticeable was the large full moon that appeared to hang right over the lake house. The lake reflected the moon's light and the water was still. The wind was strong and loud outside the house. David placed the game behind his back sat down cross-legged opposite of Dwayne and Rosa. He saved a spot next to him for Bridgette for when she returned from the bathroom. Both Dwayne and Rosa were asking David what game he selected. David told them to hold their horses; he would reveal the game as soon as Bridgette came back. Bridgette had entered the room and glanced at the game box, realizing the game David had selected.

"No way I'm playing that demonic game!" Bridgette shouted.

David quickly turned around, upset with his poor job at hiding the game. He looked at Bridgette and said, "Relax, Ouija is just a game. You don't really believe in all that nonsense. Do you?"

David placed the game on the cocktail table that was moved between himself, Dwayne and Rosa. He was surprised that Dwayne and Rosa were willing to play.

Dwayne looked at Bridgette and said, "Come on...it'll be fun. Who knows, we may even actually talk to a real ghost. If we can conjure one up, we might find out about the afterlife or maybe learn where Jimmy Hoffa's buried."

After ten minutes of debating, David looked at Bridgette and said, "Okay, if it gets weird, we'll stop. I don't think anything will happen; this game is really just a bunch of bull."

Feeling that Rosa and Dwayne would side with him, David decided to try a democratic approach, "How's this, we take a vote and if we tie, I'll choose another game. Agreed?"

Dwayne looked at David and said, "I'm in."

Bridgette didn't wait for someone to ask her opinion, "I'm a definite no!"

Dwayne looked right into Rosa's eyes and said, "Well, what'll it be?"

Rosa raised her hand as if she was answering a question by one of her teachers, "I'm in too," she declared. She was uncomfortable being the deciding vote. She didn't want to upset Bridgette, but she did want to play.

David looked at Bridgette and said "You're the only one not in."

Bridgette was feeling annoyed by David's comments, "I don't care if I'm the only one not in. You guys can play without me".

The discussion between David and Bridgette became personal. Dwayne and Rosa did not move, enjoying the discussion as David attempted to convince Bridgette to play.

"You're being ridiculous," David said to Bridgette.

"Why? Because I don't want to play that evil game?" She spoke each word slowly. "Besides, why am I such an important player? I think you can do this with three people," she said sarcastically.

David was getting frustrated with her resistance. "You know, if it's not something you want to do, you don't care about anyone else... you say 'its stupid, why do you need me'. I'm so tired of this. For the last time, are you playing or not...and don't play if you don't want to, every party needs a pooper," said David, displaying his annoyance and anger to everyone.

Bridgette sighed loudly. "Fine, lets play and let our journey to hell begin."

David pulled the top of the box off; his elation of finally winning a battle of wills with Bridgette was not well hidden from view.

"I agreed to play the game, not proclaim you master of the universe," she said, noticing his elation.

"Whatever, all I know is that we're playing and I talked you into it."

"I think you're about to watch me go out on the dock if you keep this up."

"Okay, I'll stop. On second thought, I want a moment longer to bathe in this moment."

"I'm going to make you bathe in something else."

"I'm done."

David tossed the top off to the side landing near the television. He took out the game board and laid it so that the letters were right side up towards him. Bridgette came and sat down next to him. David then took the widget that allowed the letters and answers to be revealed.

"If we're going do this right, we'll need a pad of paper to write down the letters so we can see what is spelled out." Bridgette said, as she got up and walked into the kitchen. David and Dwayne had a quick laugh over her comments. It didn't take long for her to take charge. Meanwhile, Rosa was becoming more nervous over this and questioned her commitment to playing.

"I don't know if I still want to do this," said Rosa. Dwayne looked at her at gave her a reassuring pat on her back.

"I'm here to protect you, you got nothing to be afraid of, it's just a silly game, let's have some fun with this."

"Whatever, you can barely make your bed and you're going to protect me," she said mockingly as she shoved Dwayne, causing him to teeter to his left.

Bridgette searched the kitchen drawers and finally found two pads of legal paper and two pens. She quickly sat down next to David and handed the pads and pens to Rosa and Dwayne. "Okay, you guys write down the questions and the answers while David and me do the grunt work."

Rosa and Dwayne looked at each other, shrugged their shoulders and agreed.

At once Dwayne stood up and said wait. He ran into the bathroom opened up the closet and rummaged through it until he found what he was looking for. He pulled out six candles and a lighter. Four of them were scented mango mandarin and the other two bamboo and aloe leaf. He came back into the large room cradling four candles and the other two side by side over the other four candles.

"We need to set the mood". He placed the candles by Bridgette and instructed her to light them and went around the house and made sure all the lights were turned off. This made the moon appear closer and more menacing. The candles were placed around the board. Bridgette looked at the clock on the kitchen wall noticed that the time was 11:16pm.

"Let's get started."

Bridgette and David placed both their hands on the widget. The widget was slowly beginning to move around the board. Bridgette asked the first question, if there is a ghost in the house. Everyone except David laughed.

"We need to be serious," said David angrily.

Agreeing with David, Bridgette asked four more times and finally the widget landed on the yes.

Bridgette asked the ghost its name. As the widget moved around the board, Rosa was writing down each letter that Bridgette and David stopped on. The letters spelled out the name Jonas Bearden. Rosa said the name out loud. Bridgette's face turned pale. She remembered the name from the last time she played Ouija. David looked at her in shock; he realized that the name was familiar to Bridgette.

"What are you thinking?" Asked David.

"That name came up the last time I played this game at Angela Parlini's house back in 8th grade."

Dwayne looked at her and said, "You did that on purpose."

"How could I have, David is holding on too," said Bridgette. "David, did I force the letters?" Bridgette continued staring at the board.

"Nnno. I would have felt if she did," stuttered David.

Rosa's scared attitude changed to anxious. She wanted to find out more. She directed them to ask if he was the same person from the last time. The widget went right to the yes. All four bounced from the ground to a standing position. For a moment each of them were frozen, staring at the board, then looking around the room and finally at each other.

"Let's try it again," said Bridgette.

"Are you nuts?!" Shouted David.

"What, scared? Mr. don't play this game if you don't want to," Bridgette said mockingly to David.

"No fear, ask away."

They each went back to their sitting positions. David looked at Bridgette and said, "You first."

David and Bridgette placed their hands back on the widget. Bridgette thought for a second and asked the ghost, "how long have you been dead for?" The widget revealed 118 years.

Suddenly a blue orb came through the window. David immediately noticed it. He let go of the widget and quickly jumped on to the couch. Bridgette removed her hands from the widget and turned to David. As she did, the blue orb vanished.

"What's up, dude?" Dwayne asked David with a confused look.

"A blue light thing came through the window," said David rapidly, in a frightened tone. The other three looked at the window and saw nothing.

"Knock it off," said Rosa angrily.

"I swear, I saw a blue thing floating through the window," retorted David, sternly.

"Where is it?" asked Dwayne.

"It disappeared right after I saw it."

"You see it and then its gone, maybe since we both let go of the widget it vanished. We should try again, but this time Rosa and Dwayne work the widget," suggested Bridgette.

"Sounds good. While we ask questions, don't write anything down and just look around if something shows up," instructed Rosa.

They all accepted the different roles and Dwayne and Rosa repeated the same questions. For the next twenty minutes nothing happened. They changed partners to David and Rosa and again nothing happened. Dwayne and Bridgette paired up. As they asked the third question, the blue orb entered again from the picture window. This time noticed by all. Dwayne released his grasp on the widget. Bridgette however did not. The orb floated above them and then directly in front of Bridgette. The orb circled Bridgette, stopping and hovering in front of her. As the orb finished its rotation around Bridgette, she released the widget and it disappeared.

"It's you!" Shouted David. "That thing has some connection with you."

Dwayne and Rosa were at a loss for words, they simply nodded in agreement.

"I don't know?" questioned Bridgette.

"Do the math, it doesn't show up with anyone, only when your hand's on that thing. It comes back when you're on it with Dwayne, he lets go and you're holding on to it and that thing comes to you, circles you and leaves after you let go of it." David said.

They agreed on each of them sleeping in the large room together. They spent the rest of the evening inside. They decided that they would not play the game again and spend more time out on the lake. The next three days they relaxed and enjoyed the great weather, their company, and most importantly, the freedom of making their own decisions. They each agreed that the odds of anyone believing them were slim to none, and decided to keep the strange encounter to themselves.

5

SIGNS

Michele and Jean Leflore were driving their car from the countryside of France to Paris. They were having a general conversation when suddenly there was a loud thumping on their car.

Jean cried out to Michele, "Look out!"

Without warning, hundreds of birds fell from the sky and landed on their car and all around them outside. The road was covered with black birds. The birds lay only on the two-lane highway that led into Paris.

Cars on the major highway were swerving and smashing into one another. The birds did not fall one at a time; they all came down at once. A motorcyclist crashed into the rear of the car in front of it, and the Cyclist flew directly into the back window. The driver of the car had slowed as it had entered into the section of the fallen birds. The motorcyclist was fortunate to been wearing a helmet.

In London at four in the afternoon in the English Channel there were roughly a hundred boats in the northern part of the Channel. Thousands of fish came afloat, after suddenly dying. Passengers on each boat looked out in utter disbelief.

It was three in the afternoon across the world in the small town of Cortale, located in the Province of Calabria in Italy. Cortale is nestled in a mountain chain that cuts through southern Italy. The sun was starting to set and cool down the day's temperature of around 84 degrees. The town was divided into two sections; the lower part was the older section. It reflected its age. It had been there since the days of the Roman Empire. The higher part was more modern and showed its 20th century growth. The town's church was located in the middle region that divided the two parts. The citizens of Cortale joked how the Stamens brought the new and the old together, although there was a degree of truth to it.

Dr. Antonio Santini was walking back toward his office. He had made a house visit to a family in the lower section who had invited him to stay for lunch. He often would show up unexpected to visit the families living in the southern part of town for an impromptu check up. At the young age of 72, the doctor had never learned to drive a car. He believed that his legs could get him to any part of the small town that he wanted or needed to visit.

Santini stopped at the Five Fountains, which ran constantly, for a quick drink of water. It didn't matter what time you went there, water was always available. The entire fountain portion was made out of brick; the water came out of five pipes that drained into a large brick basin for each fountain pipe.

The fountain dated back to a time when Rome ruled the civilized world. There was no way of knowing the exact date, but by looking at the formation of the bricks, the Roman arch of the individual sections, and the curved indentation, it indicated it was constructed roughly around Augustus Caesar's rule. At the top of the fountain was a fresco painting of two ancient Romans enjoying a drink of water. About fifty years ago, the townspeople built a large, rectangular cement pool where the excess water was channeled. The area was ten feet long by eleven feet wide and two feet deep. The townspeople of the older section, mainly the women, went there to do the family's laundry in the back portion.

Santini would sit there for a few minutes to have a drink of cold water, and he would look at the Five Fountains and the same scene would always come to mind. He would reflect on the day that a boy named Calogero came to drink from the fountain for the first time. Young Antonio was around seven or eight. Santini could not remember his exact age since it happened over fifty years ago.

Calogero had walked up to get some water, and stared at the young Antonio Santini. Calogero stuck his tongue out at Santini and proceeded to climb the fountain to get a drink. Young Antonio asked Calogero if he needed help to reach the water, but the boy said no. The boy lost his balance and hit his mouth. Little Calogero ended up getting several stitches on his bottom lip and chin. He grew up and was a very productive citizen of Cortale; he served as the town's mayor for 25 years. Santini returned to the present. He took one last handful of water and started on his journey back to the Stamens building.

As he was nearing his office, he slowed his walk, looked upwards and directly into the sun. He looked up for around twenty seconds, and then dropped to one knee. He was feeling tightness in his chest, and in his left arm he was feeling a pain starting at his wrist and rushing toward his shoulder. He stopped breathing for a moment and fell to the ground. Suddenly, the world around him went black. Santini could not believe that his life was coming to an end.

As he was thinking about his life, he saw the image of a figure standing next to the Five Fountains. The figure was leaning against the side of the fountain, staring at him. The figure then started walking towards Santini. Confusion was now consuming Santini. He had no idea who or what this figure was. The figure stood approximately six and a half feet in height. He came within several feet from Santini, and it became evident that the figure was a man dressed in an ancient Roman warrior's battle garment. The man had on thin chain mail with brown padding underneath it. The figure was an extremely handsome individual with black hair, and eyes as dark as night. Santini tried but could not figure out who he was. Nonetheless, he felt a sense of recognition. He believed that he knew the man and had seen him before, and he struggled with the thought of where the encounter happened.

Santini looked around, trying to see if there was anything different. As he did, he noticed that everything in the small town was in its proper place. The only thing missing were the people. Standing in the area of the Five Fountains was just Santini and the strange man. He tried to utter some words, but could not speak. It surprised him that the fear he had felt was gone.

The man extended his right hand toward the elderly Doctor. As he shook Santini's hand, the man smiled and said, "So we meet again."

Santini became confused; he could not remember ever meeting him, though the familiarity of this man became haunting. He thought to himself, I know I'm over seventy years old, but I always remember a face.

The man spoke to Santini in a deep, distinctive voice. He started answering Santini's thoughts. "Oh, but we did meet, except I did not take this form. I was a priest; we were outside, here by the Five Fountains. I approached you and asked if you were a devout Catholic. You answered yes."

Santini did not have any recognition of this encounter.

"You were a young boy, twelve years of age," the man said, "Here, allow me to assist you."

Suddenly Santini had a flashback of the encounter of which the man spoke.

"So you do remember our encounter, such a friendly encounter."

Santini remembered the encounter he had with the priest. "I was surprised that a young boy was so connected with nature."

Santini was unable to speak, but his thoughts continued to be understood by the stranger.

The man started laughing and continued his laughter as he spoke, "I too, refer to him as God. Though I have never formally met him. I believe he exists on another plane."

The man stopped laughing and said, "Now do you know who I am, Antonio Santini? Is this a more familiar look? Do you know me? Do you, Antonio Santini?"

Santini knew this person. He was shocked that he was feeling no fear as he stood in the presence of this strange person. He looked directly at him.

"What do you want from me?"

"I am actually amazed by your gift. But let me assure you, I am not Satan and I have no ties to him or the one you call God. You can refer to me as Seeker."

Santini did not understand what Seeker was referring to.

"Do you know what that gift is, Antonio Santini? Think hard, for it will come to you," said Seeker. Santini stood there thinking.

Seeker waved his hand in front of Santini and nodded his head. "Yes, I know. Except it is not a gift, rather a responsibility bestowed upon the senior Stamens of this village. I am the one that will inform the proper people of your presence in the world."

Seeker was surprised that the old doctor was able to surmise his gift so soon. "Impressive. Antonio Santini, you are quite amazing, you truly are a messenger of the Stamens, but you are no prophet. That title belongs to another."

Santini, believing that his life is about to end, listened in earnest to Seeker. He expected to receive some sort of blessing or guidance into the afterlife.

"You are being given the opportunity to deliver your newly learned message, for you are not dead, and I will not be taking you today, or at any point in the future. I have revealed myself to you not by choice, but by rule," said Seeker.

"Rule? What do you mean by that?" Santini asked, finally finding his voice, and relieved that he would not die this day.

"You see the Universe is made up of Governing Rules. One of the rules is that when the Book of Knowledge is opened, and the plans for the real new world order are put into motion, I must reveal this to you. You see my dear Antonio Santini; our plans are already in motion. Soon our time will come."

Seeker paused for a moment and then continued, "The time of the Burning Tower is upon you."

Seeker looked upward and ascended into the blue sky and out of sight.

Church bells started ringing. The decibel level of each ring grew louder than the one preceding it. The ring before the final one awoke Santini from his vision. He became aware that several people surrounded him, crying over what they assumed was his death. But Santini did not have time for conversations; he knew exactly what he had to do. The first, to assure his patients that he was alive and well. He thanked all of them for their concerns and started on his way back to his office.

"You should go to the hospital," a parishioner said to him.

Santini placed his hand on the side of the man's face and said, "God has told me my time to join him has not arrived. Thank you for your concern, but I am fine and will need a ride to Catanzaro."

There were several protests from the crowd, as many wanted their doctor to go to the hospital. Santini said to them, "Please do not try to convince me of what I should do; I truly appreciate your care for me. But you see, I have a mission that I must fulfill." Santini managed, as usual, to convince the people that he would continue on with his intentions.

Domenico Carveli, one of the locals, said "I'll take you to Catanzaro."

"Thank you Domenico, but we have to hurry. Go get your car and meet me at my office."

Domenico agreed and started a steady jog to his house several blocks from the Five Fountains.

Santini made the walk to his office in seven minutes. He impressed himself, walking at a pace that reminded him of his thirties. Once inside, he called for his eldest son Calogero, named for the mayor that he had long ago encountered, causing a pain in his throat. Calogero ran to his father. He heard the screech in his father's voice and was immediately concerned about his health.

Santini walked directly to his personal office and went down onto his knees and said a quick prayer. Calogero called out to his father. He reached him as Santini was finishing his prayer. Santini sprang to his feet as if he was a child being told he was going shopping for a new toy. He started to explain his encounter with Seeker. Calogero stared at his father with a puzzled and confused look on his face.

Santini asked his son if he had his cell phone on him.

"Yes, I have my phone with me," Calogero said.

Santini walked to the statue of Christ on the Cross and reached behind the area of Christ's feet that were nailed to the cross. He felt around until he found what he was looking for. He removed the paper and unfolded it.

Calogero was perplexed by Santini's actions, and asked, "How long has that been there?"

Santini knew that he had to take some time explaining to Calogero what was happening. He figured that if anything happened to him on his way to London, Calogero had to relay the news.

Santini asked Calogero to relax and to listen closely to what he was about to tell him. "Calogero, it is important that you listen and listen well. This paper has the direct phone line to the Order. I don't have time to explain the Order to you. As soon as I leave, go to my room and in the dresser next to my bed, in the top right drawer toward the back is my diary. In it, there is an explanation of the Stamens' role with the Order of Seven. Read it and you will understand what I am doing. I want you to read the entire diary. It is important that you learn my role here and the important role I play with the Stamens. One day you will replace me, and you will need to know all that I know and all that I have experienced."

Calogero tried to ask a question, but was quickly silenced by Santini.

"There is no time for questions. I have just had a vision in which Seeker is planning on coming to our world. I need you to call the phone number. Please, dial the numbers, and as soon as someone answers, read to them the last sentence on this paper."

Santini was now speaking at a hurried pace, "Quickly, you must do this quickly, no time for questioning," He paused for a second, and finished in a quiet voice, "...or doubting."

Calogero made the call. The other end of the phone was answered with a soft "yes". Calogero read the last line, as instructed, then handed the phone to Santini. Santini started talking to the person on the other end, explaining how he had grave information to pass along. The person on the other end of the line gave instructions to Santini. He explained that there would be a plane ticket waiting for him by the time he got to Lamezia Terme, the airport in Catanzaro.

A white Mercedes Benz pulled up to Santini's office. Domenico honked his horn several times, before noticing the old man exiting the

Building, and walking towards his car. Santini journeyed on his way to the city of Catanzaro. As he arrived at the airport, he thanked Domenico. Santini exited the white car and headed towards the airport gates that lead to the flights. Santini kept reliving his encounter in his head, so he wouldn't forget any details. He wanted to inform the members of the Order of Seven with all the information that he could.

He reached the counter and asked the attractive brunette for the next flight to London. She said that the next flight was leaving in several minutes but that the next plane after would leave in three hours. Santini calmly said to the woman that he was in the midst of important business. Surprisingly, she knew that he was coming.

"Are you Antonio Santini?" The woman asked, quickly typing on her keypad while she spoke to him. He nodded.

"We knew that you were on your way here and headed to Andrews Castle on important business. We received a call forty minutes ago that it is imperative that you take a private flight," she said, never looking up until she finished her typing. Once she finished, she handed him a printed ticket.

Santini was stunned by how fast the Order had worked on arranging this. He now knew that the brief explanation he gave was taken seriously. He also began to realize that something on a large scale was about to take place. He boarded the plane, sat in his seat and prepared himself for the half hour flight to Rome.

Back home, Calogero made his way into his father's room. He walked over to the dresser and pulled the drawer he was instructed to open. He fumbled his way around until he came across the book he was looking for. He hesitantly removed the book from the drawer. He sat on his father's bed and stared at it. He felt awkward going through his father's diary. Calogero had to fight the feeling that he was invading his father's private thoughts and feelings. He reminded himself that his father had instructed him to read about the Order of Seven.

As he thumbed through the pages, he realized that his father had lived an active life. Calogero started his intrusive reading at the beginning. He learned that his father was married once before being married to his mother. Curiosity got the best of him. He continued reading and learned that his father was a member of the Stamens before he married his mother.

Rummaging through his father's life, he finally found what he was looking for. He found a faded, colored paper, folded up and attached to the back portion of the diary. He removed the paper from the diary, and stared at it in astonishment. In his hands was his first encounter with an ancient Stamens document. Prior to this document, he had only viewed them in published books. Calogero carefully unfolded the old, faded paper and began reading. At the top of the paper in caps read THE ORDER OF SEVEN.

1025, the year of our Lord, this document has been enacted. This document is in the possession of the head messenger, who does work in the Stamens name and who has been selected by the Order of Seven. The role of the head messenger is to act as a communicator to the Order, and to contact the Stamens when an unnatural occurrence has taken place. At no time should the messenger make a determination on his own in regards to the handling of the matter. The Order members will review the matter. They will determine if action should be taken. The Order will monitor the existence of true evil when it shows itself on Earth. The existence of the Order must be kept secret from members of all religions. Only members from the selected Stamens will be made privy to this information. Though he may know of the Order, the messenger is not a member. Secrecy is of the essence. Faith is of the individual. Triumph against evil is the purpose of the Order of Seven.

Sullivan

Calogero folded the paper and placed it back on the page of the diary and returned it to his father's dresser. He sat on the bed, imagining for a moment the day he would be trained for a greater role within the Stamens.

6

STARTING TO ACT

Andrews addressed the group as he neared the table. "Good evening everyone, so glad you could come on such short notice."

The group acknowledged the two gentlemen before taking their seats. Andrews directed everyone's attention to Santini.

"Everyone, this is Antonio Santini, he is the reason why I have called this important meeting. Let's get things started. Introductions are in order. Santini, please take the seat at the head of the table."

Santini walked to the chair located opposite from Andrews's seat at the other end of the large table, and gingerly sat down.

Andrews stood by his chair and began introducing everyone. "I've already introduced you all to Santini," Santini nodded his head as Andrews looked directly at him.

Andrews then glided his hand with his palm up toward the seat directly to his right, "This is James Stewart," Stewart stood and nodded his head to Santini, the rest following suit. "To his right is Susan Sullivan, and to her right is Maria Rodriguez. We are still waiting for John Williams, who will be seated next to her."

Everyone's attention went toward the empty chair. They all wondered why he would be late for such an important meeting. Andrews then motioned towards the people on his left, "Adam Richards, Julia Bernard, and to her left is Emily Stone."

Andrews again focused his attention toward Santini, "This is the Order of Seven minus John."

Andrews reached for one of the pitchers of water and filled his glass. He took a sip and started to explain why they been summoned, "Ladies and gentlemen, we have entered a dark time. It has been made evident by Santini that the one called Seeker has started his attempt at ruling Earth." Andrews motioned again toward Santini. "Would you please describe your vision."

Santini took a drink from his glass, cleared his throat and began speaking in English with a strong Italian accent, "Yes, I did have an interesting encounter, as I relayed to Andrews. I was walking back toward my office, and as I got to the Five Fountains, everything went black. Suddenly a figure dressed in Roman armor came down from the sky. He was an extremely handsome individual. At first I thought that I had passed and an Angel was coming to escort me into Heaven," Santini started to shake as he recalled the image. He picked up his glass and quickly chugged the rest of the water.

Santini continued his description; "Then Seeker introduced himself to me. He also said that he was forced to reveal himself."

Everyone at the table began to talk at the same time. Andrews made a fist and hit the table with his right hand. Everyone stopped talking. "People, please allow the good doctor to finish his story."

Santini felt calm and at ease after Andrews settled the room down. Santini continued describing his vision, "Seeker was in front of me," he paused for several seconds and then continued, "Seeker said that the vision I was having was caused by the Rules of the Universe. I thought from God, but he claims I was wrong. He said that he did not want to warn the world that he was planning something."

Santini got up from the chair, walked around it, placing both his hands on the top of the chair. He shut his eyes and then opened them again and said, "He said his plan was already happening and the time of the Burning Tower was upon me. That was the end of the vision," said Santini.

"It ends there? There is nothing revealed there," said Adam.

"The message is that Seeker is planning something, and has either entered our plane of existence, or has humans aiding him," said James.

"Where do we go from here? I believe that Santini's vision is a true message warning us that Seeker has found a way to penetrate our plane. The real question to be addressed, is who is Seeker," said Julia.

"I think we need to discuss Santini's vision more. We do need to act, but before we overreact, we should discuss if this is a real message or simply an image created in one man's mind. No offense Santini, I don't mean to be rude, but we need to examine what you saw and try to verify that this was a true vision," interjected Emily.

Emily's suggestion that this might be a false message caused everyone to go silent. There was an uneasy feeling in the room. Everyone with the exception of Andrews seemed to agree with her. Before Andrews and Santini had entered the room, the group had discussed the possibility that this may be a false message. Now they had to deal with a being they had no knowledge of or where to start looking.

Andrews noticed that the group doubted Santini's vision. He decided that he needed to interject. He stood up and began to address everyone, "I know that hearing this story could cause you to discount it. This feeling of doubt is my fault. I should have had more meetings. There is some information that you are lacking that would have made this account most believable."

"Excuse me," asked Maria, "are you saying that there is information regarding this matter that we know nothing about?"

"Yes. First, Seeker is a mythical figure from Scrutatore mythology. I came across his name while examining the Book of Knowledge. I now fear he is a real being on a parallel universe from ours," said Andrews.

Once again, silence came over everyone in the room. Emily was the first to break the silence. "Well...please... explain if this vision is accurate and if we are in store for a fight."

Andrews walked toward the wall in front of him, stopped and waited for a moment, then turned and faced the group at the table. "As you all know, the Order of Seven has been in existence for a great many years. There are many documents that have survived throughout those years. Some of these documents explain how the ultimate battle will be revealed. In the document written back in the 1100's by Antonio Arivomandi, he explains how the messages will be revealed to a Stamen living in a town in the Southern part of Italy that has the Five Fountains. The fish will stop swimming and the birds will stop flying. These are the signs that have to happen together."

Santini was astonished that there was a document that spoke of his hometown. Andrews continued, "The document was titled 'The Coming of Darkness,' and in it, not only does it mention where the message will be revealed, but it also gives a clue as to what the dark forces will do."

"All we need to do is a little research, and we will catch up on the information we are lacking. If you could get us the documents, we'll be able to read and gather all the information." said James.

Suddenly Andrews' facial expression displayed concern. Julia picked up on his expression right away. "How many of those documents are still in existence?"

Andrews bent his head forward and closed his eyes, and paused for a moment and then looked up, "The documents are kept in the Order's underground section of this Tower."

Some groaning started around the table. Andrews continued, "There is more. I have only seen notes on the documents, and I do not know what the dark forces are looking for or trying to do. Locating the actual documents will take time."

Susan interrupted, and everyone's attention turned to her. "I don't know why I didn't mention this before, but earlier today five thousand fish suddenly came afloat in the English Channel."

Julia didn't stand up but added, "Today, on a highway leading into Paris, five thousand birds dropped from the sky. It could not be explained why they fell or why were there so many black birds of different species flying together."

Each person started commenting on the two incidents. Everyone was speaking at the same time. No one was listening to what anyone was saying. Andrews attempted to gain everyone's attention, but failed. The group continued to grow louder.

After several minutes of this, Adam stood up and shouted as loud as he could, "PLEASE, EVERYONE BE QUIET!"

Adam's voice succeeded in quieting the room down. He continued speaking, "We need to listen to Santini's vision again and try to find a clue that may exist that we have overlooked."

The group agreed. The Italian Stamen from Cortale once again became the focus of their attention. Santini retold his encounter with Seeker.

Emily expressed her opinion on the encounter, "The only thing mentioned that we could use as a starting point, is the Burning Tower portion. That is what we need to focus on, in my opinion."

As soon as she finished, the large group again began talking at once. Andrews brought the group to order. "Settle down everyone, we need to discuss how to get organized and who should do the research needed."

Everyone's attention became distracted. The door to the room opened. Everyone's attention turned toward the door. A man garbed in a long, dark trench coat and jeans walked into the room. He was wearing a faded pair of converse shoes. His face was sporting a five o'clock shadow.

Andrews stood from his chair and introduced the stranger, "All of you, except for Santini, are familiar with John Williams. Nice of you to finally get here."

John walked directly to Santini and shook his hand. He turned his attention back to Andrews. "What can I say, I fell asleep in my hotel room. Thanks for leaving the information of the meeting on my phone."

7

DEPTHS OF ANDREWS CASTLE

Andrews briefed John on all that had transpired prior to his arrival. John placed his elbows on the table and rested his head on his hands and turned toward Santini and said, "So, you're the reason we are here. Did this giant creature have a name?"

Santini was slightly taken back by the man's mannerism. He answered, "Yes, I had the vision; he revealed himself as Seeker and he was not a creature."

John turned towards Andrews and said, "The vision is correct and we have no time to waste."

The rumblings started up at the table again. Andrews managed to settle them down, yet again.

Julia turned and said to John, "So convinced in such little time?"

"I don't need time to decide if this man's story is true. He has no reason to lie," John responded, and turned his attention back to Santini, "Are you from one of the Stamens that is designated to inform the Order?"

"Yes," Santini answered his question, "the Stamens organization located in my town is one of the oldest and we have this responsibility."

John looked directly at Julia, "There you go, not only is he telling the truth, but this is a town with an ancient Stamens Fountain built during the time of the Roman Empire."

Emily was annoyed with John's quickness and confidence. "Impressive, your being able to figure it out so fast. What would we do without you?" she said sarcastically.

"Well, when you've had as much experience with the underworld as I have had, it's not that difficult," replied John, "you all know I understand the forces of the supernatural and how to defend and attack those that are."

Andrews interrupted John, "We need to move to the Order's archival section of the Tower." The words that he uttered rang through to everyone except to John.

The other Order members began agreeing with John. "Skepticism comes easily to people when they hear something like this. However, this is no ordinary circumstance. Thirty minutes ago, an old man recounted a tale that seemed preposterous. We do have a place to start searching. An understanding behind how the Order came to be may hold the clues of where to start."

Andrews knew the origin of the Order of Seven. He was very well versed in the stories regarding the Order.

"Renaldo Sullivan was the man who formed the Order of Seven. The year was 1025. He had warned the Pope that something evil was about to enter this plane of existence. He was right. An Order member was back in his home country of England, in the forest hunting deer. He suddenly came across a large boar. The creature charged him. The animal had markings on it. The Scrutatore symbol was branded into its entire left side. The boar spoke to him and told him that the Dark One was planning to take over all of humanity on this plane. He defeated the boar, but not before it delivered a devastating blow. The creature had stuck him in his abdomen with one of its tusks. He became unconscious from the wound.

"When he awoke, he was in a small wooden house. His wounds had been healed by a cleric who lived there, who had special healing abilities. The cleric told him that he would live and that he needed to head back to London. On his way was when he encountered the one called Seeker. The Seeker did nothing and only said who he was. When Sullivan arrived in London he explained to Sir Andrews that he was healed by a cleric and of the encounter with the boar and Seeker. It is from that conversation that Sir Andrews formed the Order of Seven."

Emily commented, "Now we know that Seeker is immortal."

Andrews tried to answer, but Emily continued enthusiastically, "We need to decipher Santini's vision and plan how to combat these forces and whatever else there is to come."

"We need to start as soon as possible. I offer my assistance in finding them," said Adam.

"A few of us should search the records for any information on the Scrutatores. Except for Dr. Santini. You should go back to your village and contact us if you have another vision," said Andrews.

"We need to develop a plan to prepare and train," said John.

"Andrews, I believe we should organize the Order here," said Maria, "the sooner we train and do the necessary research, the closer we are to defeating the forces that are upon us. But before we can train, we need to know what we are training for."

The other Order members voiced their agreement with her. Andrews had been listening intently to Maria's concerns. Even though he agreed with her, he knew that rushing in and haphazardly putting a plan together would not result in success.

"I know that time is of the essence, but we have more to discuss here, not all of you will be going to the archives," said Andrews. There was some confusion on the faces of his colleagues. "Once the records and documents have been discovered, the next order of business will be to decipher them and correlate them with the Book of Knowledge. If those of you assisting here could stay longer and help uncover the needed documents, it would be appreciated."

All of them agreed to stay and help. They would be serving a greater cause by assisting.

Emily spoke up, " I agree with Andrews, it makes sense that we search for as much information as possible before trying to decipher the vision. I can help here in locating the records."

"I can offer my assistance along with Emily," said Julia.

John interrupted, "Actually you two are going to Sicily to work with Franco Pastalini."

"We are?" asked Julia, surprised.

"Who decided this, and what role will we play in Sicily?" Emily responded more forcefully.

Andrews began explaining. "He knows the techniques of the cleric. He learned the procedures from the Book of Knowledge."

Emily and Julia looked at each other. "Why us?" asked Emily.

"You both have the cleric's ability," Andrews explained.

Emily and Julia felt a little unsettled that someone knew of a skill they had that they did not know about.

"Both of your mother's, who were prior members of the Order, had informed us that you had displayed the healing ability when you were younger.

"We're not going to refuse...well, at least I'm not," said Julia, while looking at Emily.

"I'm not either, I would just like a further explanation," said Emily.

"Franco is going to work with both of you and teach you the ancient techniques," said Andrews.

"Those of us who remain, will assist each other in our own training and education," noted John.

"What do you mean education and training?" asked Maria.

"Some of the Order members have the ability to be true healers. A true cleric healer is different than a regular cleric. Both of you," John indicated to Emily and Julia, "will train in discovering the essence and nature of your hidden healing powers."

The idea of learning the skills of a cleric was appealing to both Emily and Julia. They each had a plethora of questions, but before they could ask their questions, Andrews commented, "You'll both need to leave quickly if you are to conclude your training within a quick time-frame. This process will take time to learn and then more time to perform adeptly. He will have you ready and equipped to achieve this task."

Julia tried to ask another question, but Andrews, knowing time was of the essence, cut her short, "Come now, there is no time for further explanations you need to get on your way, now!"

The two ladies looked at each other; doubt was no longer an option.

Andrews addressed John. "John, we need to make our way to the archives."

John addressed everyone left in the room, "I agree. This will take all of us working together. Finding the documents will take several days, maybe sooner maybe longer, but we will need to work together."

"You're probably correct," said Adam.

"You were thinking this also?" Asked John.

"I was."

"Go figure, we're actually agreeing," laughed John.

"It's weird," agreed Adam.

All the members made their way towards the exit. Andrews whispered an aside to John as he guided the people out before him, "We also have another mission."

"What is this other mission?"

"Making sure that Santini does not on end up on Seeker's plane." quietly responded Andrews.

John waited for everyone to leave the stairwell. "Explain."

"Once we acknowledge the attempt on our world, Santini will be at grave risk. The book speaks of this Seeker. If the doorway between the planes is opened, they will need to eliminate the messenger. The first move is an obvious one," said Andrews.

"Failure is not an option," said John.

The two of them reached the top of the stairs. Standing ten feet from the secret passageway was Santini.

Andrews stopped in front of Santini, "My dear friend, you will be taken back to the airport to head back to your village. Emily and Julia will escort you there. Make sure that you stay in contact with us." Andrews handed Santini a business card.

The unknown was now upon all the members of the Order. They knew the importance of finding as much information on the Scrutatores as they could, and that time was no longer going to be kind to any of them. Each member now had specific duties that they would need to complete in order to combat the forces that were rising.

The Order members that were to work on the research were making their way to the Tower's archival section. The archival section was secret to the world and even to Stamens members, with the exception of the Order members, Andrews and his staff. The elevator leading to the underground area was located in Andrews' office, in a different part of the building. They made their way to his office first. Once there, they would enter the secret elevator that would take them below ground.

In order to enter the elevator, one must go through two procedures; the first being a numerical code that was to be entered on a keypad located behind Andrews' desk. Once the code had been entered, an eye scanner rolled out from the wall. The special elevator traveled directly to underground passages, which led into two directions. The path to the west led to the archival section. The second path led to the castle's parking garage. The walk from the elevator to the archival section took fifteen minutes. Outside of the archival section was a nameplate off to the side of the door. The nameplate said: Library of the Supernatural.

The underground library had air pumped into it from another section of the castle. The area underneath, which had been designed for the Order of Seven, had been modernized. Ancient stonewalls adorned the office area. The Order allowed no one into the special archival section unless they worked directly with Andrews. The décor of the room was very modern. There were Apple computers at the fifteen cubicles, and twenty phones scattered throughout. There was a large, seventy-inch flat panel television placed at the northern wall. The entire archival area totaled ten thousand square feet. Bookshelves ran along the eastern and western walls of the large room. On those bookshelves were documents and records that have been recorded by the Order throughout the centuries.

There were five doors that led to different rooms. Each room connected was massive in size. These rooms that were adjacent to the large library served different purposes. One room was for the development of new weapons and a sparring course for training. Another room's purpose was dedicated to the creation of potions and remedies for serious wounds and disease. A third room was devoted to the research and discovery of ancient artifacts; there were maps and computers throughout the room. The fourth room was a hub for tracking and following paranormal activity, and the final room adjacent to the central library was used as housing quarters for members working for an extended length of time. There were fifteen cots, four showering units, and a large kitchen.

Once the meeting ended, the Order divided themselves into three groups. The first group consisted of Adam, Susan, and Maria, who were to search for any documents pertaining to the Order and the Scrutatores. The second group consisted of Emily and Julia, who were on their way to Sicily to learn the technique of the healing cleric. The third group consisted of James and John, who were traveling back to Chicago to study the Book of Knowledge. They are searching for specifics regarding the Scrutatores and the existence of other planes.

8

MURDER IN THE MIDST OF SAFETY

Adam, along with Andrews, guided their group into the Order's facility. Andrews looked exhausted. The sixty-seven year old man had been working nonstop since the Book had been discovered, and all the subsequent occurrences since then. His energy level was kept high solely on the importance of the new and obvious upcoming missions. The fact that the world was in grave danger, and his recent success in finding the Order members was only the first stage of his mission.

"Man, you look like you've gone months without sleep," said Adam to him.

"Well, that is exactly what I have done. I've gone years with little sleep," uttered Andrews.

"I have been able to get several hours here and there," said John with a tired grin.

Adam and the other two Order members expressed concern about the process and the true effectiveness of an Order that had not had to fight a real threat of any kind for centuries.

"I need some clarification," said Maria to Andrews, "I'm curious, if we are successful on knowing where the Scrutatores live, how are we going to know if they are the ones we are searching for?"

"Well, Maria, that is the hard part."

Maria displayed a concerned and puzzled look on her face. "Please explain the process." Maria asked.

Inside the large underground facility, Andrews asked the three of them if they knew the history of the Order of Seven. Andrews started telling the history.

"It was centuries ago that the Order came to be. Europe was entrenched in the dark ages. Chaos and lawlessness existed everywhere. The year was 1100 A.D. and much of Europe was consumed in the conquest of the Holy land, Jerusalem. After the fall of the Roman Empire, the Empire became a series of independent pieces of land that eventually became the countries we know today. Evil rulers had taken control of different areas. Your ancestors had witnessed this and would have been able to testify to the madness that existed throughout Europe."

Not wanting to interrupt, each of them nodded their heads in agreement. Andrews continued, "Sir Andrews had been approached by a Scrutatore that needed to leave the group. Sir Andrews asked him if he was willing to accept God and the teachings of Jesus. The man agreed and the Stamen offered him protection from the Scrutatores, in exchange for attempting to convert them to Catholicism. At the time the Stamens were still the Knights Templar. The man told him that this was not possible, that the only way to deal with them would be to kill them. He informed them of his secret abilities. Of course, Sir Andrews did not believe the man. But once they were in a secure location, the man displayed the magical ability of the Scrutatores. Sir Andrews was shocked and amazed. Seeing how beneficial this could be for the Stamens, he asked the man if there were other Scrutatores that he could trust. The Stamens were known as the Knights Templar. It was after their persecution and after they went into hiding that they became the Stamens. There were only six men that he had complete faith in. The man also explained how the other men were more powerful than any of the other Scrutatore. He explained to Sir Andrews that only a select few could perform magic. The rest had different abilities. Some could speak with the dead; some could predict future happenings. The leaders of the Scrutatores could use magic and needed to be eliminated. Sir Andrews agreed to help the man, in return for his group of seven to assist the Stamens in special matters. The man agreed."

Andrews believed that the members of the Order should know and understand why they had left Europe and separated from the Church.

"The Order members have always been devout to the cause of good. They would follow any order passed on to them from the Stamens, provided it was done in the name of Stamens for a greater good. The Order's first task was to assist in the capturing of Jerusalem. The Crusades were fundamentally about freeing the Holy Land from Muslim rule. This was a task that the Order members could easily become involved in. They were assigned to work closely with the leaders of each Crusade into the Holy Land. They began to work closely with the Knights Templar from France. The Knights Templar were sometimes a little too ruthless for the Order members, but they managed to work toward the goal of freeing Jerusalem. Greed had unfortunately also been the Kings' motivating factor in agreeing with the Templar on the invasion of Jerusalem. Many Muslims were wrongly executed during the Crusades. However, the Muslims were also merciless toward the Crusaders as well. The three Crusades proved to be enough for the Order members; they believed that they were being exploited for their excellent fighting skills and their magical powers. Not one Order member was killed or captured in any of the Crusades. The Crusades spanned three generations of Order members. It was said that each Order member had warned the upcoming members not to be fooled into participating in a Crusade into Jerusalem. The end of the third Crusade disenchanted the Order regarding the Crusades. The appetite for wealth and power was the primary reason for them breaking and dissolving from the Templar and the Church. The Order members were confused as to why the Templar became involved with the likes of King Richard. This is one reason we have such a hard and daunting task before us."

Andrews continued his pacing "Before I continue, let me try and answer your questions."

Susan started the question session, "I am curious as to how the Order of Seven stopped assisting the Church."

Andrews shut his eyes for a brief second, opened them and started explaining the situation regarding the painful end of the Order. "The year was 1315, the members of the Order became angered by how they were being utilized."

The pain that Andrews was feeling became noticeable in the tone of his voice. He began to speak a little quieter, and at a slower pace. "The members were upset that they were fighting for the attainment of wealth. The Crusades had come to an end. They were assisting King Richard the Lionhearted in his quest for the Muslim rule of Jerusalem.

"I don't necessarily agree with the true reason for the Crusades. The acquisition of wealth was a driving factor. The original Crusade was for a noble reason of recapturing the Holy Land, from a religious point of view," said Andrews, his voice and pace returning back to normal.

"What disturbs me is that back then, no one understood the importance of each religion," said Andrews, regretfully.

"Could it be a possibility that the Order left because of the Church's involvement with the Kings and the people of nobility that wanted to increase their wealth and possessions?" suggested Susan.

"Yes, that was one of the aspects that caused the rift between the Order and the Church. The answer is deeper than just disillusionment with the Church in dealing with men of greed and power."

Andrews continued with his recounting of the historical portion of the Order, "The final blow to the relationship between the Order and the Church came in 1309. In that year there were as many Cardinals from France as in Italy. The Order members knew that their allegiance was forever linked with the Catholic Stamens. In 1309, came the Great Schism. The Cardinals from France wanted to move the Papacy to Avignon, located in France. The Italian Cardinals were against it. Clement V moved the Papacy from Rome to Avignon. In doing so, it had caused suspicion to arise within the Order. The Order members did not trust Clement. He was the Pope that ordered the end of the Knights Templar. The Templar were a great asset during the Crusades. The Knights Templar, remember, worked closely with the Order of Seven.

The two had a commonality of being skillful fighters and devout religious individuals. The Order had to be kept from the general knowledge of the average person. The Knights Templar was in full awareness of the Order of Seven. They often assisted the Order in different situations regarding evil when they arose. They were also the financial backing of the Order. The Knights Templar, along with being a fighting organization, also had an economic portion to it that was quite successful.

"Clement was under great pressure from Phillip IV of France to disband and end the existence of the Knights Templar. Phillip was in debt to the Templar. He needed his financial situation with them to be resolved. The Templar had an initiation ceremony, and Phillip had convinced Clement that the ritual being conducted was sacrilegious. The persecution of the Knights Templar lasted from 1309 to 1312. Templar Knights were arrested and put to trial. They were brutally tortured into false confession. Once found guilty, they were executed by being burned at the stake. Then, in 1312, Clement V disbanded the Knights Templar, effectively eliminating Philip IV of France's debt to the Knights Templar. That's when the surviving Templar went into hiding throughout Europe and became the Stamens.

"The Order of Seven viewed this act by Clement as acting like a ruler, instead of the religious leader he was supposed to be. The Order then began to suspect the Pope's intention regarding them. Phillip convinced him that the Order might attempt to assassinate him, and managed to convince the Pope to act on the Order. Phillip's influence led Clement to disband the Order and ordered them to be put to death.

"The Order of Seven was made privy to this information by the Council of the Supernatural. The Council members were the Church's defenders against the unexplained. The Council also worked closely with the Order. The Order had set up a meeting to discuss their options amongst themselves. They had come to the conclusion that the Order needed to leave the countries each of them lived in. They decided to hide in Germany. The two groups believed that in Germany, they would be able to live their lives in anonymity from the general public and the Church. The Order was to remain in contact, and gave their word that they would keep this knowledge from the current Pope and all Popes that would follow. This promise was upheld and will continue to be upheld. The secrecy of the Order of Seven cannot be revealed to anyone outside of this room and our colleagues."

The current Order members were overwhelmed by all the information revealed to them. This was a lot to take in. The room fell silent from all the thoughts racing through each person's mind. The notion that the Church had at one time betrayed the group that was assembled to protect the world from evil forces was troubling to them as a group, and individually. However, that was in the past and current affairs within the Stamens were in great contrast. In the past, the Church was strongly connected with political affairs. This had changed greatly. The elevator door opened. Everyone turned, expecting to see either James or John. To their surprise, a man dressed in a grey suit, carrying a suitcase, stepped out of the elevator and walked towards them. Adam, Maria, and Susan turned towards Andrews.

"This is one of my assistants, Eric Wrightwood. Good to see you, Wrightwood. How have you been?" asked Andrews.

"Doing well," said Wrightwood.

"Why is he down here with us?" asked Susan.

"Mr. Wrightwood has been my closest assistant. He is the one responsible for deciphering most of the Book of Knowledge. If it wasn't for my need of him here, he would be in Chicago assisting John and James."

Wrightwood placed the suitcase on a table, facing everyone in the room. He glanced at everyone for a brief second then opened it. Andrews became curious as to what Wrightwood was up to. He started to walk toward him.

"Please, stay where you are. I have some important information to show and tell you. All of you."

"What are you talking about?" asked Adam.

Wrightwood removed three documents in a clear protective wrapping from the suitcase. He walked the documents to a nearby table. He placed the documents on the table, and walked back to the briefcase. Adam, Susan, and Andrews each picked up one of the documents. Maria moved closer to Andrews and the two looked over the document together.

"How did you come across these documents?" Andrews asked.

"Well, while you were all upstairs having your meeting, I spent the last two days searching for what you were about to start looking for."

"You did not have permission to be down here," protested Andrews.

"Since you set me up with the procedure to enter, I didn't need your permission, now did I?"

"What are the documents?" asked Maria.

"They're about all the ancient council...that used to assist the seven special ones," said Wrightwood.

"Wrightwood, you are betraying your oath," warned Andrews.

"No, one can only betray an oath if one intends to follow it. Besides, I made another oath long before I ever met you," said Wrightwood.

The three Order members looked at each other while Wrightwood was talking with Andrews. They had decided to rush Wrightwood and bring him down.

The three stopped their charge when Wrightwood reached into his suit coat, thinking that he had removed a gun. Adam realized right away that there wasn't a gun, and continued with his charge.

"Attono," said Wrightwood, keeping his hands flat and aimed at Adam. A red beam of light came out of his fingers. The red light struck Adam on his chest, sending him off his feet and onto the ground. Maria and Susan ran to Adam. He had been knocked unconscious.

Wrightwood looked at his hand. A sudden rush of power engulfed him.

"Attono!" Maria shouted. A red beam of light came out of her fingertips. The red beam missed Wrightwood striking the wall and causing an explosion.

"You're a Scrutatore?" Susan asked, angrily.

"Yes, I am. He'll be fine in fifteen minutes. Well, he'll be very sore. But at least he is not dead," laughed Wrightwood.

"What do you want from us?" Maria shouted. As Maria yelled at Wrightwood, Susan attempted a stun spell at him. Wrightwood quickly waved his hand and deflected the stun spell to the ground. The spell caused the table next to Wrightwood to splinter. Wrightwood was knocked across the room several feet. While Wrightwood lay on the ground, he needed to gain his composure. He placed a protective shield around himself and levitated off the ground. Despite themselves, Susan and Maria were impressed with his ability to use magic spells.

"I want nothing from any of you. My purpose here is to eliminate you."

"Why?" Andrews asked.

"I am a member of the group that you want to destroy."

"There is no group we want to destroy!" Susan exclaimed.

"Enough of your lies! The Order hunted down and killed most of my descendants. Now I will begin the retribution that we have waited for, for over a millennium. The documents that are on the table explain how it was done. The directive to hunt us came from the Pope, and the steps that were taken by the Order. We did not believe that any of this information existed. But once the Book of Knowledge was discovered, we knew that the world would pay for their decisions and actions against our ancestors, the Scrutatores. We have returned. The opening of the book caused a realization in each of us. Our numbers will grow. We may be small for now, but in the not so distant future, we will grow. The start of a new order has begun! "

Maria and Susan each fired a stun spell at Wrightwood. Wrightwood's shield grew in brightness as the spells were absorbed into his shield spell. Wrightwood was laughing from behind his protective spell. Wrightwood's laughter grew louder and louder.

He floated over to Maria and Susan. The two were on their knees, holding Adam by his head and waist. Andrews moved himself over to them. Maria and Susan attempted another stun spell that had the same result as their last spell.

"Please move against the wall, Mr. Andrews," said Wrightwood. Andrews moved to the back wall of the room. Wrightwood raised his hands and aimed it at Susan.

"Mortem!" He shouted. A blue light shot from his palms, striking Susan and knocking her backwards onto the ground. He then aimed at Maria, and again shouted "Mortem!" The same result driving Maria onto her back. Adam's body dropped to the ground. Wrightwood directed his attention back to Adam. He looked at Andrews for a brief moment, before he returned his attention to Adam.

"Watch as I eliminate the third Order member." Wrightwood paused and raised his hands, aiming at Adam. "Mortem."

The blue light shot at Adam. Wrightwood returned his stare back to Andrews. He was speechless. He had just watched his assistant and confidant murder his friends.

"Amplus Attono." A thicker red light shot at Andrews, knocking him into the wall and back down to the ground. Wrightwood turned and retrieved the documents and placed them back into his briefcase. He walked toward the research room, and rummaged through the room, unable to find what he was looking for.

Wrightwood floated down to Andrews. "I now have the documents I am looking for, which confirms one thing for sure. I'm telling you this because I am looking forward to a face-off with the Order. But I must let you know that the world is not ready for the illumination of the evident transformation. At least not yet, but they will soon. Take care my friend, and good luck in finding us."

Wrightwood leaned toward Andrews' left ear and whispered, "The Scrutatores have returned to claim what is rightfully ours. I am Droken, bearer of knowledge." Wrightwood placed his right hand on Andrews's head.

"Oblivisci. Unfortunately Andrews, you will only remember what happened here and not who caused this."

He straightened up and made his way toward the elevator.

9

A STRANGE MEETING PLACE

The clock next to the bed displayed three a.m. on the digital display. The room was pitch black. Lannar was rolling from side to side on the large king-sized bed.

Standing in the graveyard, the wind blew, and the chill from the air caused him to shiver. A figure descended toward him. All around were tombstones and mausoleums. Trees were sporadically placed throughout the graveyard. The wind caused the leaves on each tree to rustle. There were four Celtic crosses connected in a row, making one singular tombstone. The moon was bright and full, with a halo effect around it. The clouds formed a straight line through the moon, and some appeared to be painted by a single stroke of a painter's brush. Despite the clouds, the moon still provided plenty of light.

The figure circled its way closer. Thunder started to boom, becoming louder as the figure neared the ground. Directly behind him sat a body of water, a small man-made lake. At the center of the lake stood a large, marble structure that resembled the Parthenon. The structure had six columns that supported a flat top. There were no walls to hide what was inside. Underneath the covering lie six marble coffins.

Around the structure, willow trees provided partial camouflage from the land across the water.

The gliding figure came toward him. It had a majestic pattern to its flying, and Lannar eagerly anticipated what he now knew was Seeker's landing. Seeker changed position from a prone position to one standing upright.

"My Lord," said Lannar, as he dropped to one knee.

"Rise, Lannar. I appreciate the gesture but I do not require you to bow down to me. That will be reserved for the other creatures of this beautiful plane."

Lannar stood up and shook the outstretched hand.

Seeker walked toward the lake, behind Lannar. Lannar turned and walked next to his Master.

"Have you assembled your team with loyal followers?"

Lannar turned his head to face Seeker as they continued their walk, "Yes, I have four devout Scrutatores descendants from the four major families."

Seeker faced Lannar. His remarkably handsome features stood out in the moonlight. "Good, your total number is seven. How appropriate."

Lannar was confused about the number comment. He wondered about the significance of the number.

"I can sense your confusion about the number seven. The resistance will come from a group of seven. They are descendants of the original deserters of our faith. When they left, they became the protectors of this plane. Because of them, I have not been able to make any attempts here, for many centuries. Once the portal is opened, and with the completion of the transformation, I will be able to send many different assaults upon this world. Once this world is conquered, I will be able to come and rule it."

Lannar understood the importance of the role he played in Seeker's plan. "I will not fail you, my Lord."

The two had reached the edge of where the land met the water. Seeker was pleased to hear his servant's respect. He stretched out his right hand and pointed to the small island. "Over there is all you will need to open the link between our planes."

Seeker took the first step toward the island, stepping on the water. Lannar hesitated to follow. Seeker stood on the water, and gave a devilish grin at Lannar. "Don't fear the water. It will not stand in your way. At least not here."

Lannar listened to his Lord, and walked out onto the water without any further hesitation. He walked up to where Seeker was standing. The two resumed their walk toward the large structure on the island.

"I can only communicate with you in dream, until the connection is made through the transformation. Here is where I can give you instructions, and show you what you need to do."

"Why is that?" asked Lannar.

"These are the parameters set up by the universe," replied Seeker.

They walked the rest of the distance across the water in silence. Lannar liked the sensation he felt, walking across the water. They reached the small island.

"There you will find the location of the tower. You also have the instructions on how to conduct the ceremony to complete the transformation," said Seeker.

The two made their way to the large structure. As they reached it, Lannar noticed that there were four more columns than what he first thought. All of the columns surrounded the four marble tombs inside.

Seeker glided to the center two marbled coffins. "This is where you will find all of the information that you will need."

Lannar tried to remove the top, unsuccessfully.

"This is a dream, but you will remember all that we have discussed, and all that you have seen."

"I will have my team come with me and retrieve the items inside."

Seeker walked to the front of the individual's tomb. "You will not be able to enter this cemetery, for if you do, a message will be sent to the messenger. He is the individual assigned to receive these clues. Share only what you need with your cohorts. They are not to know more than is necessary."

"They have sworn an oath to our cause," protested Lannar.

"I am well aware of that. However, they have free will. If they choose to turn or are captured, they will divulge."

Suddenly, they are standing in front of the cemetery. Seeker pointed to the name: DONOVAN. "You are familiar with this name. Send them at night. I will provide them with sufficient evening lighting," finished Seeker, laughing a deep, sinister laugh.

"Yes, my Lord."

"There is one more thing that needs to be done." Seeker glided on top of one of the marble tombs, "Eliminate the names retrieved by your assassin. They must not live."

Lannar nodded his head, acknowledging his Master.

"Send someone who will be able to do the job with no hesitation."

Lannar again just simply nodded his head.

"Yes, my Lord, it will be done."

Lannar awoke and searched for a pad and paper and wrote the names down that Seeker told him.

10

PLANNING

Lannar and three of his cohorts returned from some time spent at one of the Indiana Casinos. As they traveled down interstate 94, they commented on how they loved the view of the tall buildings that formed the Chicago skyline. No one in the car gave a second thought to his or her outcome at the casino. The view of downtown Chicago when driving in from Indiana offered a perspective of how large the downtown area really was.

"Watch it!" yelled Kantra from the back seat of the Lexus. Lannar was admiring the buildings and had briefly lost focus on his driving. He quickly swerved back into his lane.

The GPS guided them to Willis Tower. They all hated the name, but the GPS no longer recognized 'Sears Tower'. The large skyscraper, the tallest building inside of the United States, was now known as Willis Tower. Lannar commented about how American capitalism robbed the country of its historic importance.

As they reached the building, they parked the vehicle in the Madison Avenue parking garage, located across from the tall building. Lannar pulled into one of the reserved spots. The clothing that adorned them was not common dress for the weather. At ninety degrees and sunny, all black would cause most people to be rather hot and uncomfortable. The tall, dark haired woman was dressed in a black dress. The three men were dressed in black Armani suits. One was wearing a black fedora.

Kantra, an attractive, successful and extremely wealthy businesswoman, led them to the entrance of Willis Tower. Kantra was born to blue-collar parents. Love was not a shortcoming in her house. Tragically, she lost both her parents in a car accident, and was sent to her aunt and uncle on her mother's side. She enjoyed a relatively normal childhood and teenage years. She earned a Bachelors and Masters degree in business from Northwestern University. Kantra now ran a realty conglomerate that purchased land and buildings, then had William Donavan's company design and develop each building. She also had grand political ambitions.

Ulra had known Kantra since they were children, growing up in Villa Park, Illinois. Ulra was two years younger, although both had attended the same schools in a western suburb of Chicago. Ulra earned a finance degree from Northwestern University, and after graduating, landed a job through a friend of his at a business firm located in Paris, France. He worked and lived in France for five years. He reconnected with Kantra in Chicago through a chance encounter at the Harold Washington Library. They discovered they were both searching for reading material on the Scrutatores. They had both found out that they were descendants of an ancient group from Europe. This fact made both of them believe that there was a purpose for this reunion. That was the start of their renewed friendship, which led to a brief romance. However, after their romantic feelings subsided, their friendship blossomed into a tight and strong bond.

Macnar was a large, muscled male. He was Kantra's assistant in her realty company. He spent six years in the U.S. military as a Navy Seal, and had served in several wars and skirmishes. He received several commendations for valor in the line of duty. After his time in the military was up, he enrolled for classes at Northwestern University. Kantra was a guest lecturer for his class on Business Ethics. It was there that their association began. Kantra admired his ambition and once her career in realty started, she figured that he would be the perfect person to run her office. Macnar left his Catholic upbringing and joined Kantra and Ulra into the world of the Scrutatores.

Lannar leaned close to Kantra and whispered in her ear, “There is no time to waste, we need to get started.”

“We need to get to my office. You can inform us of our missions there,” she responded.

Lannar looked at her, slightly angry. “I'm growing impatient at the pace that things have been unfolding up to this point.”

Kantra tried to lighten the moment. “Then maybe we shouldn't have stopped at the casino,” she said lightly.

Lannar interrupted her. “There is a time and place for everything,” he said in a more forceful tone than before.

Kantra's joyful demeanor had faded. She quickly realized that Lannar wanted to move indoors. “This way, I'll take us to my office. It's the weekend, so there will be no one there to interrupt us,” she said.

“Good, we have a lot to discuss before we can execute our goal,” said Lannar.

With that, Kantra started walking toward another entrance, around the corner from the tourist entry. As they walked toward the protected entry, Kantra started to get the rushing feeling of embarking on the ultimate crusade to usher in a new reign over mankind.

As they reached the entry door, Kantra searched her purse for her ID card that granted her access to the building and then she suddenly realized that she left the ID at home. She had thought that they would be going to her condominium in Trump Tower. Lannar's sudden need to get inside made Kantra feel nervous, and now she was in a quagmire. She did not want to come across as incompetent or unreliable.

Macnar pulled out his entry card from his wallet. “Here you go Kantra, it must have slipped your mind that you gave your entry card to me, to hold onto.”

“Oh, thank you Macnar, with all the excitement I did forget that I gave you the card,” said Kantra gratefully, relieved and thankful that he had his card with him and that he had covered for her.

Lannar commented, “I must say, I too have had forgetful moments. I'm glad to see that you have competent assistants.”

"Yes, Macnar runs my real estate office," said Kantra.

Macnar swiped the card and pulled open the door, like a bellhop at a hotel. Macnar was the last to walk by Ulra.

As he walked by, Ulra said, "Fast thinking, bro. I'm glad you had yours, I left mine at home," he added.

Macnar followed Ulra inside. The door automatically closed itself. He looked at Ulra and said, "Luckily, I didn't take it out of my wallet like I usually do at the end of the week."

"Let's say that sometimes it's better to be lucky, than good," Ulra finished.

Macnar chuckled and agreed. "Yes it is, yes it is."

Everyone had followed Kantra inside. They made their way toward the security desk; sitting there was Tyrone Johnson. Tyrone had worked as a security officer at the Willis Tower since the building was built. For thirty-six years, the not-so-slender African American had been in charge of Tower security. He had admired Kantra for a long time. Not just for her beauty, but also for the way she treated him. Since leasing her office space in the building, Kantra always treated Tyrone kindly and with respect. She never acted like a rich, arrogant person around him. It didn't matter if she was alone or with a client, a conversation of some sort always happened. She always remembered him on his birthday and also during the Christmas season by giving him a rather modest monetary gift.

From behind his desk, Tyrone stood up to greet Kantra and her guests. " Good afternoon lovely lady, if I may, you look as beautiful as ever," said Tyrone in a pleasant tone.

"Good afternoon to you, Tyrone and thank you for your kind compliment," she replied.

"Not used to seeing you in on a Saturday, ma'am." Tyrone continued talking as they reached the desk, "Don't worry about ID's, I've known you for twenty-some years ma'am."

"You are so sweet, Tyrone. They'll be in and out of the building. I was wondering do you have an extra swipe card? This gentleman is Lannar, and he'll need a temporary access card," said Kantra.

Tyrone started fumbling around the desk. He opened the top drawer and pulled out a stack of swipe cards. "You'll need only one." Tyrone removed a card and activated it by swiping it into the computer on his desk. He typed in Lannar's name and handed it to Kantra.

"Thank you, doll," she said.

"Anything for you, ma'am," said Tyrone.

Ulra and Macnar addressed Tyrone as they walked past him, and he responded with his usual greeting to them. "Hello, gentlemen," he said.

The elevator was about forty feet from the security desk. The large foyer area was adorned with different pictures and paintings of Chicago, and was well lit with large, bright lights. There was plenty of seating, with different types of furniture throughout the foyer. Macnar informed his new associates that they were about to enter one of the fastest elevators, and warned them that their ears would pop.

Kantra pressed the button for the ninety-eighth floor. As the elevator reached the seventh floor, it had reached its top speed. At this moment, their ears started to pop. Kantra was the first to exit the elevator. She turned left and started toward her office. The rest followed. On her way, Kantra reached into her purse and searched for the key, then inserted it into the lock. She instructed everyone to wait outside, and as she entered, she closed the door behind her. Next to the door to her left was the keypad, where she entered the code to turn the alarm off. She opened the door and each of them walked in.

The large, open office had two desks in the foyer to greet business associates upon entering. It resembled a large studio condo unit, in that there were no walls inside of the large space. Toward the back were two conference rooms and three large offices.

Kantra led everyone into the largest of the conference rooms. Lannar sat in the seat at the head of the large table in the room.

After a brief prelude, Lannar stood and walked over to a map of Mexico on the wall and pointed explaining, "Here in Mexico there is an object that we need in order to complete our mission."

Everyone focused on the map, with great curiosity. They started to wonder what item could be so important that was located in Mexico.

"You all can see that there are maps of two other places," Lannar pointed to a map on the southern wall from the door. "That one is a map of Greece, and there is an object we need there as well."

He pointed to the wall on the opposite side of the room, "That is a map of Paris and there is also something we need from there."

Before he finished his sentence, he started walking back to his seat. "That's what we have to discuss; how and when we retrieve the items needed to accomplish our goals."

Ulra is the first person to speak. "I believe that we should first discuss the significance of each item, so that all of us will understand the importance of each one."

Everyone at the table nodded their heads in agreement.

"I also believe that we should discuss the process of retrieving these special items, Lannar," continued Ulra.

Lannar squinted his eyes and in a peculiar manner directed his gaze toward Ulra. "Ulra, I appreciate the respect you have given me," said Lannar in a calm and assuring voice, "However, there are forces that are here on this plane that will attempt to stop us. I have already taken the first steps in weakening them. The specific items I have mentioned are needed to complete the mission our ancestors could not complete, but they are not all needed right now. We will retrieve them and I will discuss the importance of each item at that appropriate time. However, in Mexico is a special and powerful artifact," he said.

Each time Lannar talked, he gained instant attention from all those within the range of his voice. Lannar was a very charismatic individual. His strong good looks and the soothing deepness in his voice were capable of captivating any audience. All in the room were listening intently to what he was saying.

Lannar paused for a brief moment, felt the curiosity in the room but no question arose, so he continued, "In Mexico, within the ruins of the Mayan Empire, is an artifact that will aid us in the transformation and the opening of the gateway."

Excitement in the room started to become evident with the word 'transformation'. "Our first mission is to retrieve this special artifact."

Ulra was the first of the captive audience to speak, "Lannar, what is the specific need for this special artifact? Whom will be assigned this task of finding it, and how?"

"Well, the artifact is the key, or I should say, has the power, to unleash a devastating plague."

Kantra's curiosity was piqued. "Lannar, how does a plague help us in our mission of transforming the world for Seeker?" she asked Lannar.

Lannar had been waiting for this specific question. "I'm glad you asked that. Yes, we are preparing this plane for Seeker's coming, and in order to do so we need to place the world in a state of fear. The first step is unleashing a devastating plague. None in this room will be affected by the plague. You will all be in the room where the ritual will be taking place. Therefore, the artifact will protect all of you."

Macnar, whose place in the group was toward the bottom of the totem pole, spoke up enthusiastically, "If I may, I would be more than willing to help with the search in Mexico."

Lannar spoke directly to him, "Once I met you, I knew you would be heading there. Do you speak Spanish?"

"Yes, I do," replied Macnar.

Lannar continued speaking directly to Macnar, "You will have someone from our current group here, or one of the recruited members accompany you. Together, you will locate and retrieve the artifact, and bring it back to Chicago."

Lannar walked to the overhead projector placed in the room. He looked at Kantra and asked her, "Are the pictures I asked you to locate for me ready to be displayed?"

Kantra walked over to the laptop, "I will start up the laptop and go to the website I found regarding the artifact." She turned the laptop on quickly logged in.

Ulra arose from his chair and walked over and dimmed the lights in the room. Kantra had brought up the site. Lannar paused before he began. He passed through a series of ancient Mayan artifacts until he reached what he was looking for.

Everyone sitting around the table watched in awe as the picture projected onto the large screen. They were extremely curious as to how the object contained the power to devastate the world by unleashing a terrible plague. The image was of a solid gold plate with intricate art-work on the layers throughout it. There were eight large pyramids that started on the second layer, and the points of them shaped into the start of the first layer. They pointed to specific actions by humans, committing terrible atrocities.

In the center of the plate was a large, engraved image. The image was the Scrutatores symbol. Inside the Scrutatore symbol was a Mayan farmer harvesting his crop as the Sun was about to be eclipsed by the moon. The farmer had a look of despair and pain oh his face. Engraved in the background were human bodies, laying face down on the ground, and standing over them, a skeleton with a giant sickle.

Lannar's face displayed a large grin. The picture on the screen captivated him. "That, my associates, is the item we need to retrieve."

Ulra asked, "Do you know where it's at in Mexico?"

Lannar divulged the remainder of the information that the group needed to know. "The artifact is somewhere in the jungles near Chichen Itza, Mexico. This area is also called the Yucatan Peninsula. We will need to form a team to retrieve the artifact from there."

Lannar knew he needed to explain the power of the artifact, and he knew that this would work as a motivating factor to expedite the mission. "This particular artifact was believed to have been destroyed. My friends, this is a false belief. The plate does still exist."

Lannar poured himself a glass of ice water from one of the pitchers on the table. He was able to feel the anxiousness of the group, to find out the story behind the plate. He began by saying, "A terrible plague had been ravishing the Mayan people. The Mayan priests believed that they needed to pay homage to the plague in order to revert it. The priests had no idea what they were doing. They believed that the plague was a curse placed on the Mayan people by their god. They figured that if the plague were given some sort of recognition, or offering, that their god would relieve the people from their suffering. The reality is that the plague was brought on by the practices of one of their priests."

The people sitting around the table are completely drawn into the recounting of Mayan legend by Lannar. The group listened intently as Lannar continued speaking. He began explaining who the Mayan priest was and his intention for starting the plague.

"The priest was known as Tentatuin. His name means 'destruction of light'. Tentatuin wanted to change the god they worshiped from Quetzalcoatl. The new deity's name was Yum Cimil, the god of death. He was believed to be a lesser, but still a very powerful god by the other Mayan priests. They felt that the god's main goal was to devastate and destroy all that he came in contact with. Yum Cimil brought on plagues and wars and many other forms of violence to the Mayans. The Mayans, being a religious race, believed in pleasing their gods. The responsibility of keeping the gods happy and content for the Mayans belongs to their priests."

Lannar began the part of the tale that involved Tentatuin's actions. "Tentatuin was not the High Priest, but his desire however, was to become the High Priest. The only way this could happen was by eliminating the current High Priest. The two were the same in age; outliving him was not an option. In order to eliminate the High Priest, he started praying to Yum Cimil to take the High Priest's life. The Mayan priests believed that human sacrifices were the best way to gain favor with any god. Tentatuin knew he had to offer human sacrifices to Yum Cimil, in secret. Tentatuin himself would be sacrificed if they knew he was performing these sacrifices without their approval."

Lannar loved when he had to explain about human sacrifices. This was very evident in his tone of voice. "His sacrifices consisted of young children, because they were easier to lure and take outside of the city. Children also represented pure innocence. Sneaking a child out of the city in daylight would prove to be difficult. Tentatuin would have the child drink a concoction that would cause them to fall asleep within minutes. The children would vary between ten and twelve years of age. Mayan's did not usually perform human sacrifices with children.

Lannar was fond of Tentatuin and it showed, as he explained the sacrifices with great delight. "Tentatuin brought his victims to an altar he had constructed, not far from one of their pyramids. Once there, he performed the sacrificial ceremony before he offered their lives to Yum Cimil in order to gain his favor."

Lannar began explaining the process Tentatuin used on the victims. "Tentatuin would have the victim drink a potion that would cause a mind-altering state that would make them numb to the procedure of the sacrifice."

The mere mention of potion excited Kantra.

"The victims would have their throat slit first; their blood would flow into a gold pot. The blood would be boiled with the victim's intestines. The final part of the ceremony was to drink a cup of the mixture, then burn the body in offering. He would do this twice a week."

The explanation of the sacrifice made the three feel a bit queasy.

Lannar explained how devious Tentatuin was. "Tentatuin had tricked priests into forging a plate and pot out of gold. He explained what was needed on the plate. The pictures served the purpose of praising the activities of Yum Cimil. Tentatuin had told the priests that the plate would work as a deterrent for plagues and other forms of evil. Tentatuin knew that the plate had to be forged by a different priest than the one practicing the sacrifices."

Kantra loved hearing about an individual that could easily manipulate others to work for them. She also was in awe over how Lannar was telling the tale of Tentatuin.

"He knew that the younger priests could be misled into making the plate. To keep the High Priest from finding out, he had instructed them that it would be gift to the High Priest. Naturally wanting to be obedient to their superior, and impress the High Priest, the priests went along with Tentatuin's plan without ever questioning it."

Ulra was also impressed with the way Tentatuin was able to execute his plan. As Lannar's general, he understood the necessity to have a plan and have the plan carried out.

"Tentatuin instructed the priests on what was to go on the plate and the procedures in making the plate designed to gain Yum Cimil's favor. The plate was completed in several days. The gold needed was in the Empire's reserve and all priests had access to the gold, as long as it was used to serve a religious purpose. Tentatuin had paid off the guards to keep quiet."

A grin appeared on Macnar's face as he heard the part of paying the guards off. He had performed this action many times for Kantra and Ulra.

Lannar's speaking became intense. "Tentatuin needed to complete seven sacrifices by the new moon. The plate was completed in several days and Tentatuin needed the plate at each of the sacrifices. The plague began several days after the last sacrifice. A person that contracted the plague would first become easily fatigued, followed by unexplained bleeding. The person would then contract a high fever and migraine headaches. The next phase was excruciating muscle pain. In the final stages, a person's skin would become severely dry, and then in the final days, all organs would stop functioning, bringing on death. The plague caused the person to suffer unimaginable pain for only a week, but itself lasted for several months. It ended when the altar was discovered and Tentatuin was executed.

"It was traced back to him because of a personal article of clothing that he had inadvertently left behind; his priest garment used during the human sacrifices. Tentatuin was put to death. With his death the plague had come to an end. The priests had divulged the information on the plate. History writes that the plate was destroyed with the altar, but it is believed that the plate was buried with Tentatuin.

Lannar divulged a small portion of his plan to the group, "The plate will provide us with the ability to open the doorway between this plane and the former plane. By opening the doorway we will have the ability to conjure many different mythological creatures that no longer inhabit this plane."

Kantra and her two assistants had a hard time believing that a doorway could be opened to bring creatures that are not real to life.

Lannar picked up on their thoughts by their facial expressions.

"I see you doubt this. I understand you have limited understanding of the worlds around you. It's expected, I would doubt this too, if I were any of you."

Lannar motioned for them to stop their questions. "I understand, because I have been contacted by the Seeker. You need to believe me. We all came here from another plane and on that plane, the creatures that humans believe are not real actually exist."

Lannar saw their acceptance of what he was saying. He used this as an opportunity to continue, "Tentatuin did not fully understand the power of the plate he had created. Through the sacrifices and his lust for power, the plate became a doorway to Seeker's plane. All this was written in the Book of Knowledge. We will also have the ability to unleash a terrible plague onto all of humanity. The plague is the first step toward descending the world into our control. Humanity needs to be weak to doubt all they have believed to be true. There are other measures that we will need to accomplish, but that will be for a later date."

The notion that a plague could be unleashed in such as manner stunned everyone sitting at the table. For Ulra, it seemed inconceivable to accomplish such a feat. Lannar did not detect the doubt that Ulra was feeling, and even if he did, he would not have cared.

"The area we will target first is the continent of North America. We will discuss the procedures at a later date. For now, we need to focus on the retrieval of the plate. We need to find the burial grounds of Tentatuin. That will be a difficult task, but a task we must complete. We also need to retrieve the Book of Knowledge. While one group goes to get the plate the other will get the Book."

Lannar finished his presentation. They all left the Willis Tower in anticipation of their next meeting.

11

TIME FOR THE YOUNG

Summer was now over. Well, at least for teenagers about to start college. Moving day was tomorrow, and the first day of school was only a week away. Dwayne, Bridgette, and David decided to relax in the large family room on the second floor inside the orphanage. Dwayne was sitting in the recliner in full reclining position. Bridgette was stretched out on one of the three couches, and David was throwing darts at the dartboard. All three of them were reflecting on the past summer and the years spent in the Catholic Orphanage. This evening was their last in the large house. They never questioned why they were the only ones in the facility, as it had been explained to them that there were more children there prior to them arriving, and that the number of children they could take in had declined due to lack of funding, and that they were the last. The facility would be closing down upon their departure to college.

"Where's Rosa?" asked Bridgette, as she played a game on her new phone.

"I think she's breaking up with that Conrad guy she met at Starbucks a few months ago," said Dwayne, as he was staring at the bright blue ceiling. "I met that guy two weeks ago...talk about a creep."

"I didn't have the honor of meeting Sir Conrad," said David in a sarcastic tone. "The eve of the start of our college years, and she's breaking some poor saps heart. What a shame."

Once they returned from Michigan, David had started working at the Field Museum. His long hours on either the day or night shift prevented him from enjoying the remainder of the summer. He had gotten some free time on several weekends, but nothing compared to his friends, or rather, his family. The bitterness of not being free to explore the city before he left bothered him a little. But he did enjoy working on the Book of Knowledge display. He had been introduced to several important and prominent Chicagoans.

"Conrad made her happy...for a little while at least," said Bridgette.

"Dave, you need to relax, you're the one that chose to work this summer," said Dwayne, reminding David that the decision to work on a project at the museum that he loved was his doing. "How long did they go out for?"

"Several months," said Bridgette enthusiastically.

"I bet that she couldn't stand his need to always be right," said Dwayne.

"I don't know," said David.

"Hey Bridgette, how long did you date Mr. Personality for?" Dwayne asked.

"I'd say about five months, most of senior year."

"Who dumped who?" David asked.

"There was no dumping it was mutual. Besides he could have been the most boring guy on the planet."

The door to the room opened and Rosa walked in. She didn't say a word, just walked over to the couch that Bridgette was sitting on and dropped onto it. Rosa stared at the ground. Bridgette, David, and Dwayne looked at each other, confused by Rosa's demeanor. They were under the impression that she had planned on ending her summer fling.

"You okay?" asked Bridgette.

No one said anything; they just waited for Rosa's response. Finally, she ended the quietness in the room.

"Yeah, I'm fine. It's just that he didn't care. In fact, he actually broke up with me. Can you believe that?"

Dwayne could not control himself. "He dumped you?" said Dwayne, followed by his laughing.

"Shut up, Dwayne," said Bridgette, looking at Dwayne with a scowl on her face. In a quick reversal, she turned back directing herself to Rosa. "Seriously, Conrad dumped you?"

"Yeah, he did," said Rosa slowly. "It was weird. He picked me up around seven, and he had planned on dinner, but I thought that we should talk, because I didn't want him paying for dinner. That would make me such a bitch."

David placed his darts on the Ping-Pong table and walked to the brown leather couch, across from the girls.

"I asked him to drive to the lake first," continued Rosa, not pausing for David's movement. "I really wanted to have a nice place to discuss our relationship, well actually the lack of any relationship. At the lake, he started talking about how he was getting involved in an important role in a group he was joining," continued Rosa, "He then said it's nothing that I did, and the group was going to work somewhere in Europe, and that he would be going to Cambridge instead of UIC."

"How did Conrad get into Cambridge?" asked Dwayne. "There is no way. That boy's family must have some deep pockets to get him in there."

David started laughing before Dwayne finished his sentence.

"I agree, he's dumber than a box of rocks but he was kind and sweet," said Rosa. "That's one of the reasons I wanted to end it with him. Intellectually, he's not even close to Dwayne."

Rosa and Bridgette were now laughing with David. Dwayne sat there for brief moment and then joined the laughter at his expense.

"Okay, it's over, let's talk about tomorrow," said Bridgette.

Before they could begin, they heard someone knock on the door. As the person walked in, it became evident that none of them knew this person. The man looked to be about six feet in height and in good shape. They wondered why he was wearing a long black leather jacket in August. Dwayne got off the chair and moved next to David on the couch. The man walked over to the fireplace in front of the furniture arrangement where they were sitting. The man placed his right hand on the mantel and started talking to them.

"I'm sure you are all curious as to who I am, and my reason for being here."

"I'm actually wondering why you're wearing a leather jacket in August," said Dwayne.

The man chuckled at Dwayne's comment. "My name is James Stewart." The mention of his name did not mean anything to them. None of them were able to recall the name or his face. A bald man with a thick mustache would have stood out.

"I am here to inform you all of a change in plans. You are not going to the University of Chicago tomorrow, or in the visible future."

All four of the young teenagers began speaking at once in loud voices. As they are all speaking they did not notice head mistress Mary walk in. She walked up and stood next to James.

"Please stop and listen," said Mary, "I know this is a shock, and I truly wish that Mr. Stewart would have been a little more tactful as he broke the news... but it is true. Before you continue your talk, I want to let the four of you know how much I love and care for all of you." Mary said, fighting off her tears. "I would never trade the last sixteen years for anything. No matter what you will learn about yourselves, I will always be there for you." The onslaught of tears was unstoppable. "I need you all to know I love each of you as if you were born from me."

They each gazed at Mary. They had always viewed her as their mother. Each had expressed their feelings before, except that this time there seemed to be something happening.

"How about an explanation?" Bridgette demanded. "We are entitled to one."

Another person walked into the room as Bridgette asked her question. He walked quickly toward James and gave him a strong hug. The hug lasted for a few seconds and they each patted the others back as they ended their embrace. The man turned and gave Mary a strong hug as well. “Thank you, Mary, for everything. I should have thanked you a long time ago. Thank you.” The man turned to face James.

“John Williams, good to see you. Real good, my old friend.” said James.

“Likewise,” said John.

The news of the deaths of their associates and friends reached them a few hours ago. Their first order of business was to assemble at the house of the first Order member to live in Chicago, the house of James Sullivan I, and retrieve and protect the future Order members.

Bridgette reflected for a brief moment, about the fact that she had the same surname as John. She quickly pushed the thought aside, for if he were related to her, surely she would have seen him before.

12

BACK TO LONDON

John and James were fighting their grief over the loss of the three Order members, and were working toward getting the four teens safely to London. John looked at the teens, but he avoided looking at Bridgette directly.

"We need to leave right away. Get all your bags." John is unable to finish any further thoughts, as Bridgette interrupts him.

"Excuse me? We're not going anywhere, and who are you two?" She said pointing at John and James. "Before we go anywhere I need a better explanation as to why I'm not going to school tomorrow," Bridgette said, talking loudly and with an authoritative tone in her voice. John and James shared a brief smile. It was obvious to them that Bridgette inherited much of her father's traits.

John's attempt at avoiding eye contact with Bridgette has now become unavoidable. There have been a lot of feelings he's had to deal with. The first was the loss of life that happened several hours ago. Now, standing in front of him was his deceased brother's daughter. The niece he has had to stay away from, for her safety. While he looked at her, he was amazed at how she had grown. When he dropped her off at the Andrews "orphanage" she had just celebrated her second birthday, the last event with her parents. He accepted the teaching position at the University of Chicago to keep a watchful eye on her and the other teens.

The other teens were also present at her party. All four teens were descendants of past Order members. There was speculation that their parents' deaths were not accidental, as they had been ruled. There was never any proof of foul play, however the deaths of four people related to Order members was highly suspicious since their bodies were never retrieved or found. John was fighting back his emotions as he addressed Bridgette.

"I agree, you deserve an explanation, it's just that this is not the time nor the place."

Time was unstoppable. John had to move quickly. He paused for a moment, and thought of how to move the situation forward. "You, all of you, are part of an important group," said John.

"What? I asked for an explanation and this is what you offer-- some confusing speech?" Bridgette said angrily.

David stood from his spot on the couch. "Can you give us a brief explanation?"

"Brief? We deserve more than that," interjected Bridgette.

"John, just tell them so that we can move on," said James.

"Fine. I know we are asking for blind faith in us. I know that none of you know us, and we are asking a lot from you without any proof."

John moved from the fireplace to the couch Bridgette and Rosa were sitting on. He sat between them. "All of you were brought here right after your parents died. That was done for your safety. All the questions you have regarding your past and your family will be answered. All of you have a special gift that only a handful of us have. James and I have the same ability, and your parents had this ability."

John now moved himself from the couch to where James was standing. "The two of us are part of a group that is responsible for fighting evil whenever it makes itself present, and it has. If any of you want to be a part of this group, and find the answers to all of your questions regarding your family, then come with us. The decision has to be yours."

Bridgette and the others sat silently. Each of them was in deep thought trying to take in and make sense of the information. Dwayne, David, and Rosa looked at Bridgette to deliver their decision.

Bridgette stood up again. She looked directly at each of her fellow teens, one at a time, before delivering the message that she knew they were in agreement. Turning to John and James, "This is getting weird."

"Are all of you are willing to come to London, and decide from there what your future will be?" James asked.

"Not until we have proof of this special ability you're talking about," said Bridgette, calmly.

"James, I'll show them." James nodded his head in agreement with John. John placed both hands in front of him. His action caused David and Dwayne to chuckle. John was looking at the Ping-Pong table.

"Tollere," said John, motioning with hands in an upward motion. The Ping-Pong table was raised from the floor.

"Movere," was the next word he spoke. He moved the table from one end of the room back to its original spot with the motion of his hands. The teens went from a sitting position to standing. They were in awe of what John was doing. John looked at the four standing teens. He had a grin on his face. "Each of you has the ability to do what I just did and so much more."

"So, you guys want to come to Britain and learn some magic and fight off evil?" Interjected James.

All four teens replied affirmatively.

"Great, let's get going then, shall we?" James finished.

"You four go get your things, everything. None of you will be coming back here to live," said John.

"Fine. But I still want a better explanation when we get to London." Bridgette said, and as she finished, the others got off the couch to collect their belongings.

James, John, and Mary helped them load up the two vehicles. Marry assured them that she would collect the belongings that they didn't pack and send them to London through a secured route.

John traveled with the teens to London. James went back to the Field Museum to continue his work on the Book of Knowledge. The flight to London was a quiet one. The four young adults were gathering their thoughts and questions regarding their parents, and perhaps wondering what their special abilities were. The other thought rested on what group John was referring to.

John himself contemplated how he would explain and answer all their questions. He was also concerned with how his niece would react to learning that he was her uncle, and that he had stayed out of her life for the last sixteen years, a choice that he believed needed to be made for her safety. This decision had caused him great pain. Each time a picture or video of a birthday or any event of hers passed, it caused the pain to reemerge itself. Now the pain was accompanied by guilt. In the afternoon, he and the four teens would be arriving in London. John was excited, hopeful, and nervous at the prospect of finally establishing a relationship with his niece.

13

FLIGHT

As the plane landed, the silence continued as Bridgette, Rosa, Dwayne, and David exited the plane. John had spent the entire flight thinking about how to explain to Bridgette that his absence in her life was not intentional. Intentional or unintentional, each of them was feeling frightened, confused, and lonely. None of them had ever felt emptiness like this before. Even though they were about to learn about their families, the information had already started to create a cavern in the pit of their stomachs.

The evening sky displayed a bright moon. There were some clouds, but it was a relatively beautiful evening. The weather in London resembled Chicago's weather. Waiting several feet away from the plane was a black limousine, and John entered the car before the four teens. Andrews had made all the security arrangements since the incident in his castle.

As they entered the limo, John received a text message from Andrews, informing him that there was much to discuss upon their arrival. John realized that Andrews' text was intended to serve as a reminder that there were more important matters to discuss with

Bridgette than her parents. John texted back letting Andrews know that he understood. Andrews replied with a text informing John that Emily and Julia were grasping the cleric ways rather quickly, and their arrival was anticipated. Also, he mentioned that James needed to stay in Chicago to watch over the Book of Knowledge. John was not pleased with that turn of events. He had been planning to examine the Book of Knowledge himself, and record information extracted from the important discovery. The book was John's greatest find. The idea that he was unable to examine it further bothered him. As the limo pulled out of the airport's private section, he looked over at Bridgette. Without speaking to her, he made an easy inference that she was hurting. He was brought back to the important things in life. He knew that she was more important than any find and he desperately needed to express this to her.

The trip from the airport to Andrews Castle was a forty-minute ride. The limo pulled up to the castle, and standing outside the main entrance was Andrews. He was anxious to see and welcome the four teens. He hadn't seen them since they were toddlers. The entire perimeter of the castle was set up with the lights ten feet apart from the next light. The bright lights brought out the white colored stones of the castle. The limo pulled up to Andrews. He was standing outside the walls that surrounded the complex. Inside the limo, John opened the door and Andrews climbed inside. He introduced himself to everyone, as the limo drove the remaining fifty feet to the main door.

As they exited, the teens looked around inside the complex. The inside was as well lit as the outside. They noticed how well kept the grounds were. As they entered the castle, they were amazed by the splendor inside. They had never seen as much marble in one place before. As they moved further into the main room, they noticed a large spiral staircase that ended at the exposed second floor. The main room had a large, white grand piano and fancy couches.

Andrews asked everyone to follow him into the main dining room. He walked quickly toward two large oak doors. John followed directly behind him, walking slightly slower than Andrews. The four teens followed, looking around, impressed with the amount of wealth throughout. As they entered the large room, they noticed the largest oak table they had ever seen. The table was set with expensive china. Twenty-four chairs were around the table. Hanging directly over it was an extravagant crystal chandelier. The lighting in the room was set at low. Towards the back of the room was an immensely large fireplace.

"Everyone take a seat, you must be hungry," said Andrews. "The cook has prepared a light soup for you."

Bridgette and the others gingerly took a seat at the table. Once seated, David examined the silverware. "Man, check out how much these things shine."

John looked over at Andrews and nodded his head, signaling their agreement. Andrews pushed his chair back and stood. He turned his attention to the teens.

"I want to properly welcome you to my home," said Andrews. "I would also like to take a few moments to inform you of your options. All of you will have to make an important decision. I'd like to apologize in advance for the directness I will be taking on the topic soon to be at hand."

Bridgette, Rosa, and David were listening intently to Andrews. Dwayne, on the other hand, was paying more attention to the healthy bowl of soup he was eating. Hearing the slurping sound next to her, Rosa delivered an elbow shot to Dwayne's side. The instant shock and slight pain effectively brought his attention back to the other three.

"Each of you are part of an ancient lineage, a group that has existed since the dawn of humankind," said Andrews. "You are each a potential part of the group known as the Order of Seven. If you decide to join, you will need to participate in a small ceremony, it's really quite simple."

"This is moving way too fast," said Bridgette. "I believe I'm going to speak for all of us, when I say, we want information regarding our parents. I'm not interested in a group, not right now. I want to learn about my parents, I want to know my heritage."

She looked directly at John. "I want to get to know my family. I don't think I'm asking too much. I said 'I' a lot, but I meant 'we' need to know," ended Bridgette.

John walked around the table directly to Bridgette. He kneeled down on one knee by her chair. He extended his hand to hers, and Bridgette placed both hands on his.

"I promise I will tell you all I know about your parents," said John. "But as much as this may hurt, you are going to have to wait for us to talk about all that. There are matters that require all our attention and efforts immediately. The one bit of information is that each of your parents were murdered on the same day."

Each teen looked at each other. They were under the impression that their parents died in an accident on different days of the same year.

"We now feel that the matter at hand is connected with your parents' disappearance. There was never a recovery of their bodies." John explained.

Andrews tapped his walking stick on the table. John stood up and walked toward him. "For now, eat and we can talk after you have finished."

Andrews turned his attention to John. "You stay here, I'll return when everyone is finished." Speaking in a low tone, so only John could hear him, "You need to start bonding with all of them. You and the other members will need to train them, if they decide to join." He didn't wait for John to reply. He stood from the table and made his way out of the room.

Andrews had gone down to the underground portion of the far tower to gather some material. He had spent an hour locating the indoctrination ritual. When he came back into the portion of the castle that his guests were in he met John in the kitchen. John was sitting at the kitchen table drinking a cup of coffee.

"I love the coffee you have here."

"Good to hear that, I spend an obscene amount of Pounds to have that imported from South America," said Andrews as he placed a large book on the table.

"What's this?" John asked, as he moved the book in front of him and opened it in the middle.

"That is the ceremonial book needed to conduct the indoctrination of new members. "

"Wow, this thing is thick. I don't recall the ceremony taking much time and by the size of this book I'd say it will take a week to conduct."

Andrews laughed at the comment. John continued thumbing through the book.

"No, your ceremony did not take that long. If you remember, you replaced your brother. In the book there are special ceremonies for different reasons that a member is replaced. There is also a ceremony for a natural indoctrination."

John looked up from the section he was reading. "Natural indoctrination?"

"Yes, when a member of the Order has passed away from natural causes, the replacing member is indoctrinated for natural reasons. Therefore that ceremony is conducted differently than when replacing for an untimely demise."

"I see. However, there are only three members that have been assassinated and we have four members to indoctrinate."

"Well, that's the part I've been reading up on. It appears that since they come as a foursome, each are to be indoctrinated under the untimely ceremony and for the time being the Order of Seven will be made of eight members."

"Can we have eight members?"

"My brief search in the archives uncovered a time for a very short period that there were nine members at one point in the Order's history back in the 1400's."

"Nine members. I can only imagine how those meetings went." John commented, causing the two men to breakout in laughter.

Andrews walked over to John and asked for the Book of Ceremony. He opened it to the page of the ceremony they would be conducting. "John, familiarize yourself with this spell. You will need to cast it as we walk outside. I think the back portion of the castle will suffice."

John spent the next twenty minutes familiarizing himself with the spell. While he was reading about how to cast the spell, Andrews brewed up a new pot of coffee. Andrews had two cups by the time John understood the procedure for the spell.

"Ready," said John.

"Good, then would you be so kind as to go and gather the future Order members? I would like to finish my coffee."

"On my way." John left the kitchen and headed for the second floor.

As he walked, he started thinking about the inexperience of the soon to be new members. John realized that the circumstances had led to them being indoctrinated tonight. His emotions were mixed.

John led them down to the kitchen were Andrews was waiting for them. Andrews asked for everyone to join him in the large room adjacent to the kitchen. In the room was a long table. On the table were six black robes. He handed a robe to each new member. John recognized his robe by the Order symbol. His robe was also black. The only difference is that his robe had the Earth and seven swords piercing through it. The Earth resembled a pincushion with swords in it instead of pins. Andrews' robe was white with a red cross in the front portion and one in the back. The Templar connection was evident from his robe. Andrews was the first to place his robe on. His pride beamed as he tied and smoothed out his robe.

"At each ceremony a Knights Templar has always been present and tonight's ceremony is no different," Andrews proudly proclaimed. John patted Andrews on his back.

"There will never be an Order without the Templar."

"You're a Knights Templar?" David asked excitedly.

"Well, technically yes, but we do not go by that name any longer," said Andrews in a somber manner. "We are now Stamens. We exist throughout all of Europe and in the Western hemisphere. Our role with the Order has not changed or wavered. We will always be there to assist and aid the Order with all our means," he said proudly. "Now, if you will all follow me outside."

Each teen was feeling nervous. They had made the decision to join. In part because they believed it's what their parents would want for them. They also felt a sense of loyalty and honor to be a member of the Order. Another aspect was that they were excited about learning how to use magic.

John was the first to enter the enormous back portion of Andrews' castle. From the glass doors one could not see the back portion of the ten-foot stonewall that circled the back portion. There were two small buildings three stories in height at the very back end of the large yard.

There was a cemented driveway that led to the two buildings that ran alongside the stonewall.

Andrews and the teens stood behind John, as he was several feet in front of them. John stretched out both his arms. He had his hands straightened and his palms facing the open space in front of him. John started speaking in Latin, referencing the deaths of those before, and the new members stepping up to fulfill their new roles. Only Andrews understood what he was saying. None of the teens had learned the ancient language.

"Sun and moon bring to us the needed light," chanted John. As he finished he waved his arms while maintaining his hands in the same position the entire time. Suddenly, a large altar appeared. John and Andrews started walking toward the stone altar. Andrews turned and waved for the teens to follow. John and Andrews reached the altar. John walked directly behind the stoned object. Andrews went and stood to his right. Standing in front of the altar, side by side were the four teens. Twenty-four hours ago they were preparing to start college. Now they were preparing to make a lifelong commitment.

"The four individuals in front of this ancient structure have agreed to pledge themselves to the cause of protecting humanity from any onslaught of evil. I ask you all, are you each willing to accept the role that will be entrusted to each of you? Are you willing to pledge your life, your remaining time on this planet to any cause that may arise? Are you willing to follow the code of the Order of Seven? Your answer to each will be conducted as an individual; your participation will be as a group member. The decision is yours to make. The answer you give will be the answer that represents the decision that only can be made by you."

Andrews translated the words spoken by John. The teens answered all of the questions posed to them. They each answered with a confident yes.

"Welcome, my new companions, in the fight against evil. You are each now a member of the Order of Seven."

14

THE SEARCH

Saturday morning arrived quickly. Andrews was using Bridgette and the others to search for any historical documentation on the Order's use of powerful magic. Andrews' encounter that led to deaths of three Order members and the erasure of his memory of who did the dastardly deed demonstrated the strength of spells used. Andrews had never come across any document on this topic before. While Andrews was leading the search in the castle, John headed back to Chicago where James was searching the Sullivan House. They figured that Sullivan would have placed that information in a secret and private place, perhaps his personal journal.

They had also concluded that the house he died in might be a good place to start. In the early 1900's James Sullivan had moved the Order headquarters to Chicago. Many of the Order members had continued to live in Europe, but the meetings and general business he moved outside of Europe. It wasn't until his death in the late 1980's that Andrews moved the headquarters of the Order back to London.

Andrews addressed the four new Order members in the document room underneath the castle. "I hope you all are awake and ready to start searching. If you need energy, there is the coffee pot and in the fridge are some cans of Red Bull. Help yourself with anything. At lunchtime we'll head up."

They spent the next seven hours combing through many documents. They were unaware that they had spent the last seven hours with no break or stop. Bridgette was surprised that David, Dwayne, and Rosa had stayed focused the entire time. She came to the conclusion that the seriousness of being an Order member and the excitement of working on an important mission had led to their ability to focus.

"Do we have any findings to report on?" Asked Andrews.

"Yes, I think we found a document that dates back to the Avignon Schism," said Bridgette.

Andrews was pleased by the hard work of the new members. Lately, anything in the form of success had been difficult to come by. Attention had now shifted to what Rosa found.

"The paper is a decree from Pope Clement ordering the disassembling of the Order, and it also marked them as fugitives."

"This is good?" Asked David.

There was now official confirmation that the Order were marked thought Andrews to himself. "I think all of us need to look in the section where you found this document," he said aloud.

Bridgette led the group to the area where Rosa had discovered the document. They all put on the necessary white gloves when handling the documents. Each person removed a large book from the shelf and started thumbing through their selected book. This development had given them hope. Even though it was a small development, it was a development nonetheless. Optimism had been eluding them since Santini delivered the message of the assault on Earth and the deaths of the three members.

As they continued searching, attention moved toward Dwayne. He was looking at a document with great attention. David turned to Bridgette who was standing next to him.

"I think Dwayne found something."

Andrews stopped his search, tossing aside a document written by Father Durante Alighieri, best known as the writer of the Divine Comedy.

Bridgette turned towards him, "I think Dwayne found something good," she said.

Dwayne continued reading the document, oblivious to what anyone was saying. He read the first paragraph, and called Andrews over. "I think I found what we are looking for!"

Andrews motioned to Bridgette, "Bridgette, walk with me, the rest of you continue your searching. Chances are we will need to find more documents."

Andrews and Bridgette walked over to Dwayne. Bridgette was excited as they waited for Dwayne to reveal what he had found. It had been a long time since Dwayne had been excited about something, with the exception of the ring he found at the lake house over the summer, he had been disconnected since the knee injuries.

Rosa and David made their way to the table as well. They too, had noticed Dwayne's excitement and wanted to see for themselves. Andrews noticed that they paid no attention to his request.

"I'm glad to see you are acting like seasoned Order members," said Andrews in a wry tone. Dwayne looked up and startled by everyone staring at him.

"Come on man, tell us what you found, or do we have to wait until a message is delivered by God?" David said sarcastically, but with some impatience.

Bridgette and Rosa darted looks of inappropriateness toward David. Unintentional as the comment was, it served the purpose of comic relief and allowed everyone to release some of the stress they were feeling.

Dwayne stood from the chair he had been sitting in. As he stood up, the others occupied the nearest available seats. Dwayne started to feel nervousness, stemming from the important matter he was about to read. Dwayne breathed in deeply and started reading the document.

This letter is intended for whoever may be looking for members of the Order of Seven. Pope Clement V has deemed the men of the Order of Seven outlaws. His Holiness has made his decision based on the encounter the Order had with King Philip of France. The Order had threatened the King in his dealings with the Knights Templar. The Order had accused the King of France with treachery and deceit. The threats made by the Order on his majesty did not sit well with his Holiness. The King of France has said the Order has threatened to assassinate him. All of the accusations made by the King of France have been proven to be empty of validity. There is no proof of the comments or of any meeting between the King and the Order. The King has stated that the threats were made in front of his court. The members of his court have been interviewed. Members of his court and members of the Council of the Supernatural and their accounts collaborate what the King has stated. I find that the recounting had been rehearsed. I also believe that the Order had never made any of those accusations. The responses made by the Council of the Supernatural interviewed did not corroborate the Kings' accusations. The Order does not act in that manner. The Order members have been condemned by the Pope and placed on high alert to be arrested and put to death by order of Clement V.

I am disregarding what the Pope has ordered. I am assisting the Order in hiding themselves and their Book of Spells throughout Europe. I will not be mentioning where they are, or where I placed the book in this document; that will rest with the lead Order member. I will only mention that I am the person to contact if there is need of the Order of Seven. I will also keep contact with them and I will pass along their place of residence to any priest that follows me, and so on. I am placing all my faith in God that a good and honorable man will continue with the whereabouts of the Order. I do not feel as if I am betraying the Church. In fact, I believe that I am honoring the will of God and the protection of the Church's greatest combatants against evil. May the grace and will of God guide you to me if you are in need of the Order of Seven.

May God be with you,
Father Giovanni Messeneo
Head Priest of the Church in St. Catherina, Sicily

"This is the document we needed to find. It is evident now that what we are looking for is not here, but in Sicily," said Rosa.

"We are quite fortunate that the Church is in the same area that Franco is at while working with Emily and Julia," said Andrews. "I will place a call to Franco and see if he can retrieve the information for us.

The good news about all of this is that the secrecy of the Order has obviously been passed on throughout the years, because Franco had no idea of this, also the location of the Book of Spells is either in Chicago or Sicily, one of those two places," said Andrews.

Andrews placed the phone on speaker and started dialing the number.

15

RETRIEVAL

Suddenly the Order is in a peculiar situation. The use of powerful magic has been confirmed with the deaths of three members. The retrieval of James Sullivan's diary had divulged the area where the Stamens had hid documents that explained how to use the Book of Spells. Now, they had to search for those documents. Sergio Mastelo was born one hundred and eleven years ago. At the age of twenty he was introduced to James Sullivan. For the following sixty-eight years, Sergio and Sullivan worked together in locating and fighting disturbances in the world of man. They also became close friends.

Sergio was never a member of the Order of Seven. He was and still is a Stamen. Sullivan wrote in his diary that Sergio, or whoever should replace him in the Stamen's administrative center in Sicily, was who possessed the information regarding the ancient use of spells.

The phone rang for several rings. There was no answering machine or voicemail, because Sergio figured that at his age, rushing around the house was not a good idea. On the twelfth ring, he finally reached the phone. This must be an important call since usually the phone stopped ringing before he reached it. The usual procedure consisted of Sergio missing the call, checking the caller ID and then returning the call.

"Hello. Yes, this is he. Who is this?" Sergio paused, and suddenly a look of disbelief appeared on his face. "Jonathan Andrews, Jonathan Andrews from London? Yes, of course I know who you are."

On the other end, Andrews finished asking for the documents. "Sergio, I would like to thank you for your assistance and for guarding the sacred documents."

"I am humbled by your recognition. However, I am only fulfilling my responsibilities of being a Stamens," said Sergio.

"Are you aware of the documents in particular I am in need of?" Andrews asked.

"You are in need of the location of the Book of Spells, I assume since you know who and where the Order members are."

"Yes, I am."

"I suggest that someone comes here and retrieve the documents. I am far to old to journey out to where they have been kept for centuries."

"I will be sending you two Order members. They are Emily Stone and Julia Bernard. Both are in their late twenties. They will retrieve the documents and bring them back to me."

"Understood."

"Well, thank you, I'll talk to you soon Sergio, take care." Andrews said, and hung up.

Sergio had asked Franco to come by, and at the moment, they both sat in the chairs and contemplated the important task they were about to start. Franco knew that Emily Stone and Julia Bernard were already in Sicily to assist them. Their training was complete. The two of them had learned the spells and potions rather quickly. Franco believed that their calling in life was to be clerics/conjurers.

"Sergio, where are the documents?" Franco asked.

Sergio had a disappointed look on his face. The look on his face gave away what he was feeling.

"You do know where the documents are, right?" Franco continued hesitantly.

Sergio spoke in a low tone, "Oh, I know where they are, but retrieving them won't be as easy."

Franco's frustration was evident in his voice. "Will not be as easy as it sounds? Are you saying that they are not here?"

Sergio pushed his chair back from the desk. He pulled the drawer on the right side out. He fumbled his way to the back section and pulled out a folder, moved his chair back to its original positioning and waved Franco over.

Franco moved closer to Sergio. He was eager to see the contents of the folder.

"Well, that wasn't that difficult, you got the documents," said Franco in a joking manner.

Sergio gave Franco his usual glare, "Franco, in another life you may have been a good comedian." Franco's face now displayed a large grin. "But you would have to work on your timing," said Sergio in a joyful tone. His tone returned to the seriousness he had earlier. He removed the contents of the documents that were inside the folder.

"What I have here is a map and the blueprint of the building that the documents are in."

The news that the documents are in a different building than the Stamens, and that a map is needed to get to the building, did not please Franco.

"My friend, you are too old to go to this building," said Sergio.

Franco was not too fond of the comment. "What do you mean too old? You are too old, I'm only sixty-three," said Franco, the agitation elicited from Sergio's remark being evident.

Sergio turned around to face Franco and patted Franco's large stomach, "Yes, too old and too fat," he said, with a large grin on his face.

Sergio opened the document he had referred to as the map. He opened the middle drawer of the desk and removed a pair of reading eyeglasses. He put the eyeglasses on and exhaled loudly and looked at the map. He pointed to it.

"Here is our location," he said. He looked throughout the map. He reached to his right and picked up a ruler. "We need to go...over...here."

Franco is shocked by how far the area Sergio pointed to is from St. Catharina.

"How far is that from here?" Franco asked.

"The map is old, but let me place the ruler, and I'll give you an estimate. I think its fifty kilometers from here. But let's be sure."

Sergio measured the distance with the ruler. "Yes, it is a little over fifty kilometers."

"Can you please explain why the documents are so far from us?"

Sergio stood up from his chair, walked by the door and turned and faced Franco. "The documents were removed from here for their protection during World War II. Giuseppe Cantante decided that it would have been too dangerous for the documents to be here. They feared what could happen if they fell into the hands of Adolf Hitler or Benito Mussolini. So I was assigned the task to hide them in an old abandoned monastery."

Franco squinted his eyes at Sergio and tilted his head to his right. A movement he often made when he was puzzled by information he came by. "Yes, but you told Andrews that the documents were nearby."

"I told him I knew where the documents were and I could get them to him."

Franco's frustration was growing. "You misled him," said Franco.

"No, I did not," said Sergio, his voice becoming louder.

"Have you gone to the monastery in the last sixty-some years?" Franco asked, matching Sergio's tone.

"My dear Franco, I have not been there since I brought the documents there. But I do know the building is there, and I had sent someone shortly after the war's end to make sure the building was still standing and that the inside had not been disturbed by the Americans or the Germans. Since the building has not been disturbed, there is no reason for me to believe that the documents are not there," explained Sergio.

Franco was thinking to himself that Sergio's age had affected his rational thinking. "Sergio, do you understand that no one has gone to check if the documents have been destroyed or even ruined over time?"

Sergio started growing weary of the conversation and wanted it to end. "I have no doubt that the documents are there and intact," said Sergio.

"I have faith too, and to be safe, I will pray that they are there and in one piece and readable," said Franco.

Sergio is glad that the back and forth had come to an end. He respected Franco a great deal. But those that have had the privilege of being around the two of them, the bickering back and forth were nothing new.

"Franco, there is no way you can go on this journey. Maybe you can have the two ladies you been working with retrieve the document. They are part of the Order."

Franco is taken aback that Sergio figured out that they are part of the Order.

"Before you ask, I figured that you were working with them when Jonathan Andrews called a few weeks after you had returned from the Andrews Castle. This was not a difficult leap for me," said Sergio.

"You are perceptive, my dear friend," said Franco. "Honestly, why do you think that this journey will be so difficult for me?"

Sergio gave Franco a glare, as if saying "have you looked in a mirror lately?"

"My dear Franco, I am not trying to be rude, but the location of the monastery is too difficult for a man of your age and lack of conditioning to make the journey. Myself included."

Sergio pushed the phone on the desk towards Franco. "Call them and instruct them to come to this office."

Franco dialed the cell phone, and Emily answered. He instructed them to come as soon as possible.

Fifteen minutes went by, and Emily and Julia were standing at the office doorway.

"We're here," said Emily.

"Hello," said Julia.

"Hello ladies, my name is Sergio."

"This is Emily Stone," said Franco, pointing to the thin, attractive blond with bright blue eyes. Emily waved to Sergio. "This is Julia Bernard," he continued, now pointing to the thin, attractive brunette. Julia extended her hand to Sergio.

Franco was not very descriptive about the nature of the call. Emily and Julia both had a suspicion that they were going to be asked to do something. The introduction to Sergio was the final confirmation for them, since the nature of them being in Sicily was to be kept secret.

"We have important information for you to retrieve," said Franco. Suspicion confirmed.

"Whatever you need from us, we'll do," said Emily.

"What are we to retrieve and where do you need us to travel?" Julia asked.

Franco moved away from the desk and directed them to move closer to it. Sergio placed the map with directions on top of the other documents.

"You will need to travel to the outskirts of Caltanissetta." Sergio was pointing on the map. "There you will need to travel to the southern part of the city. And from there, you will need to continue out of the city for about five kilometers."

"How far is Caltanissetta from here?" Asked Emily.

"You'll go for about fifty kilometers to get to the place you need to go," said Sergio. "Driving is the easy part. Well, it will get a little rough as you go off the road outside of Caltanissetta," continued Sergio. "The road you are looking for as you exit Caltanissetta is marked by a large black rock with a red, painted cross on it. There you will turn left and travel until you come to the end of the road. From there you will need to hike about five kilometers until you reach the ancient monastery," Sergio finished.

Emily and Julia stared at each other. "Well, nothing like a long ride followed by a long walk on a hot summer day," said Emily. "I think that the two of us can manage this, and we will have our phones and laptops with us. We can do this and not raise any type of suspicion."

Sergio pulled the blueprint of the monastery from underneath the map. He unfolded it and placed it on top. "This is the hard part, searching through a building that has been abandoned for over eighty years," said Sergio.

"Once you reach the building, you will need to find an entrance. Inside you will need to locate where you are and start searching from that point to the section that the documents are in. The path to the documents is highlighted, so once inside it will be easy to follow. Remember, this is an old building that has not been in use for some time. The building will be in shambles, so be careful," said Sergio.

Julia and Emily's emotions were mixed. They were excited about contributing to the cause and nervous about completing the task.

"I will give each of you a copy of the monastery's blueprint, in case one gets damaged." Sergio reached again under the stack of documents. He pulled out a third document. "The documents you are looking for are all in the same place and have this seal on each folder," said Sergio.

"What information are we getting for the Order?" Emily asked.

"You are both retrieving the documents that will inform us where some special resources are," said Sergio.

Emily was puzzled as to why the documents were not stored safely at Andrews Castle. "Sergio, I'm in need of some clarification, why are these important documents kept so far from the Order?"

Sergio had neither the desire nor the patience to retell the story. "I will be more than happy to explain why when you return. Time is of the essence, they need those documents yesterday," he said, obviously agitated.

Emily was a bit put off by the old man's tone. "Okay, I'll listen to the explanation another day," she replied.

"The two of you need to go and pack your equipment. You will need the climbing gear, and to be safe, bring the weapons and potions you've been training with. Meet me in the back of the office in a half-hour," said Franco, speaking rapidly.

Emily and Julia left the office and made their way to the apartment they had been occupying for the last month. Franco also exited the office, making his way outside to get the vehicle ready.

Sergio started making copies of all the contents inside the Order file.

16

SEARCHING SICILY

The sky was painted with dark, luminous clouds at two thirty in the afternoon, covering the sun. This was not a perfect day to be traveling, especially long distance. Franco just returned from filling the gas tank on the Dodge Durango. On the top of the vehicle, usually used to hold luggage, was camping equipment in case they were forced to camp somewhere overnight. Inside the vehicle there was all the modern luxuries, blue tooth capabilities, fine leather seating, ports to connect a lap top, internet accessibilities; this vehicle was designed for the comfort of any person on a long road trip.

Franco exited the large SUV and made his way to the stone steps leading to the rear entrance of Sergio's building. The back portion where the car was parked was lacking in space. This was not uncommon throughout the Italian town. There were the steps, and then an area large enough to fit the SUV and that was it. The ancient Roman design of the stone streets accented the slick, black roughness of the vehicle. Franco sat on the steps, admiring the brand new vehicle imported from the States.

The truck was purchased by the Andrews and delivered to the Stamens' office three days ago. Franco had never driven such a luxurious truck. The fun he could have driving this truck through some off-road portions of Sicily, he thought to himself. Even though the rest of the world might refer to it as an SUV, to Franco Pastalini it was a truck.

"This is too big to be a car," he said out loud, to himself.

The rear of the Stamens building was at the bottom portion of a hill. The vehicle was pointing forward toward a narrow alley, lined with residential buildings made of a rust-colored brick and mortar. The ancient quality of the buildings exemplified the old beauty that was transpired by the buildings. Usually on a sunny day, neighborhood children would be kicking a soccer ball around. Since this was a gloomy, cloudy day with no traces of the sun, no one was outside behind the buildings.

Franco looked at his watch. He realized that less then twenty minutes had gone by since they broke from the office. Suddenly, he noticed two individuals walking down the stoned alley road. As the figures got closer, he realized they were Emily and Julia, arriving ten minutes before the agreed upon time. The two of them started waving to Franco.

"Wow, this is a nice ride," said Emily as she stroked the SUV's hood, taken aback by the aesthetics of the vehicle. "It's a V8 Dodge Durango with all the bells and whistles. I love this ride."

Franco was sitting on the steps, rolling his eyes at the attention a truck was receiving. He thought to himself, this is just a truck. It goes from point A to point B. Franco slowly raised himself from the stairs, making a low grunting sound as he rose from the stoop and made his way to where Emily and Julia were standing. He placed his hand on the hood of the large SUV and ran it along as he moved toward the two of them.

"Before you leave, I need to talk to you both about the importance of some of the dangers you will face," said Franco.

"Honestly, Franco, this is not a difficult mission," said Julia, a smile on her face.

"We'll be in and out, and back before you miss us," said Emily.

Franco motioned for them to come closer. In a low voice he started explaining the possibilities of what they may encounter.

"I must warn you...you might encounter a force there that you may have to fight in order to get into the monastery." Franco is now standing right next to them. "I don't know if you'll face an actual foe, or some form of evil presence that will affect your thinking."

Emily and Julia are now paying close attention to him. They had believed that this would be an easy retrieval. They figured that they'd be doing physical actions, but not in the form of fighting. Since the murders of the other Order members, they should have realized that they needed to be cautious in their decision-making.

"You know Franco, you trained us well. If we do encounter something of that nature, we'll be ready," said Emily.

"Shh," said Franco, gesturing with both his hands as if he were pushing something down. "We don't know what presences there are around us. We could be listened to, right here and now," said Franco.

"We'll be fine and careful," said Julia, reassuringly.

"Remember your training." Franco led them to the back of the car. He opened the hatch and started to inform them of what was stored in the car.

"I have placed two laptops back here, along with a tent on top, in case you need to stay there overnight. Make sure that your phones are charged. There is a charger you can use in the truck if you need," said Franco.

Emily started giggling, "Franco, this is not a truck. It's an SUV," she said.

"This is not a car, it reminds me of a truck or a bus," he said. They all started laughing at the comment. "I think the world is becoming too technical," said Franco.

Franco walked up to each of them gave them a hug and wished them luck on their important mission. "I have faith in both of you. As soon as you arrive there, call me. Also, call once you are on your way back."

Franco paused for a moment, and then continued, "As soon as you find the documents, it may cause a break in the planes' continuum. This may happen and it may not. It may inform our unknown enemies that something significant has taken place. That is why you need to call while you are in route back here. If detected, you may be in danger. Do not stop unless you need to gas up this mammoth car."

The two Order members acknowledged his request. For the first time since their training in Sicily began, they were a little nervous of their mission.

17

A STRANGE CONVERSATION

Emily and Julia hugged Franco a second time, and got into the black Dodge Durango. Julia sat in the passenger's seat and Emily the driver's seat. Julia placed the information of the city they were traveling to into the GPS. Emily gave Franco a wave and placed the car into drive, pulling the car into the main street at the end of the alley. Julia was more than happy to have Emily drive; she had never been fond of driving. She preferred public transportation or riding a bike to wherever she had to travel. As an environmentalist, she would like to see all gas-powered automobiles removed from the planet. Admittedly, some wishes were less likely to come true; she may be an environmentalist, but she was also a realist.

As they left the little town, they were both taking in the scenery. A Durango in Italy stood out like a sore thumb. Most of the cars were much smaller. The beautiful mountain ranges seemed to encircle them. They would pass through roughly twenty towns before they reached Caltanissetta.

The two exchanged small chitchat as they drove. They both avoided the ever-present question: how the other was dealing with the pressure to succeed. The ability to function while pressured from within was difficult for any person. But there was no time for self-doubt or questioning what dangers may lay ahead. There was an important task that needed to be completed.

They stopped in a small town within an hour's drive to Caltanissetta and got a room at a bed and breakfast for the night. They didn't stay for breakfast the next morning. They awoke around seven o'clock and resumed their travel. As they pulled into Caltanissetta they admired it's curved bricked streets. The old buildings lined up in rows one right next to the other. They drove for a short while and stopped for some coffee at a small café. Emily dropped Julia at the curbside as she looked for a place to park. Julia loved the look of the quaint little café.

This café in particular had exposed brick throughout, and antique tables inside. There were only five tables and to her surprise, no one was inside having an espresso. She made her way to the counter and ordered two cappuccinos. She informed the barista that she was sitting at one of the tables outside.

While walking back outdoors she noticed several paintings on the wall. An entire section of the café wall was dedicated to Dante's inferno. Julia thought nothing of it as she figured that she was in Italy and that didn't seem odd to her. There were three tables in front of the large picture window. She exited and selected the middle table. As she sat there, she pondered why no one was there having a coffee. Julia noticed another café across the street was much busier, and wondered if the coffee was not as good at the café they had selected.

Julia spotted Emily walking towards her. She stood up from the table and waved to her. Emily waved back and started a slow jog to Julia. While they were in training with Franco, they spent their free time getting to know each other. By the time the training ended, it was like they had known each other for decades instead of a few months.

"Did you find a parking spot nearby?" Julia asked.

"Not too far, a little over two blocks away."

"I ordered us cappuccinos," said Julia. She pointed to the café across the street. Emily turned in that direction and noticed the busy café.

"I hope the coffee is good here, it seems like the one across the street is more popular," Julia commented.

Emily looked around at their current setting and noticed the name of the café they where at. 'Nasondiglio de Diavolo'. "Well I think the name of this place might have something to do with the lack of customers," she said while pointing at the sign above the large picture window. "I didn't notice it when we pulled up."

As Julia looked at the sign she gave its translation, "Hiding from the Devil."

The server came outside with their order. The old man also brought each of them complimentary biscotti. Speaking in Italian, Emily asked the server the reason for the name. The man gave Emily a puzzled look. It was evident to him that Emily and Julia were not from Sicily, or Italy for that matter.

"The name was chosen because the Devil is everywhere."

The man's reasoning caused confusion within Julia. "I don't understand, the object of opening a business is to attract customers, using 'devil' in the name may keep people from coming in," she said.

"The Devil is everywhere, and to not understand that is foolish, I don't want to have those foolish people come in here," said the man. "For centuries, this town has been plagued with his doings. Look across the street."

The man walked two feet from the table and pointed across the street. "Do you know the name of that café?" He asked, "Casa del Agrifolio is the name of that place."

Emily said, "House of the Holy."

"That place is anything but holy," said the man.

"Really? Why do you say that?" Julia questioned.

"The people that own it are one with the Devil. They have fooled the people of this town by hiding what they practice. They think that there are other existences besides ours."

"Have you ever witnessed their practices?" Emily asked.

"No," admitted the man.

Julia started chuckling. "Then how can you make such an accusation?"

Emily tasted her cappuccino. "Wow, good coffee."

The man pulled a chair from one of the tables and sat with them. "Their eyes. They have dark eyes. They hide under the name, but their eyes say it all. The young people of this town and other towns love going there. They play music and do a lot to attract the young people. They have been in business for about two years. Right after they opened, a flock of birds died as they flew above their shop. Two people died while having coffee there, heart attack."

"That could be just coincidental, don't you think?" Emily said.

"All in two years? No. Not possible," said the man.

Sensing that the man is becoming aggravated by the conversation Emily changed the topic back to the coffee. "This is really good coffee," she said.

"Thank you," said the man.

Julia, however, could not let the topic go. "I noticed that you have a lot paintings regarding Dante's inferno. Couldn't someone make the same accusation on you?"

"Well, yes, if all one sees is Hell in those paintings. But the purpose behind the story is Dante's travel to get closer to God," said the man.

Emily felt that she needed to end the conversation and return to their mission. "We would love to continue this, but we need to get going."

"Yes, I hope I didn't frighten you?" Asked the man.

"No, of course not," said Julia.

"Please come back when you want good coffee, or to continue our conversation." The man stood up from the chair he occupied and started to head in. As he reached the door he turned and faced them again. "There are many paths that lead to God. No one knows how to get there, but the roads and paths are always forked. The individual decides the path they will follow. Some paths lead to the light and some paths lead to darkness. You both have a safe journey wherever you are going. It's been a great pleasure speaking to you both, and I look forward to you coming back. Good bye."

"Good bye and thank you," said Emily and Julia.

As the man walked inside, Emily and Julia started discussing the strange conversation. “What do you make of what the man said?” Julia asked.

“I think that he’s right. The occurrences are rather peculiar in such a short span of time.”

“Exactly what I’m thinking,” replied Julia.

“We better be on our guard, something tells me this isn’t going to be as easy as we thought,” said Emily.

With that, Emily left three Euros on the table and they made their way to the car.

18

LOCATING THE BUILDING

Emily and Julia walked the two blocks to the car. The weather was beginning to turn; the sun was now blocked by a series of grey clouds. They both considered the strangeness of their coffee stop.

"That was a bit weird," said Emily.

"I agree," said Julia.

"I think that we need to look into what the café owner was talking about."

Julia turned to her with an incredulous look on her face. "And where are we going to find the time?"

"I know, I get it, we're busy doing all this," Emily responded. Emily paused for a brief moment, and then continued, "It just seems to me that there is something going on here that needs to be looked into. It might have something to do with all that's going on now."

Julia decided that she should just let this go. They did not have the luxury of time on their side. Over the last month or so, Julia had grown close to Emily, and vise versa. The two had become like sisters. They had learned a lot about each other, both personally and emotionally.

They continued on their ride to the rock landmark. They drove on the curving, winding roads of Sicily, and took in the beauty of the small island, its majestic mountain range, colorful plains, all woven in together. There were no cars to be seen for miles. The rock stood nearly ten feet in height and twenty feet in diameter. Emily brought the Durango to a complete stop. Julia reached in back and pulled forward a backpack. From it she pulled out a pair of highly powered binoculars. She looked forward and back from the passenger side.

"Let me go out and look down that dirt road for a possible clue to make sure this is the right way."

"Good idea," responded Emily.

"Wait here, I'll be right back."

Julia exited the car and walked to the rock, standing in the path made by other vehicles that had driven on it. The area was a brownish color with the undisturbed areas a lush green. On each side of the path was a grassy area that had grown quite tall. Julia thought to herself that this particular type of grass must be native to Sicily. She peered down the pathway with her binoculars as far as they could assist her viewing. She could barely make out the object that the pathway appeared to lead into. As she walked back to the Durango, she noticed the dark clouds rolling in. She stopped at the front of the car and looked up, facing west. She was amazed by how fast the clouds were coming in. This is the fastest she had ever experienced a storm rolling in. The clouds reminded Julia of a painting she had made years ago. She had named her painting 'Storm Front'.

"I wish I would have seen this before I started my painting," she whispered to herself.

Within minutes the sun was virtually gone. Julia went to the driver's side window.

Emily rolled down the window. "Don't you think you should come inside?"

"Bring the car to the rock, I'll get in there."

Emily placed the car in drive and turned down the path.

Julia walked back to the car and handed Emily the binoculars. "Look down that path and tell me what you see?"

Emily stepped out of the car and walked to the front of it. She brought the binoculars to her eyes. She looked in the direction that Julia had pointed in.

"Well?" Julia prompted.

"It looks like there's something down there. Let's go for a ride, this has to be the place," said Emily. Just as she finished her sentence, the rain started to pour.

They both ran to the car and got in as fast as they could. They ended up getting a little wet from the rain.

"This will make the drive a bit more difficult," said Emily.

"Ya think?" Julia said, in a sarcastic tone.

Emily turned to Julia and started laughing. "Sarcasm, well done," she said, with a large grin on her face.

The car's windshield wipers were moving back and forth as fast as they could. They were fighting a losing battle. Emily was driving less than twenty miles per hour, and the rain was coming down so hard, it made it seem even slower. The drops were large and hitting the car with a strong force. Emily turned the headlights on.

"I've never experienced such darkness in the middle of the day," said Emily. Suddenly thunder exploded with a booming sound. Both of them were startled by the sound. It was like a bomb went off. The sky then lit up with flashes of lighting. Twenty feet in front of them, a bolt of lighting hit the ground.

Emily abruptly stopped the car. Another loud clap of thunder happened. Instantaneously, two lighting bolts struck the ground to left and right of them.

"That's not normal, for three lighting bolts to strike in roughly the same area," said Emily.

"I know, the odds of that are astronomical," Julia agreed.

With that, Emily put the car in drive. This time she was traveling faster then before. The car was bouncing in the pathway. The rain was now coming down as if shot out of a cannon.

"Slow down!" Julia shouted.

"No way, we need to be strong and show we are not scared."

There was a loud bang that came from outside the car. It wasn't thunder. The car veered left and Emily slammed on the breaks. The car skidded for a few feet and came to a stop in the high grass, about fifteen feet off the pathway.

"What the hell just happened?" Julia asked in a frantic tone.

"We got a flat," replied Emily, in a very melodramatic tone.

"Nice job, speed racer," said Julia. Emily glared at her, not appreciating Julia's humor. The rain and thunder continued around them.

19

DISCOVERY

Julia climbed into the back of the car. She started rummaging through the packed gear in the back portion of the Durango.

"What are you doing?" Emily asked.

"It's raining too hard to change a tire, so I figured that we should move on foot." Julia replied, putting items together while she talked. "Come back here and let's see what we'll need."

Emily turned and made a sigh as she looked out the windows. "I'm on my way."

Julia spent fifteen minutes packing the backpacks. While she packed, the rain gradually stopped. Emily quickly opened the door and stepped out.

"Time to change the tire," she said as she exited the car. Emily moved quickly around the vehicle to the back of the Durango and opened the back hatch. She stood there with her hands on her hips grinning at Julia. She got a kick out of Julia sitting there, cross-legged.

"Hop out of there and let's change this tire while we have a break from the rain." The daytime sky resembled one of late night. The chances of rain starting again seemed like a sure bet.

Julia crawled toward the open hatch and rolled out of the car. Emily quickly moved some of the items in the car to the side and started to remove the panels that hid the spare tire.

"The jack is underneath the back seats. Lift the seats, get it, and bring it here, please," said Emily.

Julia quickly went and got the jack. The two were moving faster than a pit crew.

Emily was quite handy with tools. Within minutes the tire was changed. The spare was a full sized tire not one of the baby spares. They had an air pressure machine that plugged into one of the outlets that allowed them to fill the tire with air. They finished placing all the equipment into their proper place and went back into the car. Emily brought the car back to the pathway and continued driving down it.

"We do make a great team," said Emily to Julia. Julia smiled and nodded her head in agreement.

They drove about fifty feet and down came the rain again. This interval of rain equaled the earlier force.

"I think we had some timely assistance," said Julia.

"It sure seems that way... weird," said Emily.

"Weird?" Asked Julia.

Emily is back to driving at twenty miles per hour. "What I mean is that the rain stopped, giving us time to change the tire and then started again. I too think that help was sent our way, that's all," replied Emily.

The two drove the remainder of the distance in silence. The two worked so well at finding the pathway and changing the tire. But now the purpose of the journey was about to begin. Through their deep thought, the rain continued its downpour. After thirty minutes they finally reached the end of the pathway. There before them was a large building at the top of a small hill. There were around fifty steps that led up to the large, decrepit building.

Emily parked the car at the foot of the staircase. She kept her hands on the steering wheel looking upward at the building. Julia was also staring at the ruined staircase from the passenger seat. Julia opened her door first.

"Well, let's do this. Sergio was wrong about the hike thankfully," she said enthusiastically. Julia leaped out of the Durango and made her way towards the back of the car. Emily sat there for a few extra seconds staring at the old building before exiting. Then she ran to the back of the car and joined her. Julia handed Emily the plastic raingear and her backpack.

"Time to get this started," she said to Emily.

They both put on their backpacks. Emily shut the hatch and they made their way to the stairs. As they neared the stairs they noticed that the stairs were in much worse condition then what they had observed from the car. Without any hesitation, they started the ascent to the top. The climb was made extensively difficult with the rain and the increasing wind shear. Several times, each had slipped on the decrepit stairs. Though they never fell to the ground, the weather conditions made climbing it difficult.

As soon as they reached the top of the stairs, the rain stopped. They both looked at each other and just smiled. They climbed out of their raingear and placed it into their backpacks. The journey up the steps had consisted of moving around broken stairs and the weather conditions had caused them to miss the beautiful Sicilian scenery. Now was their chance and they both looked around at the beautiful landscape. The massive green hills around them were not hidden in the lack of sunlight.

After several minutes they looked at the building in front of them, the large monastery. There were four large columns that appeared to be ancient Roman architecture. As they walked toward the columns, they guessed that they were easily one hundred feet in height. They stopped at one of the center columns.

"This monastery resembles a worshiping temple," said Emily.

"Yeah, it does, we could use John Williams here to tell us which god it was built for," said Julia.

Emily directed a frown towards Julia.

"What?" Asked Julia.

"This was a temple built for Juno, queen of the gods."

Julia was surprised by Emily's knowledge on Roman gods and goddesses.

"I knew you knew your chemistry, but Roman history too? Impressive," said Julia.

"The enormity of this temple signifies that it was for one of the major deities." Emily paused for a second. She is fighting back laughter. "Also, the large statue over there gave it away," said Emily with a large smile on her face.

"We have work to do," grumbled Julia, heading towards the large doors. She wondered how she missed the statue to her left. Emily followed behind her, continuing to laugh.

They reached the large doors and Emily removed her backpack. She fumbled inside and pulled out the blueprints Sergio had given them. She unfolded them on the ground.

"Okay, let's see. We are here and need to get to...there, the lower floor. This seems easy," said Emily.

Julia tried to open the door. The door was obviously locked. She turned to face Emily. "So then you have another way of getting us in," she said.

"The only other way is for us to scale the building, walk across the roof and scale ourselves down the back."

Julia figured that Emily was trying to be funny again. "Seriously, is there another way?"

"I am being serious," said Emily.

Emily folded the blueprint and placed it back in her backpack. She straightened up and walked next to Julia with her backpack in hand. She tried to turn the doorknob and confirmed, "The door's locked."

Julia turned toward her and said, "Thanks for confirming that, I know when a door is locked. Four years at Princeton and three years working on my Masters and Doctoral degrees at Cambridge appears to have paid off."

"Relax," said Emily and kneeled over her backpack. She reached in and pulled out two items. The items looked like two thin picks.

"What are you doing?" Julia asked.

Emily didn't respond, she took the two thin metal objects and started to work the lock. Within minutes she successfully had opened the locks.

"Don't ask where I learned how to do this," said Emily.

"Don't worry, I wont."

Emily pushed the large door open. Inside was total darkness. They both reached into their backpacks and pulled out flashlights. The heavy-duty flashlights projected a strong light beam. As they looked around, they were amazed that everything was made of marble. As they slowly walked along, they came across a large marble staircase leading down, and eight large marble religious figures. Emily motioned toward the staircase. Neither of them spoke. There was no telling what they would encounter.

Emily was about to start walking down when Julia quickly grabbed her arm and shouted, "Stop!"

Emily, startled by Julia's actions, shot back, "What's wrong?"

"Look," Julia pointed the flashlight down the stairs. Halfway down the middle, a large section of the staircase was gone.

"I don't think these stairs are sturdy enough for us to walk on. The middle section is gone," said Julia.

"Thanks and there goes our intentions of not alerting anyone or thing. We need to think of another way down," said Emily.

Julia followed all of Emily's steps with her flashlight as she walked around. Julia decided to have a look herself. She pulled out her blueprint of the old monastery and examined it while Emily searched the area for something to make the descent down the staircase.

"There is no other way down, except from here," said Julia. She repeated herself louder when Emily didn't respond. She was about to repeat herself again, when Emily emerged from the darkness, holding on to two strands of thick, heavy climbing rope.

"Let's scale our way down."

"You've got to be kidding," said Julia.

"Come on, it's the only way...and besides, it'll be fun," Emily said eagerly. It became obvious to Julia that Emily was definitely the more adventurous and athletic of the two of them.

Emily wrapped one of the ropes around her waist and handed the other to Julia.

"What do you expect me to do with this?" Julia asked.

"Tie it around your waist, of course. There is no other way down," said Emily.

Julia was shaking her head. "Don't you think one of us should stay here, in case the rope comes loose from wherever it's secured?" asked Julia.

Emily took the rope and tied it around Julia. "Trust me, I know what I'm doing, I'm an experienced climber."

Julia was not keen on the idea of falling to the bottom.

"The only way it's coming undone is if someone undoes it, and since we are the only ones in here, I think the chances of that are slim to none."

Before Julia could respond, the rope was fastened around her.

"Okay, here's the plan. We are going to walk slowly down the stairs."

"We're what?" Julia interrupted.

"Let me finish. We walk down slowly, if the staircase gives way, we won't fall to the bottom. When we get to the missing stairs, we will scale down slowly."

"How does the scaling part work?" Julia asked nervously.

"It's simple, you will control the slack from here. You simply release a little at a time, until we reach the bottom. If the stairs go, we simply start scaling down sooner."

Emily knew what the next question would be, so she continued, "On our way up, this mechanism will pull us up from the bottom floor."

"Fine. Let's get going," said Julia, reluctantly.

They both started walking down the stairs at a slow pace. Surprisingly, they reached the missing section without incident.

Emily turned towards Julia. "Race ya to the bottom!"

"I don't think so," said Julia.

They both started their descent. Emily could not help moving faster than Julia.

"You've got to be kidding me," said Julia, as she noticed Emily reached the bottom in seconds.

"Just get down here, and don't think about the height," said Emily. She untied herself and quickly pulled out her blueprint to locate where they needed to go next.

Julia was moving at a snail's pace down. It took her nearly fifteen minutes to finally reach the bottom. When she got there, she expected to find Emily congratulating her on her successful descent.

"Where are you?" griped Julia as she untied herself. She took out her flashlight and searched for Emily.

"Over here," shouted Emily, from around the corner. Julia walked towards Emily's light. Standing in front of a door halfway down the hallway was Emily.

"Thanks for waiting. What if I would have fallen?"

"You didn't. So all is good," replied Emily.

Julia reached Emily. It became pretty evident to Emily that Julia was not pleased with her.

"All right I'm sorry, I should have waited. In my defense, I figured that the quicker we find the hiding place the quicker we head out of this place."

"Is this the room?" Julia asked.

"Yeah, check this out." Emily guided them into the office. On one of the desks in the room she had laid out the blueprint of the monastery.

"See, this is how I found this room. By the circled words 'Statue of Christ'." Emily then walked back towards the door. Julia was wondering if she wanted to show her the statue of Christ.

"You know, I've seen plenty of statues of Jesus, I don't need to examine this one."

From the hallway Emily retorted, "Just get out here."

Julia moved into the hallway. Emily closed the door and pointed to the writing on the door. It said "Records". There was a drawing of a statue next to it.

"What's the sense in drawing this statue, like we don't know how to read?" Emily commented dryly.

"Come on, we need to get to work and work is in here," said Julia as she walked back into the room.

They made their way to the back of the room, and spotted five file cabinets. They went to the cabinets and started searching for any markings that indicated the Order of Seven. They spent what felt like an eternity going through the file cabinets. They finally came to the last files. They found nothing. They then went through each desk. After looking through the four desks, they came to the conclusion there is nothing in the room.

Suddenly, Emily groaned "Oh my God," and ran back into the hallway.

"Where you going now?" Julia asked after her.

"Get out here," responded Emily.

Julia joined Emily in the hallway. Emily was standing directly in front of the statue of Jesus.

"This is the place," said Emily, pointing to the statue of Jesus.

"Emily, it's a statue. A solid marble statue."

"You don't see it, do you?" Emily asked.

"All I see is a statue."

Emily had grabbed the blueprint on her way out; she laid it on the floor. "Look, at the words Sergio circled."

"Yeah. I see them."

"Now look at the statue," said Emily.

"Okay, I see him pointing to his heart."

"That's all you see? Look at his left hand," insisted Emily.

"His left hand is just dangling. Just tell me what you're thinking," said Julia, irritated at the guessing game.

"His left hand is pointing to the wall," said Emily.

"Yeah." Then suddenly Julia realized what Emily was saying. "Do you think he's pointing to the records?"

"Yes, I do," said Emily.

Julia kneeled in front of the area the statue of Jesus was pointing at. She knocked around the wall.

"It sounds hollow." Emily reached into her backpack and pulled out the small hammer she had used to attach the climbing fastener to the wall upstairs.

"Here, have at it." Emily handed Julia the hammer. Julia struck the wall several times. Each strike knocked out a section of the drywall.

Inside the wall was a large plastic bag with a legal sized manila folder and a box inside it.

"I wonder why he just didn't tell us that the statue is the key to finding the records," mused Emily.

Julia reached in and retrieved the plastic bag. She removed the folder from the bag.

"Here it is." She opened the folder and found the items that Sergio had indicated would be there.

"Let's get going."

They both went back to the staircase.

Julia's happy feeling of discovering the records quickly vanished. "Back to reality," she said glumly.

"Come on," chuckled Emily, and secured the ropes around both of them.

They both started their climb and reached the upper portion of the stairs at thc same time. They climbed onto the stairs and walked slowly up. They exited the building and walked down the outside stairs. They noticed that the sky had cleared and a beautiful sunny day had replaced the lousy weather. They got into the Durango and Emily put the car into drive and they started their road trip back to St. Catharina. Julia placed a call to Franco and informed him they had retrieved the material and were headed back.

20

BEAUTIFUL ROME

The plane carrying Kantra and Ulra landed in Rome at its designated time. They exited the plane, quickly picked up their luggage and grabbed a cab to head to one of the luxurious hotels in Rome. The two checked in and made their way to a room on the top floor. They unpacked, and Kantra placed a phone call to Lannar. She informed him of their arrival. He was pleased to hear from them, and that they were in place. Kantra did not stay long on the phone with him and ended the call with, 'we'll see you as soon as we can.'

Kantra unpacked her carry on bag. She removed several weapons that she managed to get by security. Ulra was taken aback by Kantra's ability to get those weapons through.

"How did you manage to get them out of Chicago and into Rome? They searched our bags and they didn't notice them?"

"I simply put a spell of disappearance on my weapons," said Kantra.

"A spell that can make an object disappear, interesting. I need to learn that one," said Ulra.

"When we get back, I'll show you it along with some other spells. I think you are a natural and will learn them quickly. Besides, I think that someone else besides me should be able to conjure up these spells," said Kantra.

Once Kantra finished placing the weapons on the bed, she started examining each of them individually. The first was a miniature crossbow, made of cedar wood. The tension was extremely tight on it.

"The miniature arrows are laced with poison on the tips," said Kantra as she locked the wire and pulled the trigger.

"Interesting," said Ulra. The second weapon she looked at is was a set of daggers. She took out a sharpening tool and ran the daggers along it, alternating the blades angle with each stroke. After she finished sharpening her daggers, she picked up a pouch she had placed on the bed. Inside the pouch were three vials.

"This will require some up close and personal maneuvering," said Kantra, while holding one of the vials in her hand.

Ulra reached into his briefcase and removed several pictures. He placed the pictures on the bed.

"We should go over the targets, Lannar explained that these men are part of a group called the Council of the Supernatural," said Ulra, while holding a picture of Father Lopez.

"Good idea, we definitely should familiarize ourselves with the target. I'm curious about this group and their connection with the Order of Seven."

"Lannar explained to me that they at one time worked closely with them. He figures that if they are eliminated there is no chance of them working together against us," said Ulra, as he spread the pictures on one of the beds.

There was no plan on where to conduct the assassinations. Kantra had never been apart of an assassination, and she was nervous about conducting her part, both professionally and effectively. It was decided that they needed to get some rest and start their mission tomorrow.

The two had spent a week in Rome finding, and then following the targets. They needed to know their routine in order to find the best place and time to conduct the assassination of each target. The two woke up early every day. They would learn the routines of all the Stamens members in Rome. Kantra had rented a small white Fiat to get them around.

After learning the routines of their targets, the time had come to put their plan into motion.

They went down to the car and made their way to the 'Piazza de Spagna'. The morning was a gorgeous and sunny one. The temperature was sixty-eight degrees. The piazza was a short distance from the hotel. Kantra carried a large handbag, which contained all the weapons she was going to use; the crossbow, daggers, and the vials needed to accomplish their mission.

Once they reached the square, Ulra pulled over and Kantra got out.

"I'll be back here in fifteen minutes," said Kantra.

Ulra nodded and Kantra shut the passenger door. As she made her way down to the bottom part of the square, Ulra drove off. Kantra walked at a brisk pace. She didn't want to attract too much attention to herself. She was surprised to see people starting to gather at the square. As she made her way down the steps she saw her target arrive at the 'Fontella Della Barcaccia'. Father Lopez liked starting out his day with a morning walk to the square. Once he reached the fountain, he would pray, and then call for a car to come and pick him up.

Kantra had already loaded her weapon before she reached the bottom. She looked around and noticed that no one was paying any attention to her. She slowly removed the crossbow from her bag. She held the bag with her left hand and the crossbow with her right. She used the bag as camouflage for the mini-crossbow. She was twenty feet away from Father Lopez. Kantra looked around, raised the weapon and fired it. The mini-arrow sailed through the beautiful Italian morning with grace and ease. Off to Father Lopez's left, a family of four walked toward the area where he was kneeling. The young couple and their toddlers were basking in the beautiful morning. Suddenly, Father Lopez stood from his kneeling position and reached for his back. He looked up to the bright sun, with no clouds near it, and fell into the water. His death came within seconds of the strike. A man several feet away ran to him. He reached to grab Father Lopez, but he could not get to him quick enough. There was a splash in the fountain and a stream of red from his back began to taint the water. The man yelled for help in Italian. As he reached to pull Father Lopez from the water, he noticed his collar and the arrow sticking into his back. In the confusion, Kantra continued her walk back to the area where Ulra said he would be. She got into the car and they made their way to the next target.

"That went well," said Ulra.

"Yes, it did. Once I saw the arrow find its target, I knew he had seconds left to live."

"Let's get the runners," said Ulra.

The two drove through the busy part of Rome. They made their way to a road that led to the countryside, next to the large city. After traveling several miles, the next targets came into sight. Ulra pressed down on the accelerator and the car's velocity started to climb. Within seconds he bore down on the targets. As he neared them, they noticed the two men talking and laughing while they ran. Their morning run served two purposes; the first was to stay in shape; the second was to give themselves a momentarily break from the pressure of the work they were going to do with the Stamens.

As Ulra neared them, he swerved the car into them from behind. The two men were thrown several feet from the point of impact. Neither of the men was instantly killed, but they suffered many injuries. Both men were lying on the ground, bleeding.

Ulra slammed on the brakes and brought the car next to them. Kantra had her window rolled down. She had earlier removed the poison laced daggers from their protective sleeves. Kantra leaned out the window and took aim on them like an eagle on its prey. She threw the first dagger at Father Kilpatrick first. He had no time to react. The poison entered his bloodstream quickly and he died within seconds. Father Jennings watched Kantra as she threw the dagger at Father Kilpatrick.

"Why are you doing this?" He asked.

Kantra walked directly over Jennings as Ulra was protesting her exit from the car. "God is in need of your assistance," said Kantra in a cold manner. She then threw the other dagger at the priest's heart, silencing him forever.

There was no damage done to the car. Kantra ran to the car and Ulra sped off. Three of the targets had been eliminated. The next target would take them into the busiest section of Rome. It was now nine in the morning. They were making great time. The next target needed to start his day with a coffee and a newspaper. Once at the Trevi Fountain, Ulra and Kantra needed to find the café located across from the fountain. Father Abay was waiting on his order. Ulra pulled up to the café and Kantra exited. She looked for the table he was sitting at. She spotted him and noticed he hadn't received his order yet. Kantra made her way inside the café.

Kantra walked up to the area where orders were placed. She spoke to the barista in Italian and mentioned how the priest sitting outside was an old friend and wondered if she could bring him his order. The man at the counter was charmed by her beauty, and easily capitulated to her request. Father Abay was sitting outside at a table, wondering where his order was. He thought about going inside and finding out but decided that they were probably working hard and would get the order to him soon. Kantra saw his actions and thought he was coming inside and quickly motioned to the young server. He looked at her nodded his head, signaling to her that he wouldn't blow her surprise.

The server walked outside and reassured the priest that his order was coming up. The server came over to Kantra with Father Abay's order. She placed her left hand out for the server to place the tray on. With her right hand, she threw some type of dust on him. The server sneezed and made his way to the café's restroom. As the server walked away, she placed the tray on a nearby table and removed one of her vials from her pocket. She emptied the contents of the vial into Father Abay's coffee. Kantra made her way to him. She introduced herself and asked the priest if she could sit down with him. He motioned for her to sit next to him. Kantra started to speak in Father Abay's native language from the Philippines. He was pleased to hear his language, but was confused as to who this person was.

"We met several years ago here in Rome," said Kantra, hoping that the priest was in Rome several years ago.

"I'm sorry, I can't quite remember you," said Father Abay, embarrassed.

"That's okay. Let me make a toast," Kantra lifted up her tea and said, "To God and his mysterious ways of looking after his sheep."

Father Abay thought that the comment was a peculiar one. But he didn't want to insult the young attractive woman, so he drank to her toast.

Ulra had pulled up next to the curbside table.

"There is my ride," Kantra said to him.

"You're leaving?" Father Abay asked.

"Yes, I have a few more errands to get done. You have a great day and so good seeing you again," said Kantra as she made her way to the car.

Ulra was in the car, wondering what Kantra was up to. She was leaving the priest, and he was alive.

"You have a great day too, Kantra," said Father Abay. From inside the car Kantra waved to Father Abay and he returned the gesture.

Inside the car, Ulra questioned Kantra about the priest's current vital signs. "Don't worry, he will finish his drink and then die," said Kantra, coldly.

"How long will it take?"

"It all depends on how fast he drinks his coffee."

"Aren't you concerned about the server identifying you?"

"No, not a chance. I blew the dust of forgetting. It causes the victim to forget anything that took place in the last twenty minutes. As soon as the dust reaches the senses, it happens in seconds."

Father Abay was reading the newspaper when he suddenly fell forward onto the table.

21

FULL MOON ADVENTURE

Lannar turned the overhead back on, and started explaining the layout of the cemetery. On the overhead was an outline sketch of the cemetery, and at the bottom of the sketch the entrance was marked. In the middle of the outline was a marking labeled 'Donavan'.

"The lines inside the outline are the roads that travel throughout the graveyard," explained Lannar to Conrad, Macnar and Edwin.

Tonight was the chosen night for the retrieval of the items inside the Donavan Tomb. Lannar retrieved a laser pointer off the table and pointed at the screen.

"This is the entrance to the cemetery," he said, placing a red dot on the screen. "You will not be entering through the front gates. You will walk around to the back wall and scale it."

Conrad was familiar with the area. "What time are we planning on going?"

"I think the best time will be tonight at eight o'clock."

"Lannar, I was under the impression that you were coming?" Macnar asked.

"If I were to enter the graveyard, it would trigger a warning to a member of the Stamens. Our plans would be revealed prematurely and that may alter our mission," said Lannar.

Lannar brought everyone's attention back to the screen. He placed the pointer directly on a circle on the map with the name 'Donovan' on it. "Here is where you will find what we seek."

The men knew it' was a cemetery, but the giant circle for a gravesite was confusing.

"You are curious as to the circle," surmised Lannar. "Well, it's actually a small island with the tombs on it."

Lannar was not a tolerant man when it came to failure. The thought of having to cross water, then dig up items and not be detected seemed rather difficult to them.

"Lannar..."

Before Conrad could ask his question, Lannar reacted angrily. "Stop with the questions! I will explain what you need to do, and that is it. We don't have time to discuss every aspect. I will tell each of you your roles. I am expecting you to follow them without question, is that understood?"

Before anyone could answer, Lannar continued, "It's a rhetorical question, do not attempt to answer."

They were nervous to move in fear of some form of retaliation. Lannar brought his focus back to the overhead projection.

"This is the area you will enter. There is a wall and you will have to climb it."

"Mr. Wrightwood, you will wait outside and walk around the area, making sure no one is summoned to a disturbance in the graveyard. If someone, or even a group becomes suspicious you will need to eliminate the concern."

"Excuse me Lannar, just so I understand, can you define 'eliminate'?" asked Edwin, the only one out of the three able to speak with confidence towards Lannar.

"Yes, eliminate the source means killing anyone that attempts to enter or interfere with what Macnar and Conrad are doing. You will need to not make any noise. From there, you will have to quickly dispose of any bodies. You will be in a large white van from Kantra's company. Place any bodies inside the van and then dispose of the bodies at a later time. We are fortunate that the gravesite we are going into is towards the northern portion of the graveyard, away from the Irving Park entrance."

Lannar moved the laser pointer back to the large circle on the slide. "It's a grave that is entirely surrounded by water. The water is five feet in depth. There is large wooden bridge to take you there. The bridge is arched, which may cause running with all the equipment difficult."

Conrad and Macnar were anxious to start out on the evening's events. "Before Michael left for Mexico, I had him gather all the equipment needed."

Conrad interrupted, "Is there a way we can practice for this mission?"

"No," responded Lannar, obviously annoyed with the stupidity of the question.

"You will be doing this tonight after I finish, was that not clear? Please do not answer. You are all capable of accomplishing this. There will be no one expecting this to happen.

"Once inside, you will have until the graveyard opens tomorrow at nine in the morning. The graveyard closes its doors at seven. The hours between seven tonight and nine-tomorrow morning are plenty of time to accomplish this. As you are leaving the tomb, inform Mr. Wrightwood and he will return to the same site where you were dropped off."

Lannar turned the lights back on. He paused for several moments before he addressed the group again. "We have one chance at this. If you fail, there will not be another chance with the same percentage of success. But I know you will be successful," finished Lannar, pointedly.

Conrad, Macnar, and Edwin made their way to the garage. None of them spoke on their way down. They reached the van and got in. Edwin paused before he started the vehicle.

"Should we discuss our roles and how this is going to work?" He asked.

"Not here. Get going," said Macnar in a forceful manner.

"I agree, let's get rolling and talk on the way down," chimed in Conrad.

Edwin started the van and pulled out of the garage. He made his way through Chicago's downtown area toward Lake Shore Drive.

While en route they discussed their roles. Edwin would drop them off at the designated spot. He would then circle the cemetery and drive away for some time, so as not to raise suspicion from any of the residents. Macnar and Conrad would exit the vehicle and scale the wall. Macnar would go first. Conrad would tie together the two large duffle bags with all the equipment in them. Then he would scale the wall and the two would head to Donavan Island. Once there, they would locate William Donavan's tomb. They would open it and remove the instructions and location for the ceremony. The key to success would be Edwin not raising suspicion, and getting to the pickup point in a timely manner.

The full moon was in a phase that brought it closer to Earth than normal full moons this night. Driving through Chicago's downtown was always an eye-pleasing pleasure. Lakeshore Drive was a winding beauty, but driving on it was never an easy task. Luckily for Edwin there is was little to no traffic. Edwin turned right on to Clark from Irving Park. He drove down a block, and turned another right. They looked around the area.

Once again, luck was on their side for there was not a soul around. Edwin pulled over at the designated area. Macnar opened the side door and tossed out the two large duffle bags. Conrad got out from the passenger side and ran up to the eight-foot brick wall. His grafting hook gun was loaded, and fired. The hook landed in place. Macnar dropped the two bags by Conrad and quickly scaled the wall. Once on the other side, he signaled to Conrad with a poor attempt at simulating a bird. Conrad heard the sound and tied the bags to another rope attached to the hook gun.

On the other end, Macnar pulled the ropes over. Once the rope and the bags were on the other side, Conrad scaled the wall. They executed the actions to perfection. Both men grinned at each other. Conrad pulled out the map of the cemetery and located the direction they needed to precede. Macnar motioned with his hand for Conrad to lead the way. They ran in a slow jog, bent over slightly. As they cut across the cemetery, they moved around the tombstones and grave markers. After a few minutes, they reached the bridge.

In front of them was a large wooden bridge that arched across the water and onto the manmade island. The crescent moon shaped lake had large willow trees along the water shore. The trees did not block the view of the island, but it greatly diminished its visibility by about sixty-five percent. The only clear view of the island was from the bridge. The tree line nestled up to both sides of the bridge. The tombstone was a large white Parthenon-like structure. Running the length of it was a series of massive columns. They stood fifty feet in height. The same columns ran along its width.

They started across the bridge. Conrad was in front, and Macnar close behind. Once onto the island, they dashed to the large structure. As they reached it, they noticed the name 'Donavan' chiseled into the side of the ceiling. They also noticed four cement tombs. The tombs belonged to William Donavan, his wife Cynthia, and their two children William Jr. and Charles. Examining the writing on the children's tombs, it was clear that they had passed away at very young ages. The two men examined the area. They noticed that William Donavan died in 1888 and his wife in 1860. One of the sons was fifteen years old and the other was seven years of age. His wife died several weeks after their eldest and last surviving son died. The Donavan's occupied the two middle tombs with one son on each side. Conrad and Macnar placed their duffle bags on the tomb's white granite flooring.

Meanwhile, Edwin drove around the neighborhood that surrounded the cemetery. He had not encountered anyone or arose any suspicion, but was ready to do anything he felt necessary to prevent the mission from failing.

Macnar and Conrad examined the marble tomb of William Donavan. Each was on the opposite side, feeling for something that would make opening it easier. After several minutes of contemplation, they reached the same conclusion. They needed to remove the top. Conrad reached into the duffle bag and removed a large chisel and hammer. Macnar grabbed the same tools. They each placed their chisel on the section of the tomb where the top meets the base. After several minutes of striking they finally managed to chip away at the marble. Once the initial incision was made, smashing away the rest was easy. Each of them worked on the opposite end. Finally they were able to remove the top. They positioned themselves on the same side and pushed it off to the left side of the tomb. As the top slid, it slammed into the ground. Sections of the top smashed into his wife's tomb, causing chips in her tomb.

They looked inside and noticed a cement casing. It became evident that William Donavan's coffin lay inside the casing. They figured that the cement was several inches thick. Macnar removed a giant sledgehammer from the duffle bag. He jumped on top and started hitting the cement with all his force. After several minutes, he switched with Conrad and he continued the same in the area Macnar started. This back and forth continued for twenty minutes. Within a half hour they had cleared away the top and had a good view of the mahogany coffin.

Macnar and Conrad looked at each other and paused for a minute. They knew they were going to disturb William Donavan's final resting spot. The moment came when they each had to make a decision. They had to open the coffin in order to retrieve the needed material. Conrad stepped off the coffin and stood next to the tomb. He started walking around the area. Macnar had made his decision and lifted the top of the coffin. A pungent smell forced Macnar to remove himself from the tomb.

"Did you open the coffin?" Conrad asked.

"Can't you smell him?" Macnar replied, gagging.

Conrad walked around the entire structure at a fast pace.

"What is your problem?" Macnar asked.

Conrad continued with his pacing. He finally stopped, facing out toward the water. He stared out at the large moon. The moon appeared so close to him that he extended his arm, attempting to touch it. He was searching for salvation. Conrad had come to the end of his allegiance to Lannar and the rest of the group. His back was to Macnar.

"I am not sure that this is right. I don't think that disturbing this man's resting spot is right. He suffered with the loss of his family. He obviously lost faith in God when his sons died at such young ages. It's clear that his wife was so grief stricken that she took her own life after the second boy died."

Macnar did not interrupt Conrad as he talked. He simply kept encouraging Conrad to continue. "What are you saying, Conrad?" He reached once again into his duffle bag and started to walk towards Conrad. Conrad continued looking out toward the water as he talked, never turning to see Macnar slowly and quietly moving toward him.

"You get the items out of there. I can't. I'm changing my mind with the overall mission, I just can't disturb this grave any further." As he finished his sentence, Macnar was directly behind him, with a large knife in his hand that had a nine-inch blade. He drove the blade into Conrad's side, causing him to drop to his knees. He let out a loud moan. Blood was gushing from his side. Conrad continued looking out across the lake.

"I'm so sorry for my actions," he said from his knees, looking upward toward the large moon.

Macnar swung Conrad around so that he was facing him. "I like you Conrad. It's just that you can no longer be trusted to continue with us."

Conrad realized that his life was soon to come to an end.

"You're right Macnar, I can't be trusted. I can't explain what happened, but I can no longer continue with this. I no longer want to assist Lannar in this ridiculous scheme. While you were opening the coffin lid, I made peace with God and asked for his forgiveness. I don't know if I'm forgiven, but I am sorry for all of my actions."

Blood continued pouring out of Conrad's side. He felt himself becoming weaker. Macnar took his knife and slit Conrad's throat. As Conrad fell forward into him, he dragged Conrad's body to the water and threw his body into the lake. Macnar then walked back to William Donavan's coffin. He moved the bones to the side and looked around. He finally found a large envelope. The envelope was sealed in a plastic bag. Macnar took the envelope and the duffle bags and made his way back to the area where Edwin had dropped them off.

He radioed Edwin that he was on his way.

Once inside the car Edwin noticed the blood on Macnar. "What happened to Conrad?"

"He decided to not carry out his role. Now drive," said Macnar.

Edwin placed the van in drive and headed back downtown. Conrad used his right to exercise freewill. As his corpse lay there, it was uncertain as to which plane his soul would travel to.

22

RETURN TO TRUMP TOWER

Macnar and Edwin returned to Trump Tower after retrieving the information they were assigned to procure. They waited for the elevator. The two men shined with joy in accomplishing their mission. Macnar did not have time to clean Conrad's blood from his clothes. The blood had dried, leaving stains on his shirt and pants. The wait for the elevator indicated to them that the elevator was coming from one of the top floors.

Lannar stood in front of the elevator with no display of emotions. He was anxious to get a hold of the material from Donavan's tomb. He had been awaiting their arrival since he received the phone call from Edwin that the items had been found and that they were on their way back. Lannar felt empowered, knowing that he was one step closer to completing his goal. He thought back to his reading on the Scrutatores and their struggles with the established religion and the Order of Seven. Lannar reflected on the revenge that was finally about to take place.

The elevator light came on, indicating that the car had arrived. Lannar kept his excitement bottled in. He believed there were only two emotions a Scrutatore should ever display. The first is was anger and the second was pleasure due to success.

The elevator door opened. Lannar was taken aback by who was in it. Stepping out toward him was Kantra and Ulra. As the doors closed, the elevator made its way down to Macnar and Edwin. The dark haired beauty ran her hand across Lannar's face as she passed him. Ulra followed her but did not touch Lannar's face. He did shake his hand.

"Are you the welcoming committee?" Kantra asked in a joyful tone.

"I am expecting Macnar, Edwin, and Conrad. I assume you both accomplished your mission?" Lannar asked with no emotion in his voice.

"All but three. We needed to leave Rome before we finished the task. If there is nothing else, I'll be in my room," said Kantra.

"Don't be long, we are going to meet as soon as they arrive," said Lannar.

"I'll be ready," said Kantra, her voice fading as she entered her condo. "Is there anything I should do or prepare for the meeting?"

Lannar did not turn to address her. "Just your attendance is needed."

Kantra turned and walked into the luxurious condominium. Ulra walked into the condo as well, without ever saying anything.

The ride in the elevator to the top floor seemed longer than usual. The two men were nervous that Lannar would be displeased with Macnar taking action in killing Conrad. Edwin was not as concerned as Macnar. Macnar stood tall in the elevator. He wanted to exude confidence in his decision. He felt nervous, but also vindicated for the actions he felt he had to do. As Macnar ran the developments in his head, the elevator door opened.

Macnar stepped out, followed by Edwin. Lannar noticed that Macnar was carrying the sealed contents and extended his hand for them. Macnar gave them to him.

"Excellent. Most excellent, gentlemen," said Lannar, expressing a great deal of pleasure. Lannar took the contents in their plastic holding and turned and walked into the condominium. Macnar looked at Edwin, and both men stared at each other and raised their shoulders, wondering if Lannar even noticed that Conrad was missing.

Lannar was at the table where he had been conducting his meetings. Kantra heard the door close from the room she was in and decided to join them at the large table. It was Kantra who noticed Conrad was not there.

"Where is Conrad?" She asked. Lannar looked, recalling that he did not see him exit the elevator.

"Conrad is not here? Is he by the vehicle?" Lannar asked.

Macnar and Edwin started to feel nervous. The joy felt from seeing Lannar pleased was now extinguished by the fear of how he would react. Macnar believed that he had no choice in the matter. He also noticed that Edwin was staring at him.

Macnar knew that he had to explain what happened. "No, he is not by the car."

"Well, are you going to tell me where he is or should I guess?" Lannar said.

Macnar took in a deep breath and decided that the time had come to explain what happened at the cemetery.

"Conrad decided that he could not continue with our mission," began Macnar. He paused to see how Lannar would react.

"I hope you eliminated him," said Lannar.

Kantra reacted to the thought of her nephew being eliminated. "I hope you didn't! If Conrad changed his mind, which I can not believe that he would, I could change his mind back."

Lannar did not seem interested in Kantra's comments. He kept his focus on Macnar.

"Conrad is gone," said Macnar.

Lannar is angered by Macnar's statement. "Will you get to the point, Macnar? I want to know now where he is and do not speak in innuendos."

Macnar remained confident in his decision. "I killed him when he expressed that he could not continue with the entire mission."

Hearing this, Kantra broke down and started crying over the news that her nephew had been murdered. "No, he would not change his mind, he wouldn't," she sobbed.

Lannar, hearing the emotions taking control of Kantra, changed his focus from Macnar to her.

"Get control of yourself. Macnar would not have done this if there was not sufficient evidence to do so," said Lannar.

"I had no choice, Lannar. I'm sorry Kantra, but the entire mission is far more important than any one person," said Macnar.

"He made his decision. I feared that something like this might happen. Kantra, are you still on board with our mission?" Lannar asked.

Kantra had regained her composure. "Yes, I am. You can count on me, Lannar."

Lannar had started to look through the documents. He reviewed the procedures and the location of where the ritual would take place. After several minutes of reading the details, he looked up at Kantra.

"Good to hear. You are a vital part of this mission. I need to know that you have not changed your mind," said Lannar.

Kantra looked at Lannar, her eyes red and full of tears. "I am upset that I lost Conrad, but I am on board now more than ever. God has once again taken someone that I loved from me," said Kantra.

"No Kantra, God had nothing to do with this. The decision rested solely with Conrad," said Lannar. He placed all the documents on the table. Lannar kept the steps for the ritual to himself.

23

DOCUMENTS

Franco informed Julia that plane tickets to London were on hold for them at the airport. He informed them that a car would be waiting for them to take them directly to the Order once landing in London. It took them an hour to reach the airport. Their time in Sicily had come to an end. They both reflected on their time spent in Sicily. They had spent several months on the beautiful island, but never had the time to truly see and experience it.

On the plane, Emily sat next to the window. Julia sat next to her in the aisle seat. Julia didn't care where she sat; Emily, on the other hand, wanted the window seat. She loved looking out the window and envisioning herself skydiving from the plane.

"We did it," said Emily, as she looked out the small plane window. Julia was deep in thought on about the next phase they were about to embark on. Emily turned to her, surprised that Julia had not responded.

"Earth to Julia, Earth to Julia."

Julia sat there, consumed in thought by the pressure of what was on the horizon for them.

"Seriously, do you hear me?"

Julia resembled someone that had awoken from a deep sleep. "I'm sorry, I drifted off in thought."

"Drifted? You were off in another time and place. I'd say more like sucked out from reality by a giant tsunami."

Julia smiled at Emily then broke out in laughter. "I was thinking about how we are going to train Order members, and the pressure that comes with that."

Emily gave the same topic about a second of thought. "Pressure? I'd say excitement."

"How can you say excitement, we are responsible for training them and making them prepared to fight evil, and remember we need to be trained as well!"

"Well, I'd like to know why Franco couldn't train them, like he trained us. He's the best at the art of being a cleric and yet they are going with us and the little training we have," said Emily.

"I know, it doesn't make sense. I can't even speculate as to why us."

The stewardess came by and asked them if they would like a drink. Julia turned to Emily and smiled, and then turned to the stewardess, "Coke will work for us."

Emily interrupted quickly, "Diet Coke for me."

Julia shook her head as Emily ordered her drink. "What? Like I need the empty calories from that sugar-filled drink," said Emily.

"It's not like you're diabetic or fat," said Julia.

"Why start? I'm in great shape and plan on staying there for life. Besides, if we have to train and educate the new ones, I plan on staying in the shape. I'm in for as long as I can."

The plane landed in London at seven o'clock. As they exited the plane, they noticed the driver standing there with both their names on a large white cardboard sign with a moon symbol on it.

"Hey look, our ride is waiting for us," said Emily. They both made their way to the driver. They presented the driver with identification that confirmed they were who he was looking for and went to the car.

The driver presented the guards at the front gate with his identification and drove on to the building that housed the Order members. The car made its way around the large complex and stopped at the familiar building. Emily and Julia exited the car with the large plastic bag stored safely in Julia's backpack.

As they walked toward the doors, Andrews and John came out to greet them. Andrews was gleaming with hope that the information to get them started was a few feet away from him. John sported his usual unreadable expression on his face.

"I'm so glad to see both of you. I'm sure your training went well," said Andrews.

John walked next to Emily. "Do you have the material?"

Emily pointed to Julia. The four entered the building and made their way inside. Waiting around the elevator were the rest of the Order members minus James. They all appeared to be anxious for their arrival. The ecstatic youngsters, awaiting them, greeted them. The moment had come to find the location of the Book of Spells.

They all went into the adjacent conference room to the left of the elevator. Inside the room was a large table with seating for all of them.

Once inside, Julia removed the clear plastic bag and handed it to Andrews. As he removed the contents the other Order members seated themselves at the table. John took the initiative to introduce Emily and Julia to the new members. The Order members waited anxiously for the material to be reviewed. Andrews removed the five items from the plastic bag. The first item was a brown accordion folder. He thumbed through it. He passed two of the items to Julia and the other two toward John and Emily. Julia had two letters. She passed one of the letters to Bridgette, who was sitting next to her. They each started to read the letter they had. Emily was looking through a small book that was passed to her. John was looking through a manila folder.

John emptied the contents of the folder onto the table. Out poured a series of photos. The photos were of past Order members. John rummaged through them and picked out the most recent pictures.

"I'd say the most recent picture looks like to be of 1930's quality," he observed.

Emily glanced over the pictures handed to her.

"This document says that they have moved to the United States. But doesn't give a city or region," said Julia.

Andrews was looking at documents that appeared to be dated back to the 1300's. "This is it!" Andrews exclaimed with great enthusiasm. "I'll finish this document and make sure that it'll lead us to the resources."

Attention turned to Julia. Everyone noticed that she was reading the back portion of the book.

"Why are you looking at the last part of the book?" Bridgette asked.

"This is not a book. It's a diary."

"A diary?" John asked.

"Well, not a diary of one person, but of entry's made by Order members throughout the years," she said. This is a great discovery, she thought to herself. Suddenly she shouted, "Here it is!"

"Here is what?" Said John.

Julia passed the book to Andrews.

"It's written in Latin," he said as he started to read.

"The twenty-third of July, in the year 1936. I am James Sullivan of the Order of Seven. I have been selected by my fellow brothers and sisters to be the messenger between the Order and the Stamens. The Stamens are the remnants of the Knights Templar. We have been living in different countries throughout Europe since the last days of action. We have all concealed our identities from the Scrutatores and the world, although each member prior to us has informed the Stamens of our place of residency. We are on edge about some developing issues happening in Europe. The election of Adolf Hitler is a great concern to us. The growing fascist government in Italy is also a great concern. We no longer feel safe in Europe. If we fall into the hands of a demonic creature, our existence and that of our families would cease to be. After careful communication, we have all decided to leave Europe and venture to America. We feel strongly in our hearts that America is the safest place for us to live. We have selected the city of Chicago. Once we have secured an area for ourselves, we will contact the Stamens in Sicily and inform them precisely of our place of residence.

"It ends there," finished Andrews.

John is the first to ask the obvious question. "Who will join me in Chicago, and when?" He was also thinking about why he hadn't been made aware of this. He had moved to Chicago with his family from England when he was three years old.

"I have other concerns, but there is no time to discuss them," he said, looking directly at Andrews.

"The Order through the Stamens has equipped several buildings in Chicago. I will get them converted for the Order as soon as possible."

Emily was wondering what that meant. "Converted?"

"This has all come on so fast, we are not prepared to train in a particular location," said Andrews.

John felt that time was being wasted. "We need to get going," he said.

"On the last entry they wrote down the name of the special tree. It's the Grey Alder. The tree is here, in a forest located just outside the London area," said Julia.

"Who will go and do the searching?" John asked.

"You, Emily, Julia, and the new members will be assigned to gather the materials and bring it back here. I will research these documents to see if there are instructions or a person capable of constructing them. I fear that time is not on your side and you will only be able to give a partial training, then pray for the best," said Andrews.

As he finished his sentence, Bridgette stood up. "Rosa and I found another document on the Order. It says that a ring must be worn at all times. If the ring does not burn, then they are the ones you will train."

"Funny you should say that. Inside this tin box are seven rings," said Emily.

24

FALLEN FRIEND

The sun had just set as James was making his way back to the Sullivan house. The weather had switched from summer to fall. James was caught off guard by the sudden drop in temperature. He wondered if he had placed the Book of Knowledge away as he drove north on Lake Shore Drive. The museum's curator, Victor Resnik, had been working with him for the last several weeks but had not been around for the last week. In his absence, James had worked alone. The age of the book required it being stored after several hours of exposure. James had recently spoken with John and Andrews regarding the discovery of the location of the Book of Spells. The plan was for James to head to London, bring the book with him and study the section on spells. The book described how to conduct spells and mentioned several spells by name. The book was the property of the Andrews Society and James was a member. A call from Andrews to Victor explaining that the book was needed in London would allow James to escort the book to London.

James decided that he needed to return to the Field Museum to be certain that the book was placed back in storage. James pressed the button on his blue tooth.

"Call Mary," said James, initiating the call command on his iPhone. As the phone dialed the number, James decided he would inform her to head to London tonight and he would head there in a few days.

"Hello James," said Mary.

"Hey Mary, I'm heading back to the museum to double check something."

"That's fine. I'll leave your dinner in the oven, that way it will stay warm for you," said Mary.

"You are the best."

"James, I have not heard from the kids yet to see how they're adjusting to life in London. Do you have any news on them?" Mary asked.

"I've talked with John and he mentioned that they've accepted their roles in the Order and look forward to their training," said James.

"Oh, that's great. I'm glad they've made the adjustment," said Mary, her tone indicating she missed them.

"Hey Mary, I also spoke with Andrews and he would like for you to head out to London. Are you up for that?"

"I would love that," said Mary, her mood turned from down to up faster than the other direction a minute ago.

"You need to bring the James Sullivan journal to London with you. If you want I can place a call, Andrew's private jet is here in Chicago and you could go tonight if you want," said James.

"I'd love that. Will you be going tonight as well?" Mary asked.

"I'll be heading out in a couple days," said James.

"Then I'll see you in a couple days."

"I'll make the call, and if they can, I'll send you a text telling you what time to be ready by. I'll also send a cab to take you."

"Thank you, James."

"No problem. Mary, I want to thank you for all you've done for me. You've made things very comfortable for me and I want you to know that your cooking is phenomenal," said James emphasizing phenomenal.

Mary's face displayed a large smile on the other end of the phone line. "James, it has been my pleasure. I'm going to get started on my packing. I'll get the journal before I pack. It'll take me some time searching but I've got a pretty good idea where to look."

They both said good-bye and James turned his car around and headed back to the museum.

On his way back, he called the pilot and arranged the flight for Mary to London. As he ended the call, James felt good about getting Mary out to London. He knows how much she missed the kids and figured that they are missing her equally.

James reached the museum and parked his car in the parking lot next to the museum. Before exiting his car he sent a text message to Mary letting her know that she would be heading to London tonight. He also sent a text reminding her that she should call a cab after retrieving James Sullivan's journal.

James exited his car and was greeted by a strong wind blowing in from Lake Michigan. The crisp soothing air felt great to James. The museum had closed for the evening. James had keys to enter from the side doors. He walked briskly to the doors. As he inserted his key, he noticed that the door was already unlocked. He contemplated the reasons why before entering. After several minutes, he concluded that a night shift janitor probably unlocked the door to dispose of the day's trash and perhaps forgot to lock the door. James turned the doorknob and walked in and locked the door behind him.

James made his way from the side entrance to the main entrance of the museum. He was surprised to have not run into a single person from the night crew. He finally reached the main entrance area. He looked around as he made his way to the back portion. It is from there that he will reach the exhibition prep room where the Book of Knowledge was located.

"James, wait."

James turned around, wondering who was calling him. He knew a couple people working on the night crew but they usually didn't speak much with him. Once James began deciphering the book, he rarely left the room. He noticed Victor, the museum's curator, and another person.

James knew how Victor liked to bring in large donors after hours. When it came to gathering donations, no one could outdo Victor. He not only looked after the museum, he also realized that the museum functioned best with large funds collected from the private donors.

"Hey, Victor!" James shouted back. James stopped where he was at and waited for Victor and his companion.

"James, good to see you," said Victor, as he extended his hand to James. Victor grasped James' hand with his usual tight grip, and shook it enthusiastically. "This is William Donavan. He's one of our favorite museum goers."

James was familiar with Victor's codes. He surmised that William Donavan was a large donator to the Field Museum.

"Pleasure to meet you, Mr. Donavan," said James, as he extended his hand to him.

"Nice to meet you too, but please, call me William. I also would prefer no special treatment, even though Victor has spoken to you in code about my donations," said Donavan, with a wink.

James found Donavan's comment humorous and displayed it with a hearty laugh.

"No problem. Let's go to the book," suggested James.

The three men made their way to the room that the book was stored in. As they walked, they engaged in small talk regarding several topics that had nothing to do with the Book of Knowledge. James was running on fumes. He had spent two solid weeks of twelve-hour days examining the book. His main concern was to put the book in its place and return tomorrow to formally sign the book out in order to bring it to London. James did not want to discuss this with Victor now that Donavan was with them.

They reached the double door that led to the staircase. James removed his keys from his pocket and unlocked the door. He opened the door. James turned to say goodnight to the two men.

"Um, James, you don't mind if we show Mr. Donavan the Book?" Victor asked.

'Victor, I understand that Mr. Donavan is a donator to the museum, however no one is allowed in the room outside of me." James was showing his displeasure at the request.

"James I understand the rules set up for the book. However, I am museum curator and Mr. Donavan is a large contributor, I believe the trust factor should not be in question," Victor persuaded.

James thought to himself and eventually he reluctantly agreed. James believed Victor's rationale. After all, Victor was the museum's curator and a large donor would bother him to see the museum's most important exhibition in decades.

James kept the door open and held it open for Victor and Donavan. James followed the men through the door. Victor followed them down the stairs. James shut the door behind them.

Since the deaths of his three friends and Order members, James had been very cautious within his environment. The thought of someone coming into the Field Museum to take the Book of Knowledge or harm him seemed inconceivable to James but he needed to maintain tight security regarding the Book of Knowledge. They finally reached the room. Next to the door was an eye scanner. Victor was not programmed to enter the room. The only person in the country that could enter the room was James. He proceeded to place his chin in the holder and the blue beam scanned his eye. Within seconds the door became unlocked and the men entered, led by James.

Once inside, James turned all the lights on. Even though they had not entered from a dark room, the brightness of the room forced their eyes to adjust. Sitting on the table in the center of the room, wrapped in its protective covering was the Book of Knowledge. James could not believe that he had forgotten to put the book away, but was glad he came back to check. Since he was the only person that had entry, and he was the last person to exit the room, the blame rested solely on him.

"I can't believe you actually forgot to put the book away," said Victor.

"I know," said James in a somber tone. "I may need a break."

"Well, I think you will soon have the time you need to rest," said Victor.

James looked at Victor with a confused look. Unless Victor had spoken with Andrews and knew that he was bringing the book to London. Once in London, he would definitely be able to take some time to recharge himself.

Donavan walked over to the book. James was getting ready to ask him not to touch the book without gloves, when he put on white gloves. James noticed that Victor was standing by the door. Victor had taken an item off the shelf next to him a placed the item between the door and the doorframe.

"What are you doing here?" Victor said, in a loud voice.

James quickly turned toward the door. Standing in the doorway was a rather attractive woman. James had never seen this person before and also wondered why she was down here with them.

"Never mind why I'm here, Victor," said the woman.

Donavan was thumbing through the book. "This book is incredible. I cannot believe that it's in my grasp. The Book of Knowledge is finally mine," he said.

"Excuse me, who do you think you are... and Mr. Donavan, the book is not yours," said James in a forceful tone.

"Oh, how I grow tired of you and your stupid Order," said Donavan.

James was shocked that this man just mentioned the Order and knew he was a member. James was not sure exactly what was happening but he knew that danger had just gripped his throat. Not sure what he should do, he decided to ignore the woman at the door and walked toward Donavan.

"Mr. Donavan, I'm not sure why you are acting this way and I don't know what you mean by 'my Order,'" said James.

Donavan turned and faced James. "You have no clue who I am, do you?"

James took a step back from Donavan. "You are a donor to the museum. That's all I know about you," said James.

"Of course that's all you know. Now if you and your group had done the necessary research you would have learned that I am the descendant of the architect behind the Scrutatores coming to America. My uncle that lived here in Chicago in the 1800's was a Scrutatore. I'm sure you've heard of the Scrutatores, James Stewart," said Donavan.

The woman walked into the room and walked next to Donavan. She stood next to him, staring at James. Victor had positioned himself next to James.

"I think introductions are in order," said Donavan. James assumed he was talking about the woman. "The man that you know as Victor is also known as 'Ulra,' a current Scrutatore. This beautiful woman is Kantra. You may have heard of her as Susan Wellenmyer. I am also known as Lannar."

"What are you up to?" James stammered, now truly fearful about what was going to happen.

"For the record, you should know that I arranged the assassination of your colleagues," said Lannar gloating.

"You bastard, they were good people," said James.

"Oh well," said Lannar, showing no remorse or emotion over the killing of the Order members.

"What are you planning on doing with the book?" James kept talking, trying to stall and gather as much information from Lannar as possible.

"Well, take it of course. Oh, I will be using it to open the doorway between this plane and the one next to it. I also need the instructions to unleash a devastating plague on this plane," said Lannar, casually. Lannar displayed no concern at divulging this information.

"You will never be allowed," said James angrily. His tone provoked Lannar to continue his diatribe.

"Who will stop me? Once you're dead, the Order will be down to three and incapable of acting. I will have the book. I have the ability to use magic. Even though you and your friends do as well, you don't have the book. Kantra, I'm done talking to this Order member." Lannar turned his back on James. Lannar was trying to distract James' attention to make Kantra's action easier.

Kantra raised her right hand she snapped her arm straight and her palm faced directly at James. "Mortem," she shouted, and a blue light shot out from her at James.

James had prepared himself as Lannar had been speaking. He quickly countered, "Proesido Fortitudo".

A bright light became wrapped around James providing him with a protective shield. The death spell from Kantra bounced off James' shield and struck Ulra flush on his head causing him to fall backward and onto the ground instantly killing him.

James cast a stun spell at Lannar's back, driving him into the door that led into the room. The death spell drained Kantra of some stamina. She found coverage behind the large workstation the Book of Knowledge was on. James quickly ran to the back of the room, sliding behind a large tall cabinet. As he slammed into the wall he cast another stun spell in Kantra's direction. The spell went over Kantra's head and slammed into the back wall crushing the equipment on the shelves and leaving a distinct mark on the wall.

Lannar was on the ground, incapable of moving. James' stun spell struck him on his back. The spell was powerful. Lannar was unable to move for several minutes. He could hear the casting between Kantra and James. Kantra was gaining some of her stamina but not fast enough. She had brought a vial filled with a potion that gave her instant energy. Kantra anticipated that James would not go down without a fight. As she drank the potion, James cast another stun spell in her direction. Once again the spell flew over her, causing an explosion against another section of the back wall. Kantra got to her feet and shot a maximum stun spell at James. The spell struck the cabinet that James was standing next to for protection. The contents of the cabinet came crashing out the cabinets' doors. The cabinet was slammed into James driving him to the ground. James quickly cast another protective spell before Kantra's second spell struck his shield.

Lannar crawled over to where Kantra was.

"Cast a death spell over his head or off to his side. That will cause him to cast a spell our way and while he's defenseless I'll strike him with my death spell."

Kantra nodded, and attempted to cast a spell. As she stood, James had anticipated a spell coming his way and had timed his stun spell with Kantra's movement. She was struck by the thick red light, driving her into the wall behind her. Lannar cast a stun spell to the right of James. The small explosion caused another explosion to the left of James. Glass and other debris from the equipment exploding around him hit him. James noticed that he was bleeding from the side of his face.

Lannar stood and spread his arms and brought them together. He had summoned all his strength. A bright red light engulfed the room. The light came back into one and shot from Lannar, striking James' body.

Lannar walked over to James and kicked his leg to confirm that he was dead. James' lifeless body shook a little, but no other reaction. Lannar had now succeeded in assassinating a fourth Order member. Lannar turned and walked back to the Book of Knowledge. He placed the book into a duffle bag that Kantra had brought with her.

"Our work is done here. We now need to learn how and where to put our plan in motion," said Lannar. Before he left the room he glanced over at Ulra. "Good-bye, my old friend."

The two Scrutatores walked out the door and made their way back to Trump Tower.

25

A NEW SEARCH

The good news from the night before was short-lived. Before they could celebrate the discovery, a phone call from Chicago changed everything. Mary called Andrews and informed him that his friend was dead. Andrews broke the news to John. John excused himself and went to his room. James was the fourth Order member to die in the past six months. This had never happened in the history of the Order. Even during their active years.

The discovery of the Book of Spells being in Britain was a needed break for the Order. Andrews woke up early, ventured down to the kitchen and started brewing a pot of coffee. He had sent the kitchen crew home for the weekend. He often did this in order to allow himself the opportunity to manage the kitchen himself. While he was preparing the coffee, John also awakened early and joined him in the large, state-of-the-art kitchen.

"Morning, Andrews," said John, as he entered the kitchen. He sat down at the oval glass table.

Andrews brought over two cups of coffee and joined him. "Morning John, you're up early."

"I really didn't get a good night's sleep."

"Sorry to hear that. I hope the room was comfortable?"

"The room was fine, and the bed very comfortable. It's everything that we need to do before we can engage them," said John.

"I know. The loss of James is forcing us to use them sooner than we anticipated," said Andrews.

"No way. They aren't even close to being ready," said John, his tone very emotional.

"John, none of you are ready to confront them. I will examine the tape that Mary brought, but I expect that it's foul play that killed James, not the supposed heart attack that the authorities think. The evidence I expect to see on the tape combined with my experience, I'd say we have to get the Book of Spells soon. I know you don't want them to get involved, but unfortunately I think you know that they have to, in order for us to defeat them, even stand a chance," said Andrews.

"How was Mary able to get the tape, if she had no access to the museum?" John wondered.

"She told me that James had set her up with keys, and the scanner and took her through the lab and instructed her with what to do in case of an emergency, or he became ill," said Andrews.

"He was always one step ahead. What will happen to his body?" John asked.

"As you know, all of the Order members have me listed as their next of kin. Once the body comes out here, I will have him cremated. Unfortunately, you and the others won't be able to participate in the ceremony. At least I don't have to stage a car accident, like I had to for Adam, Susan, and Maria," added Andrews, as he got up to get more coffee for both of them.

"Why am I not able to participate?" John asked, as he watched Andrews pour coffee into both of their cups.

"You, Emily, and Julia are traveling back to Chicago to retrieve the Journal of James Sullivan. Mary told me that she didn't have time to search once she was notified of James' death," said Andrews.

"I see. I will mourn their deaths at a later date," said John, with a large sigh and a heavy feeling in his chest.

"So that it's not a surprise, the four of them will go and retrieve the needed materials. I will be busy bringing James home."

"I guess, what other options do we have," said John.

"None," said Andrews.

John finished his coffee and went back to his room to pack. He decided to allow Emily and Julia to sleep in. As John packed, he thought about the loss of his good friend and comrade. James had been John's best friend. He helped John during his grieving over the death of his brother and John did the same for James over the death of his father. They were both inducted into the Order at the same ceremony. James was inducted even though his father was still alive. James' father had reached an age that was too old to be an active member. They had been so excited to be members. John now had to lead the Order on his own. All of the older members, except for him, had been murdered. He now questioned the deaths of Julia and Emily's mothers. It was now up to him to be the experienced one... with so little experience. John had spent the last twenty years working as a college professor and an archeologist. He now had to make decisions for himself and the other six members. None of them over the age thirty. Seventeen years separated him from the next eldest. On top of all that was the fact that his niece was an Order member. John wanted to establish a relationship with her as uncle and niece, not as the leader of the Order of Seven.

Andrews informed Emily and Julia of their new mission. They packed and joined John in the front room. Andrews and the four youngest members waited with them for their car to arrive. To be less conspicuous, Andrews decided that they should fly coach on British Air Ways. The private jet may be monitored and could tip any Scrutatores watching the airport. They said their good-byes and got into the cab.

Andrews led the other four Order members back into the kitchen. He had prepared a large breakfast for them. He figured that they would need a good meal before embarking on their first mission. He instructed them to sit at the table, and proceeded to serve them.

"There has been a change of plans. You four are going to retrieve the materials from the Hill Wood Forest. I had the car prepared last night with all the materials you will need," said Andrews.

"Awesome," said Dwayne, with great excitement.

"Really, us?" Rosa questioned.

"Yes, you are about to perform your first mission as Order members," said Andrews.

"This sounds like an easy one," said David.

"On the surface, it sounds easy. But let's play it safe, regardless of its appearances," cautioned Andrews.

"Andrews, how can walking into a forest and gathering things be difficult or dangerous?" asked Bridgette.

"Remember that the Scrutatores already have powerful spells and they have used them. Therefore we can conclude that they had the knowledge needed and may have people there protecting the forest," said Andrews.

"True, I didn't even think of that," said Bridgette.

"I have placed several weapons in the car that you will need to carry with you. All of you," said Andrews.

"None of us have any experience using a firearm," pointed out Rosa.

"Well, you don't have experience with spells or firearms. There are four crossbows," said Andrews.

"We have no experience with crossbows either!" David protested.

"Before you leave, I will show you how to load and fire them. It's relatively easy," assured Andrews.

"Okay, no problem with the crossbows. Why don't we get started, so we can leave and be back before nightfall," suggested Bridgette.

"You will not be back before nightfall. The forest is one hundred miles outside of London. It's a total of four hours of travel there and back. Not to mention time spent searching," said Andrews.

"Let's get started then," said David.

Andrews led them into the large yard that was encased by the castle walls. A few nights ago they were being inducted into the Order in the same location. Andrews had his ground crew set up targets for them to shoot at. He spent the next hour demonstrating how to load and fire the crossbow. Dwayne and David learned instantaneously, Andrews was amazed by how quickly they caught on. Rosa also got the hang of firing the weapon fairly quickly. Bridgette, on the other hand, had a much harder time. She missed her targets on each attempt. Some of her shots went over the targets; some shots listed left and some went right.

Finally, Bridgette gave up and slammed the crossbow to the ground. "Screw this!"

David, Rosa, and Dwayne laughed hysterically.

"Man, you suck!" Dwayne shouted, in between gut-busting laughter.

"No shit, you really do suck," said David with the same zeal.

"I never thought I'd live to see the day when I'm better than you at something athletic," said Rosa, holding back her laughter.

"Whatever. Let's get going," said Bridgette, walking back to the door.

"Bridgette! There is nothing to be upset about, this is not an easy task," said Andrews to Bridgette's back as she walked toward the castle.

"I think you guys were a little hard on her," admonished Andrews as he turned and faced the other three.

"You don't understand, Andrews. She is always good at everything she does. Finally we witnessed her fail at something. Man, that's a good feeling," said David.

"Come on, let us get going. You all have an important task, so the razing needs to stop now," said Andrews.

They all met Bridgette at the car. She was going through the gear in the hatchback compartment. She looked through each backpack to see the equipment that had been packed for them.

"Hey there you are," said David, as they approached her.

"David you drive, and I'll co-pilot," said Bridgette already over her failure with the crossbow practice.

"Hey, I drive," said Dwayne.

"No way. You have a hard enough time when the wheel is on the left side," said Bridgette.

"Oh, it's a black thing," said Dwayne.

"No...It's a bad driving thing," said Rosa as she walked past Dwayne, smacking him across his chest. David started laughing as he sat himself in the driver's seat. They all got into the car. Bridgette rolled down her window and Andrews went to her side of the car.

"You all be careful. I checked the weather report and it snowed in that area last night. There are several centimeters of snow on the ground. Call for anything."

"Andrews, we'll be fine. After all, I have three people that can use a crossbow. They have no clue how to organize a sock drawer, but they can fire a crossbow. Hopefully, this will only take a few hours. I noticed the tent in case we have to stay overnight," said Bridgette.

"Okay, be careful. I'll see you all soon. Godspeed," said Andrews.

"Bye," replied the others.

David placed the car into drive and they headed out.

26

SHORT VISIT

John, Emily, and Julia had arrived at O'Hare airport in Chicago at six in the evening. They got their bags, hopped in a cab and were off to John's apartment in Bucktown. As if on cue, once they entered his apartment John's phone started to ring. He looked at his phone and saw Andrews' name on the caller ID. The two talked for thirty minutes. Emily and Julia went into their rooms for a quick nap. John finished his call and went into his room for a quick nap himself.

Several hours elapsed since John had finished his call with Andrews. John, Emily, and Julia needed to take a break from everything they were working on, so they decided to go out, but didn't want to travel far from their home base. They decided to walk across the street and have a couple of drinks at the neighborhood tavern. A stroll to the neighborhood bar would help, and 'The Web' had been a neighborhood bar for decades. It was the ideal place for them. John had been frequenting it since he moved into the neighborhood.

They left the apartment and walked across the street. The evening sky is was a clear, smooth black. A full moon was always an impressive sight, but when the moon was closer to the earth, its size was massive and intimidating.

"Check out the Perigee Moon," said Emily, as they walked across the street.

"Perigee Moon?" John asked.

"The Perigee Moon is a full moon."

"Hey thanks for that information," interrupted John.

"Can I finish?"

"Yeah, just kidding, I couldn't resist." John opened the front door to the Web and gestured for his two female companions to walk in first.

"Such a gentleman," said Julia.

Once inside, the girls looked around. The bar's lighting was on the dark side. As they walked in Emily and Julia noticed two dartboards set on the wall. John commented on how he loved playing steel tip darts. As they moved forward they were quickly in front of the very large square bar with stools and chairs around it. On the wall was an assortment of famous athlete's action photos in black and white, from an era long gone. The pictures were a mix between Chicago Cubs and Chicago Bears players. On the wall to the left were caricatures of the regulars that frequented the bar.

John and Emily sat in two stools at the front of the bar. They left the seat in between them for Julia. She was heading toward the bathroom. The bartender made her way toward them.

"Hey John, haven't seen you for a while. How you been?" She asked.

"I've been vacationing in London," he replied.

"Must be nice. I've always wanted to visit England. The usual?"

John was definitely in need of a cocktail. "I'll have a shot of Jameson with my beer. Emily what do you want?"

Emily didn't hesitate. "That'll work for me."

John was a bit surprised by her order. He didn't figure Emily as a beer and a shot kind of girl.

"What do you think Julia will want?"

"I'm not sure, but I think she'll probably want a glass of wine," she suggested.

The bartender handed them two bottles of Miller Lite and two shot glasses.

"So you were saying about the moon?" John asked Emily.

"Really? I think I'm done with that conversation."

"Come on, don't be mad, I really want to hear the rest," said John.

"I'm not mad, but if you're that interested, Google it." They both started laughing as soon as she finished her comment.

All of the hard liquor was kept on a small island in the middle of the square bar. The bartender reached for the Jameson bottle and filled up their glasses.

"You know what your friend wants?" She asked.

"Well, we better wait for her, I usually don't drink hard liquor and I'm having one," said Emily.

John gave her a quick glance at the comment she made. "Why you drinking it then?" He asked.

"It's been a long week, no, it's been a long six months. I figured I could use a stiff one."

John grinned at the comment.

"I walked into to that one," said Emily.

"What, I wasn't insinuating anything."

"Shut up," said Emily, with an embarrassed grin on her face.

Julia made her way back and sat on the stool between them. She looked at the drinks they were having and preceded to order. "I'll have what they're having."

The bartender nodded her head and set her up with the same drinks. As soon as her shot was poured, Julia raised her shot glass. "To the fallen members of the Order."

Emily and John followed suit and raised their glasses and repeated the same toast. They each downed their shot, reached for their beers and took a swig out of their bottle.

"I wouldn't have figured on either of you being a shot and a beer kind of drinker," said John.

"That's all I ever drink when I go out, another round please," said Julia.

"Not me, I prefer a glass of wine or a mixed drink. I'll probably switch to a mixed drink soon," said Emily. She then turned her attention to Julia, "When we were in Sicily you only drank wine the two nights we went out."

"That's because we were in Sicily. The wine is fabulous there."

"Yeah, it was pretty good," responded Emily.

"When in Rome." said Julia.

They all laughed at that one. John motioned for the bartender, "Amy, will you pour us three more Jameson's, please."

The Bartender grabbed the Jameson bottle and poured three more shots.

"Let's do this round to our new associates and the luck they will need on their mission," said Emily. They each downed the shot.

"Amy, can we use the bar darts?" John asked.

"Why would you use the bar darts? Your darts are right here." Amy pointed to the small area cut out of the island, underneath was a drawer that sat just below the register.

"Totally forgot." John thanked her as she handed him his dart case.

The three of them walked over to the farthest dartboard from the bar. There were twenty plaques on the wall with the names of each winning team that participated in the Windy City Dart League.

"Are you on any of those plaques?" Emily asked.

"Yeah, I'm on these two," pointed John, with great pride. Emily and Julia walked to the plaques.

"There you are, John Williams," said Julia, pointing at his name and speaking in a sassy voice.

"Not only are you a college professor, an archeologist, a weapons specialist, special trainer to the Order, member of the Order, but you are also a dart enthusiast," said Emily.

"Funny. You two are very funny. I think a stint in Vegas is a part of your future," said John.

The laughing and the sarcasm continued for the next hour. So did the drinking.

Emily and Julia took turns throwing the three darts. Several times John had asked if they wanted to play a game of cricket. Each time they responded with a resounding no. They enjoyed the relaxing evening. None of them had commented on Order matters. They accomplished an unexpected task, which was relaxation.

"This has been great, no calls, no driving, no flying around on a plane. Just what the doctor ordered," said Emily. John and Julia nodded their heads in agreement with her.

It seemed that just as she uttered the words, John's phone started ringing, interrupting their moment of leisure. The phone's ring cut through the good time like a hot knife through butter. John picked his phone up from the table. The caller ID displayed a phone number and no name. He answered his phone and realized that it was an important call.

"Back to work," said Emily, with a sigh.

John walked outside the bar to continue his call with less noise. The music wasn't so loud that they couldn't talk, however, it was loud enough to make talking on the phone difficult.

Julia and Emily stopped throwing the darts and congregated around a table, looking outside as John walked back and forth while talking. They watched him as he kept nodding his head in apparent agreement. The evening was ending in a grinding halt. John walked back in, looked at both of them and motioned for them to leave.

"It's on for tomorrow morning. I figure before we get too drunk, we should leave."

With that, they walked back across the street. On the way, they noticed the moon had disappeared from where it was when they arrived at the Web. They entered the apartment.

"We need to be up and ready to leave by ten," said John. They each wished each other a good night's sleep and went into their separate rooms.

The alarm clock started playing "I'm walking on Sunshine" in Emily's room from her iPod. She reached over and pressed the snooze button. There were two more swipes at the snooze until she finally got out of bed and headed for a 'wake me up shower'. Emily stumbled her way to the bathroom and into the shower, feeling the effects from last night's drinks. While she was showering, she started thinking about how in several hours everything was going to change. She started to feel the pressure of training the young Order members on things she was not even certain she's capable of performing herself. There was also the pressure that she would need to learn how to use dangerous spells. As her nerves grew, she turned the water off. Emily dried herself off and headed back to her room. She knew she had some time for a jog to release some stress. Emily headed out the door while John and Julia lay in their beds, waiting for their alarm to sound.

Emily had been out running for a half hour when the other two woke up. As they dressed, Emily had returned from her run and went straight to the shower. She joined the other two in the dining room. "Morning all," she said.

John and Julia smiled and returned the morning greeting.

"This day could be a long one. I think the man should call today," said John.

"Um, don't you know his name?" Julia asked.

"No. He never gave me his name and said he will call with instructions today on where and when we will meet him," said John.

"Andrews doesn't know his name either?" Said Julia.

"Nope," replied John.

"This doesn't make any sense. There is no name in the journal of James Stewart, and no name in any of the documents we retrieved from Sicily. Unbelievable," Emily fumed.

"The hard part is that we know Lannar and his followers have death and destruction spells and are using them," said John, frustrated.

"So we wait. I'm turning the TV on," said Emily.

Emily left the dining room and walked into the family room. She sprawled on the couch and turned the plasma TV on. Julia and John remained in the dining room looking over the documents they brought with them from London. They were hoping to find something that might have been overlooked. They spent the next half hour reading and rereading them. As they were about to put the documents away, John's cell started ringing.

"It's Andrews," said John, as he looked at the name on the screen. "Hey Andrews, anything new?"

"Morning, John. Hope you all had a good night's sleep." As Andrews finished his sentence, John knew immediately that there was some sort of a breakthrough and that they were going to have a long day ahead of them.

"We found his name. Well, I should say Bridgette deciphered the clue. The good news is that we have his name and have already made contact with him. He lives in Mexico City. I have already arranged transportation for him to come out here to London," said Andrews.

"He called me last night," said John. Before he could continue Andrews interrupted.

"That could not be him. I spoke with him yesterday and never gave him your number or your name. I think you are all in danger and should leave your apartment ASAP and head to London sooner than we planned," said Andrews frantically.

"I don't understand," John said.

"When James' belongings were sent to me, I could not find his cell. Then Bridgette deciphered the location and name of the Book of Spells translator. I called him and explained who I was, and he understood and had been waiting for this moment his entire life, he too is a Stamen," said Andrews.

"Okay, you found him, then who did I talk to last night? I think we should investigate and find out," said John.

"I agree, you should find out, but Lannar and his group have spells and use them. You have no defense. The video that we retrieved from the museum, before the authorities thankfully, had audio capability, but confirmed that there is more than one person with the ability to use magic. It's unsafe for you to stay in Chicago. We now know who we are up against," said Andrews.

"I can't argue with you on this one. You're right. We will head there today. Is there anything we should do before heading out?" John asked.

"No just get on a plane and get out here. I figure you and Jose Batista should arrive at roughly the same time, and we can get started in training and figuring out where the Tower is located and bring the fight to them," said Andrews.

"And avenge our fallen members," said John quietly into his phone.

"John, you can not think this way. I'm feeling the same, but if we allow vengeance to consume us, then we will fail," said Andrews.

"Okay, I'll relax on that thought. But they've killed four of our members and probably my brother, don't expect me to fully get that out of my mind," said John.

"I understand. Get packed and on a plane within the next hour or so. I'll talk to you when you get here. Be careful and be aware of your surroundings."

"See you soon," said John, and ended the call.

As soon as John hung up, he explained to Emily and Julia the contents of the call. They were both concerned over their safety and agreed they should head to London.

"Well, let's get packed and fly once again. I wish I had a frequent flyer card," said Emily. The three packed and were out the door within half an hour. John sped toward the airport. They were looking forward to learning how to effectively use powerful magic.

27

THE START OF MAGIC

Bridgette studied the map as they made their way off the Andrews compound. Dwayne and Rosa sat in the back of the Land Rover and discussed the excitement of using a crossbow. David concentrated on the road. Driving on the opposite side of the road made him feel awkward. Bridgette guided him through London to the road that would take them to Hill Wood Forest.

"Can you guys believe that we have spent three months in London?" Dwayne asked.

"I know. Our lives have changed so much since August," Rosa commented.

"Are you guys comfortable with the changes?" Bridgette asked.

"I am," said David.

"How 'bout you guys?" Bridgette asked, indicating Rosa and Dwayne.

"I am. I feel closer to my parents," said Dwayne.

"Me too," agreed Rosa.

"I don't know. I mean, on one hand I'm proud to follow in my dad's footsteps. On the other hand, I feel like I'm giving up so much," admitted Bridgette.

"What are you possibly giving up?" David asked.

"My freedom, for one. Also, I was looking forward to going to college and being able to do all the things that an average person does," Bridgette continued. She turned and faced Dwayne and Rosa. "Being an Order member complicates everything. Being an Order member will trump anything we want to do. Our lives are never going to be normal again."

"I don't think we ever had a normal life," said Rosa, quietly.

"Think about how and where we lived. We might not have known we would be Order members, but the people around us did."

"Agreed. Normalcy was never in the equation, we just never knew it," Dwayne added.

"Well, before we get excited, remember four members have died. And I mean murdered. It sounds exciting to be member but it's also extremely dangerous," said Bridgette, turning back around and facing forward. "I wonder if the Scrutatores did the same to our parents?"

The inside of the car became silent. For the next hour no one spoke. The silence was broken when they arrived at the intersection where they needed to turn. After another half hour of driving, the outskirts of the forest were reached. They finally arrived at the location where they had been instructed to park the car. Before leaving, Andrews had informed them that he was making Bridgette the group leader, and that she was to make any final decisions.

"Where do you think we should park? There is no parking lot," said David.

"Let's park inside the opening, get out the gear and head in, following that path next to that opening," suggested Bridgette, pointing to a narrow dirt path where they would have to walk single file.

David pulled the car off the road and drove down onto a stretch of grass that led into the forest. Luck was on their side for there were no other cars on the road with them. Before they left, Andrews had told them that the forest was located next to the road in one of the few remote locations in Britain. The black SUV would blend in with the trees, so seeing the car from the road would prove to be difficult. David was able to drive the car into the forest and park it in an area hidden from the main road. Dwayne was the first one out of the car.

"Let's get our gear," said Bridgette.

"On it," replied Dwayne, from outside the car.

"The trees are so tall," said David, leaning into the steering wheel and looking up.

"The trees have to be one hundred feet tall," Rosa added, standing just outside the car.

"Look at how beautiful they look with the snow covering on them. It must have snowed here last night," said Bridgette.

"Get back here and help me get the gear out," said Dwayne. David walked back to Dwayne, followed by Rosa and Bridgette.

"Should we bring the tent with us?" Dwayne asked.

"No. We'll leave it with the car and come back if we need it," said Bridgette.

"Is that a good idea? What happens if there are people in there waiting for us?" Rosa asked.

"Good point. I didn't even think of that. We should bring it with us," decided Bridgette, placing the tent next to her backpack. "Since I'm not good with a crossbow, I'll attach the tent to my backpack."

"That's a small tent," David commented.

"Are we all going to fit in there?" Dwayne asked.

"I've actually used this type before," assured Bridgette, as she started to attach the tent to her backpack. "It's a small tent, but it's big enough for the four of us and since it's cold, our body heat will help keep us warm. To make it lighter, I'm leaving my crossbow."

"Let me know if it gets too heavy. We'll switch," offered David.

"It's not going to matter. My pack has the tent. All three of your packs will have crossbows," said Bridgette.

Bridgette led the group into the forest. With each step into the forest, it became denser and darker. Within several minutes the forest engulfed them and limited the lighting. The thickness of trees and bushes were all around them. The trees towered over them. The path they walked on threaded its way through the forest. The thickness of the trees protected the ground from the snowfall of the previous night. The temperature was cold and kept the snow on the branches from melting. On occasion, a strong gust of wind knocked some of the snow onto them.

"Let's stop here and look over the notes Andrews gave us. Plus, I could use a breather. We've been walking for over an hour," said Bridgette. No arguments from the other three; they too needed a rest.

They stopped in an opening. This was the only area they came by that had presented a clear view of the sky. Around them were five large tree trunks that seem to have been dragged into the area many years ago. The tree trunks appeared to be a third of the size of the trees around them. They each walked to a trunk and sat down.

"Hey, check it out, a circle of rocks is deep in the ground in the middle here," said Dwayne. The others looked over at the area that Dwayne was pointing at

"Do you think there's been a recent fire?" Rosa asked.

David walked over to the area. He had not taken his backpack off when he sat on the trunk. He knelt down around the tip of a rock that was protruding from the ground. He searched through his backpack and pulled out a trowel. He dug around the rock tip. He proceeded to dig up five rocks, placed in an obvious circle.

"I'd say this is a fire pit, but no recent fire. Probably not for a very long time," David surmised.

"Why not a long time?" Rosa asked.

"Well, the rocks are either a little over the ground or completely covered with dirt. The dirt is tight around the rocks. If it was recent, there would be a loose fit," said David.

"I had no idea you were so smart on geology matters," said Dwayne.

"I'm not, I stayed at a Holiday Inn last night," responded David, causing everyone to laugh. "Seriously, I paid attention in Geology class and how the ground consumes objects that don't move over a period of time."

"Gotta love AP classes," said Dwayne.

"Yeah, Dr. Richards loved pointing that kind of stuff out to us," said David.

“Then this is an area people may have camped out at or used as a guard post,” Bridgette suggested. “Think about it. We can’t be too far. Let’s rest for another five minutes, and then get going. I looked over the notes and we are looking for trees with a crescent moon on them.”

“That should be easy,” said Rosa sarcastically.

The time had come to start walking. Bridgette stood and motioned for everyone to get moving. They followed the path deeper into the woods. The sunlight kept eluding them. The lack of light would make finding the correct tree difficult. Thirty minutes had passed since leaving the rest area. Bridgette noticed a tree to her right with markings on it by sheer luck. As they neared it, she noticed that the marking was a large full moon. Dwayne walked around the tree. As he did, he noticed another tree with similar markings.

“This is weird, let’s get back on the trail. Obviously the markings are purposely done to get people off the path,” said Bridgette.

“I think you’re right,” said Rosa.

Bridgette headed back for the path, with Rosa following closely. David and Dwayne looked at each other, shrugged their shoulders and followed Bridgette and Rosa back to the path. As they walked, they noticed the same markings on trees to their left and further down the path on both sides. Three hours had now passed since entering the forest. The sun was beginning to set outside and inside the forest; it had already turned to night. They went into their backpacks and pulled out flashlights. It was evident to them that spending the night in the forest was becoming likely.

Bridgette tried to place a call to Andrews. However, the denseness of the forest prevented a signal from being found. For the first time, they were truly on their own. This may have been an enticing predicament in most matters, but in this situation they were all a bit nervous.

“We need to think about finding a place where we can pitch the tent,” said Bridgette.

“We have more time before we start talking about camping in this creepy forest,” said Rosa.

“Rosa, the sun is setting and it’s already dark in here. The car is four hours away and we haven’t found anything. I noticed that some food and water is in our packs, so we'll be fine. If we find nothing by tomorrow, we'll head back and replenish our supplies and return," said Bridgette.

David and Dwayne agreed with Bridgette.

"How do we find a place to camp?" David asked.

"Let's break up into two groups and head in opposite directions," suggested Bridgette. "Rosa and I will head this way, and you two go that way. Walk around for fifteen minutes then come back."

"You think..." David began, but was quickly interrupted by Bridgette.

"Don't even think about going down that road, David," she said. "Rosa and I are more than capable of venturing off on our own. Now you guys go that way and we'll go this way," she finished, as she nudged Rosa to follow.

They made their way in the direction Bridgette wanted to go. Dwayne and David watched them for a minute and then started in the opposite direction. Both groups found themselves walking over branches, bushes and other debris.

David and Dwayne did not come across a viable area to pitch the tent. Time had elapsed and David and Dwayne made their way back. As they reached the path, they noticed Rosa standing there, and questioned where Bridgette was.

"We found an area and she started clearing it to pitch the tent. It's not far, about fifteen minutes in," said Rosa.

"Cool. We found nothing," said Dwayne.

David, Dwayne, and Rosa reached the area where Bridgette was. They each helped in clearing and setting up the tent. After a half hour, they had set up a nice area to overnight camp. After setting up the area, Bridgette again attempted to call Andrews. She figured that since there was an opening she would give it another try. This time she managed to find a signal. She informed him that all was well and that they are were spending the night in Hill Wood Forest. Andrews agreed that it was a good idea and once again reminded her that they should be cautious and careful.

David walked to the edge of their encampment facing the thick forest area.

"I think I heard something," he said, continuing to face the direction he was looking in.

"This is a forest and there are probably woodland creatures in here," said Dwayne sarcastically.

"Woodland? You could just say animals. Dork," Rosa teased.

"Two of us should check it out," said Bridgette, being serious. "Rosa, go with David and look around but don't go too far. Stay within shouting distance."

"All right," said Rosa, reluctantly walking towards David.

David and Rosa headed in the direction where David thought he had heard something. As they walked, Rosa handed David his crossbow. They both paused for a moment and loaded their weapons.

"Remember, don't shoot unless we're being attacked," whispered David.

"Then if I were you, I wouldn't startle me at any point in this search," said Rosa, also whispering. David shook his head as he looked around. Normally he would engage in the friendly bantering but he knew the seriousness of the situation.

The two walked further than they were supposed to. David noticed another opening in the woods and suggested they should check it out. As they reached the area, they realized that the sun had set, and as they looked upwards noticed the evening sky. As they looked around, Rosa came across an interesting find.

"Check it out. There are four paths spreading out from here," she said to David.

"Way to be on your toes, Rosa." said David, as he examined one of the paths. "I think we should get Bridgette and Dwayne over here. One of us should go back. I'll do whichever you don't want to do."

"I'll go, I remember the way."

"All right then...I agree you should go," said David.

Rosa ran back to the campsite. Once there, she explained to Bridgette and Dwayne what they found. Bridgette and Dwayne agreed that they should do some investigating. First to arrive to David was Dwayne.

"Hey, where are Bridgette and Rosa?" David asked.

"Lagging behind, probably talking about girl stuff," said Dwayne. "Where are these paths you guys found?"

"Right here," said David. "Check it out. They each head out in a different direction."

While David and Dwayne were examining the paths and speculating where they led to, Rosa and Bridgette walked up. David stood from his kneeling position and pointed to the paths.

"Well, what should we do, boss?" David asked, directing his question to Bridgette.

"I think we should follow them and see where or what they lead to," said Bridgette.

"Yeah, but there are four paths," said David.

"We each take one," Bridgette replied.

As soon as the words left her mouth, a realization set in. Whatever they encounter, it would be done alone. They knew that they had no experience and very little training. Bridgette had felt comfortable and confident as she suggested they go on their own. But now that the words had come out of her mouth, doubt and fear crept in to replace that confidence.

"You think that's a good idea?" Rosa asked.

"Look, I don't like this any more than any of you," said Bridgette, not sure herself of what to do, "But if we are to be Order members we need to accept the responsibility that comes with it, and the reality that this is real and that we can get hurt or worse."

"Let's do this and set a time frame to return," suggested Dwayne.

"Okay, I think that we should follow the path and if in a half hour we find nothing, return. If you find something, come back sooner and after we regroup we'll go back together," said Bridgette.

They synchronized their watches, and headed out on their path. They ventured off slowly. After several steps they would look back at each other. Finally, when they looked, there was no one to look back at them. Sounds started occurring in the woods, each of them passed it off as the wind blowing around them, even though it sounded like someone was whispering in their ears.

Dwayne was the first to head down the assigned path. As he walked deeper down the trail he was hearing the sound of someone stepping on tree branches. This continued for fifteen minutes. He was now deep into his trail. Suddenly he saw a flash of red light buzz his head and strike the tree next to him. There was a small explosion on the tree causing bark to fly around him.

Dwayne dropped and rolled. He quickly threw off his backpack and reached for his crossbow. Dwayne quickly loaded an arrow and crawled off the path and looked in the direction the light came from. Neither Dwayne nor the others had been trained how to use or identify any form of magic. This was clearly a stun spell shot in his direction.

Even though Dwayne was not familiar with spells, he was able to deduce that someone or thing was shooting something in his direction.

Dwayne walked in a slumped manner looking over the area in front of him and off to his side. Another flash came in his direction, once again striking a tree and causing the same destruction. Dwayne dropped to the ground. He noticed a hand sized rock next to him. He grabbed the rock and threw it off to his right hoping to draw the attackers attention to look in that direction. He stayed crouched in the same place waiting to see if his attacker would reveal himself to him. Dwayne spotted a man with a beard walking upward through the brush in the direction he threw the rock.

Dwayne studied the path the man was walking. It appeared to him that there was some sort of animal following him. He noticed that the creature was half man and half horse.

"A centaur??" Dwayne thought to himself. He figured his eyes were playing tricks on him. Then the centaur was in an open area, and his thought was confirmed. Dwayne raised his crossbow after several seconds, after his shaking had stopped. He had never shot at anyone or thing. His nerves were beginning to get the better of him. Dwayne quickly gained his composure and moved in on his target to have a better shot. His nerves and fears had quickly vanished. As he moved in closer he noticed that the centaur was circling the area. Dwayne managed to get closer. He was confident that the centaur's distance was in his range. He lifted his crossbow and placed it in a firing position. He pulled the trigger and the arrow sliced its way through the air.

Within seconds the arrow found its target. The arrow struck the centaur in its midsection, and it let out a howl and then quickly disappeared. Dwayne walked over to where the centaur was. He looked around the area and did not see any tracks leading away from the area, only the ones leading there. He studied the area for several minutes. After awhile Dwayne decided he needed to get back to his path and continue.

Meanwhile, Bridgette held her flashlight steady in her hand, pointing it toward the ground, illuminating the path she was following. At times she would stop and point the flashlight off the path to see what was making the weird sounds she was hearing, like a person shrieking or a loud pounding sound. With nothing but trees around her, the sounds started to make her think that the forest was haunted. She wished she had brought her crossbow with her. Even though she had a hard time firing it, she figured that she could at least use it to scare something or someone away.

The sun was now completely set and on its way to cross the Atlantic. The forest's density blocked any light from the moon or the evening sky. If she could climb one of the trees and reach the top, she would glance upon a clear winter British sky. Bridgette brought her left wrist up to view her watch. She noticed the watch had stopped. Thinking nothing of it, she reached into her left pocket and took out her iPhone and was shocked to see that the phone was dead. It was fully charged when she called Andrews. There was no way that the battery could have run down. What she was unaware of is that the same thing was happening to her fellow Order members.

Bridgette needed to make a decision: return to the meeting spot or forge on. After a brief thought process, she decided to move on. A strange smell had suddenly started. The smell grew stronger with each step she took. She wondered what the smell was. At first, it reminded her of a roaring campfire and with each step it became more prominent. The strong smell became more and more distinct until it finally reminded her of roasting chestnuts. The scent was pleasing to Bridgette. She was becoming entranced with the smell. Suddenly, she heard her name called out. Bridgette's fear disappeared. The voice sounded as if it were surprised to see her.

As she traveled further, she noticed the path had come to an end. It led directly to a tree ten feet ahead of her. She cautiously moved forward. Bridgette did not hear her name or any sound from the surrounding forest. She was now standing directly in front of the tree. She walked behind it, expecting to see the path continue, but it did not. As she made her way around the tree, she noticed an image in the tree begin to illuminate. The light became blindingly bright. Bridgette quickly covered her eyes. The bright golden light reached it zenith and then faded. As it faded, Bridgette uncovered her eyes and noticed a crescent moon. She had found the marking they set out to find.

Bridgette extended her hand and rubbed the smooth golden moon. She was a little confused because the object rendered itself on the tree as she stood in front of it. She was relieved that she found it, but was now not sure what to do. As she thought about it, the ground below her vanished and she fell down onto her back. A slight pain shot through her. As she lay there, she reached for her flashlight and shined it in the direction she fell from. Suddenly the ground above her started to close. She leapt to her feet and tried to reach the ground she fell through, but was too far down.

In a state of panic, she flashed the light around to see her new surroundings. She was definitely underground. The circular chamber she was in had a set of torches on the wall. She walked up to one of them, and unexpectedly it lit up. The same happened with the other four torches. There were three openings, and two wooden benches nestled in between the openings.

Bridgette noticed a bright blue light inside one of the tunnels, slowly making its way toward her. As she stood there, a blue orb entered the circular room emitting a loud humming noise. The orb moved towards Bridgette and floated in front of her.

"It's so pleasing to see you again, Bridgette." The voice came from the orb.

Bridgette, shocked by the speaking orb, stumbled backwards landing in a seated position on one of the benches.

"Um... who are you?" Bridgette asked in a frightened voice. "What do you want from me?"

The orb transformed itself into a glowing person. Bridgette found the person to be familiar.

"I'm your father, Richard Williams," said the ghost.

"You're who?" Bridgette asked, shocked. "You can't be, my father is dead."

"In case you didn't notice, sweetie, I'm in front of you in a ghost-like state, but I and your mother are not dead."

"Really, you're my father? Mom too is alive?" Bridgette gasped, as tears started to form in her eyes.

"Yes. Please, don't cry," said Bridgette's father. "We have limited time together. There is so much I want to say, but time will not allow."

"I have so much to ask," said Bridgette, with tears streaming down her face.

"Oh, sweetie, I'm so happy to see you."

"Dad, I love you and mom and have never stopped thinking of you," said Bridgette.

"We know, your love is always felt. In time, you will be able to speak with us. You have the gift of talking with the dead, but we are not dead. Your ability has allowed myself and three other Order members to speak with your fellow Order members," he said.

"I have a gift?" Bridgette asked, as she remembered her encounter at the lake house. She realized that her assumption was right; the spirit of Jonas Bearden had been trying to speak with her.

"I am so pleased that you decided to become an Order member. Everything you are looking for is in this room. At the right time, ask and the materials you are searching for will appear before you. Also, there is a description of how to train with spells in a building guarded by three of the Knights Templar in Chicago. Your uncle must be the one to retrieve the instructions. Will you please tell him that I am not upset with him and that I'm proud of all he has accomplished, and you need to forgive him for staying out of your life. He believed he was doing the right thing to protect you, and he was right. In time, the Order will discover how to reach us on the plane that we are at. We have been here for the last sixteen years. We have waited for a long time; we needed you to develop your ability as a clairvoyant. First you must accomplish the task before the Order, then you will need to rescue us and that is when we'll be reunited. This forest is the chosen forest of the Order of Seven. The powers that the Order has emanates from it. Protect it and treasure it. You are about to embark on a very dangerous mission. You are now ready to start your training," Bridgette's father finished.

"Dad, I will see you again right?" Bridgette asked.

"Yes, you will. Remember, your mother and I are always with you, even though you can't see us," he said as he placed his ghostly hand on her cheek. "You have turned into a beautiful young woman. I am so proud of all you've done and so is your mother."

"Dad--"

Her father interrupted Bridgette before she could finish. "I'm sorry, my time is up. Remember to relay the message to your uncle, all that he will need to locate us is in the Book of Knowledge. I love you," he said as he vanished.

"I love you, too." As she sat on the bench wiping the tears from her eyes, Bridgette noticed a light coming from each tunnel. Within seconds, standing in the entrances were Dwayne, Rosa, and David. They each ran to Bridgette. Bridgette leapt from the bench and they engaged in a large group hug. Each of them had an encounter with one of their parents, like Bridgette.

As they discussed how and who each encountered, a large wooden trunk appeared in the middle of the room. They walked to the trunk. David reached down and opened it. As he did, the ground directly above them opened up and a staircase appeared.

Inside the trunk were three separate compartments. There was also old parchment paper. At a quick glance, they noticed that the paper was written in Latin. Dwayne and David hauled the trunk up the stairs, and as the last one of them stepped onto the ground, the opening closed back up.

They headed back to their tent, and spent the night in Hill Wood Forest. They talk excitedly of their encounters with their parents. Excitement and happiness is felt throughout the night. Dwayne and the others wondered about his encounter with the centaur, and what it meant.

In the morning, they made their way back to the car and drive back to Andrews Castle. As they arrived, waiting for them outside was John. Bridgette had tears forming in her eyes as she looked at her uncle. Once the car had stopped, she rushed out of the car and ran to him, embracing him with a strong hug. Surprised by her actions, but not wanting to stop the moment John returned the strong hug.

"I love you, Uncle John," said Bridgette.

"I love you too, sweetie," John responded.

28

MAYAN EXCURSION

Macnar and Tim Stevens entered the limousine that would take them to O'Hare International airport. They decided that leaving after rush hour would make the ride shorter and more bearable. During the ride, they chitchatted about the weather and how long the flight to San Antonio would take. Tim spoke about his college days and how he had started working for Kantra. He commented on how he had overheard a conversation between Kantra and someone else regarding their religious views and found it interesting. When the time was right, he had raised the conversation with Kantra. He informed Macnar that it had only been the last several weeks that he had entered a life as a Scrutatores. Macnar was doubtful of the young man's willingness to complete the entire mission, but he decided that this was Lannar's decision, and not his, to make.

Their limo came to a stop near a small, black private plane. Before either man could move, the left passenger door opened. Standing outside the door was a lovely looking flight attendant dressed in a green outfit. She greeted the men and informed them that their plane was ready for departure. As they exited the limousine, they noticed two men take their luggage out of the trunk and carry them to the plane. Macnar and Tim walked towards the staircase, the luxury the plane presented. Macnar had never flown before. He was reminded of his first time driving or riding an elevator. He felt extremely nervous about flying. But being that they were pressed for time, there was no other option.

Inside the plane another flight attendant was welcoming them aboard.

"Welcome, gentlemen. My name is Susan and the flight attendant that opened your car door is Erica. If you need anything during the flight please feel free to ask."

She gave them a quick tour pointing to the door directly behind them.

"Behind this door is a large sleeping quarter. If either of you need to rest, the room is ready. As you can see, in front are six luxurious seats. You will have Internet access once we reach a certain altitude. The Captain and co-pilot are in the cockpit, so as soon as you are both buckled in, we will depart."

Macnar and Tim both thanked her. The men sat in the luxurious yellow leather seats. The Captain came out and introduced himself. He relayed to them that there was no bad weather in the forecast from Chicago to San Antonio. Within a few minutes the plane began its taxi down the runway.

As the plane climbed off the ground, Macnar felt the feeling of the plane separating itself from the ground. The plane climbed higher, and Macnar felt his throat reach his stomach. Within several seconds the feeling left. As the plane continued its ascent, Macnar looked out the window. He enjoyed watching everything on the ground become smaller. He looked over at Tim. He noticed how unaffected he was by the takeoff. Tim was preparing his laptop to connect with the Internet. They had agreed not to discuss any of their plans on the plane. While Tim was researching the area they are were going to, Macnar started reading a book.

The plane landed at its scheduled time. They exchanged goodbyes with the flight crew and exited the plane. The men made their way to a slick black Cadillac CTS sports sedan that was waiting for them. Tim went directly to the driver's side and popped the trunk from the key remote entry system. They put their three duffle bags in the trunk and headed on their journey to the tip of Texas. The town they were headed to was named Brownsville.

The distance to Brownsville from San Antonio was approximately two hundred and sixty miles. When planning the trip, Tim figured that they would need three hours travel time. Tim started the car and the two men were on their way. The ride to Brownsville was uneventful.

When they reached Brownsville, it was seven in the evening. They drove to a designated pier where a seaplane was already waiting for them. Tim parked the car; they grabbed their bags from the trunk and walked down to the main pier. The evening was nice and cool. The temperature was a comfortable seventy-three degrees with very little humidity. As they walked, they took in the beautiful beach around them. After several minutes, they reached the main pier. Standing at the front of the pier was their pilot. A large, plump man in his mid-fifties was waving and smiling at them.

"Hey, glad to see you guys got here okay," shouted the man.

"Great night, we should have great weather for the ride," he continued shouting.

"Why is he talking to us when we can barely hear him?" Macnar commented.

"Don't know, maybe southern hospitality," responded Tim. They finally reached the man known as Trevor Grace.

Trevor Grace had been working as a sea pilot for thirty years. He gave tours of the Gulf of Mexico and the Texas shoreline. On occasion, he would bring someone to a destination outside the United States for the right price.

"Welcome, gentlemen," said Trevor.

"Trevor Grace?" Tim asked.

"That's me, were you expecting Diana Ross?" Trevor chuckled. "Ah, just kidding guys. Here, let me carry one of those bags for ya."

Macnar was not about to let someone carry one of the bags. "That will not be necessary, sir," said Macnar.

"Sir? Call me Trevor, my pappy's called sir. Shit, I still work for my money," said Trevor as he started laughing. "Suit yourself, I thought I'd give you a hand. Let's get to my plane." Trevor led the way with Tim and Macnar following, carrying their bags.

There were several boats tied on each side of the pier. Macnar was amazed by the size of some of them.

"Hey, you two know how to swim?" Trevor asked conversationally.

Macnar thought that was a peculiar question to ask. He was now skeptical of Trevor Grace's abilities. Trevor noticed that no one was answering.

"Don't worry guys, I ask everyone I bring aboard. You guys have nothing to worry about. Jennifer passed her inspection last Tuesday."

Tim gave out a friendly chuckle at Trevor's comment. Macnar, on the other hand, labeled Trevor as peculiar, and his trust in the man was now very low.

Trevor started to beam with pride as they reached the seaplane. "Here she is, this is my Jennifer. Her full name is the Jennifer Ashton."

Macnar gave Trevor a puzzling look. Noticing Macnar's confusion, Trevor started explaining why the name. "I love that show 'Friends,' and she's my favorite character. Plus, it grabs people's attention. I like to think it helps with booking more tours for me.

"Whatever works, I guess," said Tim. He wanted to point out the misspelling, but decided not to. Macnar simply nodded his head.

"For a big man, you sure don't speak much," said Trevor, speaking directly to Macnar. He nodded his head again. "Let's get onboard."

He opened the door, allowing Macnar and Tim to enter the seaplane before him. "Just drop your bags behind your seats. The oars you requested are already loaded."

Once they were seated, Trevor climbed aboard. The plane leaned a little in the water as he climbed in. Trevor's entrance onto the plane was a lengthier process than Tim and Macnar's. They turned back and watched the large man climb into the plane and make his way to the front seat.

"Buckle yourselves in, we're taking off right away. The flight attendant will be by shortly with some refreshments."

"There is another person flying with us?" Macnar asked.

"Now I know why you don't speak much. Like I can afford a flight attendant, it was a joke," he said.

Trevor started up the plane. He turned to make sure that everyone was buckled in and moved the plane forward on the water. Macnar couldn't believe that in one day he had flown long distance to a destination, and was now on a plane that would be taking off from water. The seaplane was picking up speed. In a matter of minutes, the required speed was achieved and the plane was in the air.

"We are off to the Yucatan Peninsula of Mexico." Trevor pronounced 'Mexico' in Spanish.

Tim used the time to study the map given to them by Lannar. On the map, it outlined the route to the ancient Mayan site and how to get to Tentatuin's burial site. Trevor gave information like he was giving a tour. Neither of them paid any attention to him. It was done out of habit, and since there was no complaints, Trevor continued.

Trevor didn't ask why they needed to leave near nightfall, but it had raised some suspicion. For the amount of money he was being paid for this trip he knew he'd better not ask too many questions. He figured the less he knew, the better. The flight took nearly five hours of flight time. Trevor knew that his plane would not show up on radar as long as he flew one thousand feet above the water and followed the path a friend of his in the Coast Guard explained to him. The plane landed five hundred feet from shore. In one of the bags was an inflatable raft. Tim removed the raft, pulled a string and watched it inflate as it entered the water.

"We will give you the rest of the money after we have landed back in Brownsville," said Tim, handing Trevor an envelope.

"That's fine, you want me back here at the same time in two days, right?"

"Yes," responded Macnar, as he threw his bag onto the raft and jumped into the water.

Tim nodded his head to Trevor and jumped in. Trevor waited for both men to enter the boat and threw them the oars they had asked him to bring on board.

As they paddled away, the plane taking off caused waves in the water that made the paddling somewhat difficult. The water was relatively calm after they got past the waves.

"What do you know about him and can we trust him?" Macnar asked Tim.

"A friend of mine that smuggles in cheap labor uses Trevor. He says that he's a shrewd business man that would do anything if the price was right," said Tim.

"A man that works for money alone can never be trusted," said Macnar.

"He will be here at the designated time. The man will want the rest of his money, so he'll be here and he'll stay quiet."

"I too, think he will stay quiet," said Macnar.

Tim was taken aback by Macnar's tone. He wondered what he had gotten himself into. He didn't want to be a part of killing anyone, but he knew that if he said anything that might cause Macnar to be suspicious of him, he could be the one to end up floating in the water.

"Let's get focused on getting to shore. We'll deal with Trevor when the time comes," said Tim.

Macnar was pleased to hear Tim's response. The two men continued paddling and the raft bounced along with each wave that they encountered.

The sun had completely set by the time they landed on the Mexican shore. They exited the raft and pulled it toward an area thirty feet from the water so they could hide it in a clearing of bushes. They finished covering the raft and rearranging the greenery of the bushes, then made their way inland. Tim took out the map Lannar had marked up for them. He quickly located where they were and estimated that they were about two miles from a small village. The plan was to go to the village, rent a car and drive to the Mayan ruins.

Tim suggested they walk off to the side of the road that leads into the village. He did not want anyone to get a look at their faces in case they run into any form of trouble. The two engaged in talk regarding the mission, but mostly Macnar asked Tim about his upbringing. After two hours of walking they made their way into the small village.

The men were in need of some sleep. As they walked through the village, they came across a small cantina that was open. It was only eleven at night so the place being open was not shocking. However, being in a small Mexican village did surprise them. They walked into the small squared cement structure. Sitting at the counter was an elderly Mexican man. Tim asked the man in Spanish if he had any rooms available for the evening. The man chuckled and informed him that he had only one room and that his wife was sleeping in it. The man took them out in back of the small building and pointed to two hammocks. The man informed them that it would be ten Pesos per person. Tim reached into the duffle bag and pulled out twenty pesos, pleased by the great deal he received. They each climbed into a hammock and realized how beautiful of a night it was. There was little humidity, and a clear sky filled with stars and a large moon. Within several seconds of lying down they had fallen asleep.

A very loud rooster awakened them. Tim was the first one up. For a brief moment, he had forgotten where he was.

The pleasant morning air in Mexico made Macnar feel extremely comfortable and relaxed. As quickly as that moment came, it left. He had looked over at Tim and quickly come back to reality. Tim suggested that they have a quick meal and make their way to Chichen Itza. The ancient Mayan city was not far from the village. Tim estimated that it was just a few hours away.

Tim secured a car while Macnar picked up some food. As soon as he found out how much money he had spent on the car, he became upset with Tim. Before them was a rusted out pickup. The vehicle looked like it was fifty years old. The Ford emblem on the grill had been covered completely by rust. The upholstery was torn up and the bed was also covered in rust. Macnar opened the passenger side door. It made a loud squeaking sound. Tim's door made the exact same sound. The vehicle did not portray safety. Both man sat in their respective seats. Tim inserted the key, placed his foot on the clutch and turned the ignition. The pickup fired itself right up. Tim looked at the odometer and noticed it only read fifty thousand miles. He wondered how many times it had flipped itself back to a row of zeros. Tim drove the pickup out of the garage and they were off to Chichen Itza.

Tim commented on the Mexican landscape the entire drive. He admired the beautiful mountain chain they were driving through. He continued talking about the landscape and the gorgeous day even though Macnar had not commented once. He assumed that Macnar was just not a morning person. In truth, Macnar was growing tired of Tim. He had lost all confidence in Tim completing the overall mission. The way he talked about his family last night signaled to Macnar that Tim would not be able to continue on a mission that may kill all of his family members.

After several hours they neared the Mayan ruins. It was now noon. Macnar had now found another reason to dislike Tim; his estimation of travel time had not been stellar. Macnar was finding many reasons to dislike the twenty-three year old. They arrived at the site, and as expected the tourists had already started to gather. Five city blocks away was a parking lot. Tim paid the cashier and parked the beat-up pickup. Tim was having a problem placing the clutch in position to park the old clunker. Macnar was the first to exit the vehicle and remove each of the duffle bags from the bed. It took Tim several attempts but he finally managed to put the clutch in place. Tim got out with much enthusiasm.

"Let's do this," he said. Macnar looked at Tim and shook his head.

They made their way to the ancient pyramids. There were several pyramids at the site. Tim was looking at the map and noticed that Lannar had circled one. He also wrote the word 'tallest' next to the circled one. They made their way toward it.

"We need to get to the top and look outward. Lannar described the area where we need to search," said Macnar. "Let's get going."

As they climbed, Tim continued to talk about the pyramids, "This large slab that runs down is where they would sacrifice humans."

This topic sparked Macnar's interest. "Continue," said Macnar.

"Well, you see, up at the top is an altar and they would say a prayer to whichever God they were praying to, then decapitate the lucky individual and his head would roll down to a pit underneath the pyramid."

"Fascinating," said Macnar.

Tim had become used to Macnar's short one or two word answers. The two men finally reached the top. As Tim looked around Macnar reached in one of the duffle bags and pulled out a pair of binoculars. Tim started talking to a small family of four that were also at the top. Meanwhile, Macnar kept looking out in the direction behind the pyramid. He noticed a large wooded area. What he hadn't noticed was Tim's conversation with the young family. If he would have, he may have just snapped on Tim, right there at the top. Instead, he called Tim over to where he is. Tim excused himself from the family and walked over to Macnar. He handed Tim the binoculars and pointed in the direction to look.

"There is where we need to go," said Macnar.

Tim acknowledged Macnar's comment by nodding his head.

"Let's go," said Macnar. Tim looked over at the family and was glad that they did not overhear any of their conversation.

"Yes, time to move," he said.

The two men made their way down the large pyramid. Once they reached the bottom, they walked around the pyramid and headed toward the forest area. None of the tourists paid any attention to them. As they walked, there were several families having a picnic on the beautiful sunny day.

As they reached the woods, Tim noticed a sign. It was written in several languages. The sign said that entrance into the forest was strictly prohibited. Macnar walked past the sign, never paying any attention to it. Tim entered slowly, looking behind him to see if there was anyone paying attention to them. No one was. Tim sped up in order to catch up to Macnar.

The area was deep and grew thicker the further they walked. There were trees of all shapes and sizes around them. As they walked deeper, the ability for sunlight to enter became more difficult with each step. Tim also noticed all the sounds getting louder. There was a lot of screeching and many birds chirping. Macnar was paying close attention to odd-shaped trees and rocks. He would stop and examine them frequently.

"Hey Macnar, how do you know where to walk to?"

"Lannar had told me that there are three specific markers to look for etched with black ink and they are placed on four large boulders. The first is a circle with a crescent moon in its center. The second is a lightning bolt that has three arrows. The third and final marking is a sun beaming rays settling down on a hut."

The two men continued walking as they talked.

"Do they have any meaning?" Tim asked.

"Lannar never explained their meaning. I'm sure they have to do with the Mayans or Tentatuin."

"I see," said Tim.

They decided that they needed some assistance in clearing a pathway. Macnar reached into his duffle bag and removed two machetes. He handed one to Tim and they both walked and hacked away with each step.

"I spotted two of the three markings," said Macnar.

"Two down and one to go," replied Tim.

They had been in the jungle for over an hour. Macnar had spotted the second marking twenty minutes ago. The two men contrasted in their beliefs of finding the markers and the golden plate. Macnar had never swayed from the idea of finding the last marker. Tim, on the other hand, had doubt creping into his thoughts. He was content with being in Mexico, however he had never fully believed that the item would be found. Tim felt that finding a needle in a haystack would be easier but he knew better than to mention this to Macnar or anyone else for that matter.

"Are we supposed to continue in a straight line?" Tim asked.

"No. At the third marker, we need to walk about twenty feet to the last stop."

As Macnar slashed at some vines in front of him, his eyes suddenly lit up. He noticed a boulder directly ahead. Tim's attitude was now annoying to Macnar.

"I think we may have discovered the last marker," said Macnar.

Tim started thinking of his youngest sister. He was puzzled as to why her image popped into his head once Macnar mentioned discovering the final marker.

"That's great," said Tim unenthusiastically. Macnar turned his head toward Tim after picking up on his tone. He didn't say anything, but was questioning Tim's lack of enthusiasm to himself.

Macnar removed his compass from his pocket; he looked at it and pointed west. "We must head in this direction."

"Okay," said Tim, reluctantly.

Macnar needed to find the plate and he needed to understand the sudden change in Tim. He figured that the best way to accomplish this was to converse with Tim a little bit more.

"Soon we will have attained the final piece to our puzzle," said Macnar.

Tim came from a fairly large family. He had two sisters and two brothers. His youngest sister was an unexpected birth. She was forty years younger than their parents. He was thinking of his two brothers and his other sister graduating from high school and college.

Macnar had talked about how the spot should be fifty feet from the rock. As they walked they came across a large patch that had nothing but dirt. The two of them walked to the patch.

"I guess we won't be needing the metal detector," said Tim.

Macnar stepped onto the patch. As he did, he knelt down in the middle and ran his hand over the dirt, making a circle in the area as well. Tim was hesitant to step onto the patched area. When Macnar finished, he looked up and noticed Tim standing outside the area.

"Why are you just standing there?" Macnar asked.

"I'm...um...I'm...getting the shovels ready," replied Tim.

"Good, now would you please get them out of the bag and assemble them," said Macnar, fully convinced that Tim had lost his nerve.

Tim reached into the bag and pulled out two blue fiberglass items. They were each a mini shovel in two parts. Being made of fiberglass made them light and sturdy.

"Let's start right where I'm at," said Macnar.

Tim walked over and handed one of the shovels to him. Macnar took the shovel and started digging into the ground and removing dirt at a very fast pace. Tim matched Macnar in speed and accuracy. Within twenty minutes they managed to dig up seven feet of dirt. As Tim was still digging, Macnar stopped to take a short break.

"I need to rest for a bit," said Macnar.

Tim continued digging. Just as Macnar stepped out of the hole, there was a loud clang. Macnar jumped back into the hole. Tim carefully started spreading the dirt. Suddenly, they saw the circular item.

Macnar raised his hand in front of Tim, signaling him to stop. He knelt down and removed the large circle covered in dirt. The item lay on top of human bone remains. Macnar directed Tim to get out and get one of the duffle bags. As Tim reached for the bag, Macnar took his shovel and struck Tim in the back of his head, knocking him out. Macnar pushed Tim to the side and grabbed the duffle bag. He turned back to the plate and reached for it. He placed the plate and the bones into the duffle bag.

Macnar pushed Tim into the center of the small pit. He climbed out with the duffle bag and started to place dirt back into the shallow grave. Within ten minutes Tim was completely covered. Tim came to and frantically tried to scratch his way out. He held his breath for as long as he could, but finally had to gasp for air. With each gasp, he took in more dirt. Within minutes his lungs and mouth were filled with dirt. Tim's memory kicked in and he was at a family gathering some years ago. The gathering was before he had drifted from his family. He wished that he were with his family now. He wanted to tell them how much he cared for and loved them.

Macnar remembered the route they took and traveling back was easier and quicker than he thought. Macnar had also made sure that the seaplane would be ready and waiting. It was now night and Macnar paddled the raft out to the pickup area. He waited there for two hours until the seaplane finally arrived. Macnar climbed into the plane.

"Hey, where's your buddy?" Trevor asked.

"He decided to stay a bit longer." Trevor took off and within several hours he had Macnar back in Brownsville. Before he exited the plane, Macnar went into the cockpit and quickly slashed Trevor's throat.

Macnar drove the Cadillac back to the San Antonio airport. He managed to find the hangar where the private planes took off. As he sat in the luxury chair, he was convinced he did the right thing. In a few hours he was back in Chicago and on his way to Trump Tower. As he exited the elevator, Lannar, Kantra, and Wrightwood were there, ready to greet him. As he stepped out, Lannar reached out and Macnar handed him the now shining golden plate. Once everyone saw the plate there was little attention given to the fact Macnar returned minus one person again.

29

FINDING THE TOWER

Dwayne and David brought the large wooden trunk into the castle. They stepped back and allowed Andrews and John to examine it. Julia and Emily joined them. Bridgette and Rosa had finished emptying the car and rushed to the main room as well.

"John, I need to tell you what happened in the forest." Dwayne said nervously. Dwayne was about to explain how he fought off a centaur. He was afraid of not being believed.

"What is it Dwayne? You can tell me anything." John said sensing Dwayne's nervousness.

"In the forest I fought a centaur."

"Really, that means that the doorway has been opened for some time." John said as he turned to face Andrews.

"You believe me, right?"

"Of course we do. You have no reason to lie." Dwayne was happy to hear that he had been taken seriously.

"John, if the doorway has been open that could explain why we never retrieved any of our fallen friends."

"I know, but lets not lose our focus. We need to accomplish this task and we can discus all that on another date understood?" Everyone in the room nodded their heads in agreement.

John opened the trunk, and a bright light shined from inside. John and everyone in the room covered their eyes. He stepped back and within a few seconds the light faded.

John looked inside. Right at the top was a collection of tree branches. He called Dwayne and David over and the three of them removed the branches from the trunk. As John removed the last branch, he glanced inside the trunk and fell quickly backwards.

"Unbelievable," said John, shocked.

"What? Is there something wrong?" Andrews asked, concerned.

"Look inside, just look inside," said John.

Andrews looked inside the trunk. "What am I looking for?"

"What do you see?" Asked John.

"Branches in a trunk. What's the big deal about that? Just finish taking them out," said Andrews.

"We did. We removed all of them and now the trunk is full again with branches," said John.

"Unlimited supply," Bridget breathed.

"Bring the trunk, and the branches you already removed down to the offices," said Andrews.

Dwayne and David carried the trunk over to the elevator that led down to the Order rooms below the castle.

"It'll be safe down here," said Andrews, once they were all down below.

"Are you sure?" John questioned.

"I removed everyone from the security clearance with the exception of us," responded Andrews.

"Has the spell-translator arrived?" Emily asked.

"Yes. He is upstairs. I'll bring him down once we have figured out what we need to do," said Andrews.

"Don't take any branches out. Just move them around and see what happens," said John to Dwayne and David.

Dwayne and David moved the branches off to the side. They were extremely careful not to remove any of the branches. Once they reached the bottom of the trunk, there appeared a book bound in leather. David waved John over to the trunk. John took the book and handed it to Andrews.

"What do we do first?" Julia asked.

"The book that was in the trunk is written in Latin. Let's look through it. I think all our questions will be answered by the book," said Emily.

Since only John, Emily, Julia, and Andrews could read Latin, Andrews suggested that the younger Order members go and get cleaned up and rest a bit as they read over the book. Bridgette led them back to the elevator and they retreated to their rooms for a shower and a quick nap.

John opened the book to the first page and started reading. The book explained how to use spells. It described the technique used in conducting spells. Most importantly it listed spells and a brief explanation of each one. After several attempts of trying to read the Book of Spells it was evident why they needed the translator. The spells and the instructions to conduct the spells changed each time someone different read the passage. They spent the next five hours reading the book. When they finished, they decided to bring the spell-translator down.

Bridgette brought Jose Batista below. As they entered the main room, she noticed that Dwayne, David, and Rosa were already in the room. She was surprised because they were rarely ever on time.

Andrews walked up to Jose Batista and shook his hand. He introduced him to everyone in the room. Another person was also in the room, and he was introduced to Bridgette and the other young Order members. The man introduced to them was Antonio Santini. Andrews felt it necessary to bring Santini back and have him recount his encounter. Santini spent the next half hour retelling his experience and answering the same questions over again.

Jose was led to a separate room. He explained that in order to attain the correct version of each spell he needed to recite the passage in the correct tone. Jose explained that the book reacts to the voice procured for each spell. Jose explained that if he were interrupted at any point, the spell would just be a simple poem. Jose had been waiting his entire life for this moment. He was the first in his family, since leaving Spain centuries ago, that a Batista had been called upon to return to the trade they used to be known for.

Santini finished retelling his vision. The time had come to locate the Tower mentioned in his vision.

"There are two towers that come to mind," said John. "The first is the Eiffel Tower. The second is here in London, the Tower of London."

"How about the Tower of Galata in Istanbul," suggested Emily.

"Or the Belem Tower in Portugal," said Andrews.

"The Leaning Tower of Pisa," Julia continued.

"The two Towers of Bolonga," said Emily.

"Willis Tower in Chicago," said David.

They quickly realized that they were no closer at discovering the tower. Though they might not know the tower, they did know that Lannar's plans were still in play. They had to determine its location.

"Let's review what we have so far," said John. "First, we know that the Scrutatores are in Chicago, Rome, and London. They may possibly be in other places as well. Second, we know that a tower is in their plans. Third, we know that Lannar is William Donavan Sr., a descendant of William Donavan, the architect of famous buildings in Chicago."

"Wait," said Bridgette. "He is a descendant of William Donavan, the famous Chicago architect?"

"Yes," said John. "You have a hunch?"

"I think I know the tower," said Bridgette, smiling. Everyone's gaze in the room was transfixed onto Bridgette. Feeling a little nervous, Bridgette cleared her throat and threw out her thought. "We know who Lannar is and who he is related to. Let's presume that William Donavan, the architect of the 1800's, was a Scrutatore. Maybe that's how Lannar discovered that he was one too. You know, like in a journal or some family book. Well, if Lannar is related to him, William Donavan built a building that survived the Chicago fire."

"What building is that?" Andrews asked.

"The Chicago Water Tower," said Bridgette. "It totally makes sense."

"I think you're right," said John, beaming with pride towards his niece.

"Do we have any listings of Scrutatores?" Julia asked. "If we can confirm that his ancestor is a Scrutatore, then we know the location of the burning tower."

All the lights in the room went dark. The Order members start to murmur in panic. Could the Scrutatores have found a way to penetrate the security that Andrews put in place? As they felt around the room, a blinding bright light is emanated from the door leading into the room. Slowly the door opened. The bright light consumed the room. Before any of them could react, the lights came back on. Standing before them were seven men, dressed in 1000ad clothing.

"Who are you?" John asked.

One of the men stepped forward. He looked around the room and made eye contact with everyone.

"I am Richard Williams, a distant relative to John and Bridgette. My friends and I are the first Order members," said the transparent figure.

"How is this happening?" Emily whispered.

"We are here to inform you that you have solved the mystery of the burning tower. William Donavan, the one referred to as 'the Architect' is a descendant of the original leader of the Scrutatores. His descendant is attempting to finish what William Donavan could not complete. The information you will need to stop him, and hopefully defeat him is in the building marked by the Three Knights Templar in the same city as the burning Tower. We cannot show you the building; you will need to do it yourselves. We cannot show you how to conduct and use spells; you will have to learn yourselves. We are here because in your midst is a supreme medium." The ghostly figure pointed at Bridgette.

The lights in the room suddenly went out again. A bright light again consumed the room. Within seconds the light faded and the room's lights came back on. Just as the original Order members appeared, they had now vanished. They now knew the location of the transformation. Before they could attempt to confront Lannar and his followers, the Order members must be well versed in the use of powerful magic.

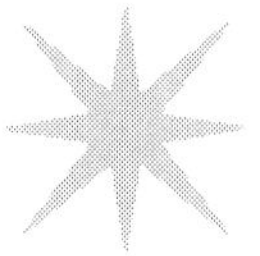

30

TRAINING

Andrews had set up the outdoor portion of his castle for training. The outdoor portion was immensely large. After the translator completed translating the entire Book of Spells, Andrews had his crew set up three areas. The first was an area with a large pool of water. The second was set up with eight cardboards of menacing looking figures. The third had four large tables with different objects on them, and a car.

John, Emily, and Julia had read the book's section on spells and had been coached by Jose. They had spent the last few weeks teaching the four other members Latin. All of the Order members were now capable of reading and speaking Latin. Though the four younger members were not proficient, they were well versed enough to conduct the spells. John had designed a program for practicing spells. Since none of the Order members had ever conducted the more powerful spells, they had spent one month in each area, practicing.

The moment had come to see if they had mastered the spells. The objective of the exercise was to move a body of water to land. The first person in the pool area is was Dwayne. He stepped up to the pool pointed his palm at the water.

"Aqua Fluctus," said Dwayne, and he motioned his hand from the water towards the left of the pool. As he finished reciting the phrase, the water rose thirty feet in the air and went left in the form of a wave. The water splashed over the area to the left of the pool.

Emily walked to the area where the water dispersed. She moved her hand in a circle while saying "aqua reditus". The water that was dispersed from the pool went back into the pool.

David stepped up to the pool, "Aqua Fluctus." The same result occurred.

Emily repeated her part and the water went back into the pool. The usage of the water spell was performed by all of the Order members and they all had succeeded.

At the second area, the first person to attempt the spell was Julia. "Attono," said Julia, with her palm pointing at the first cardboard figure of a man with a gun.

She then pointed to the cardboard of a man with a knife, "Attono Maximum." A red beam of light shot out of her hand and the cardboard shattered into many tiny pieces. She then aimed at the remaining cardboard figures each of a man holding a different weapon

"Diffusus Maximum Attono," said Julia. The red beam split and a different beam struck each figure at the same time. The remaining cardboard figures exploded.

John gestured at the remnants of the first board and said, "Interdum," and the board went back to its original form. Each one performed the same task with the same results. Confidence in each member's ability to successfully use magic grew.

At the third area, Emily was the first to attempt the appropriate spell. She went directly to the car. "Subvolvo," she said, facing her palm out, and the car began to levitate off the ground. The car moved up and down, side-to-side, depending on the direction she waved her hand. The car came crashing down.

"I stopped concentrating on the levitation spell," she said.

"After calling the spell by name, it will continue until you either end the spell, or lose concentration," said Bridgette.

"Thanks for pointing out the obvious," joked Emily.

John brought the group in for a discussion. "Remember that all spells work only when spoken out loud in Latin. Some of the spells we practiced can be used without speaking them, but our concentration must be greater. I suggest that until we are proficient, all spells should be spoken out loud. Especially when we encounter the Scrutatores. Let's practice the shield spell."

John went to an area in the backyard that had nothing in the general vicinity. Emily stood fifteen feet in front of John. She pointed her hand toward him and spoke the stun spell. "Attono." The red light shot towards him.

John pointed his hand in Emily's direction and said, "Clypeum." The red beam dissipated in different directions. Each of them took turns practicing their shield spell. They all succeeded using it.

John knew that the time had come to practice the death spell. He had Andrews' crew prepare the back portion of the yard with a large cement wall. John was the first to cast the spell. "Mortum."

The red beam shot from his hand damaging the wall. Julia and Emily each performed the spell to perfection. However, the teens did not succeed in any of their attempts. After many attempts John rationalized to them that they may be either too young or lacked the experience. Emily pointed out that neither her or Julia had ever cast any spell before today. That left youth as the only explanation. John quietly kept his content over the fact that none of the teens could effectively cast the death spell. He had strong reservations against teaching them that spell.

John felt that they had practiced enough. The Order of Seven members believed that they were ready for action. Just then, the ghost of Richard Williams appeared. The ghost floated around them and finally came to a stop in front of them.

"On the summer solstice, the Scrutatores will attempt to open the doorway between this plane and the next plane. They will also attempt to unleash a terrible plague onto this world. They will have to complete this before the end of the summer solstice." With that, the ghost vanished.

"Well, at least now we know the when and the how. We've known the where. It's time to form a plan to take them on," said John.

They stopped practicing for the day. In the coming months, they acquired a layout of Chicago's Water Tower. They continued practicing different spells. The moment of truth was near. The remaining winter and coming spring witnessed the Order of Seven becoming stronger and more confident in their abilities. They were ready to equal the Scrutatores in the use of spells. On June 20th they would find out.

31

DELIVERY

John, Emily, and Julia did not have a clue where to begin. What to do? How to start? John Williams had lived in Chicago for a long time. He knew that there were hundreds of buildings. The building had to be directly linked to the Order or the Stamens.

"We need to call Andrews and have him tell us the buildings that have a connection with the Stamens," said John. He opened the contacts list on his phone, located the entry titled 'Andrews' and dialed.

It was three in the afternoon in London. They figured that the Stamens members were busy looking through their records and ancient documents for a connection.

Andrews's phone started ringing. He removed it from his pocket and looked to see who was calling. He noticed that it was John and picked it up.

"Hello John, I hope all is well. I'm concerned about getting a call so soon after landing in Chicago."

John sensed the sarcasm in his voice. "Funny, funny. I have a serious question if you are done with the sarcasm," said John.

Andrews chuckled on the other end. "Trying to add humor to our plight, my dear friend. Things are getting frustrating here trying to find the Templar building in Chicago. We have a list of cities with prominent buildings but they are all on this side of the world."

"You're the only one? Is everyone out to lunch?" John laughed.

"No John, I've called a meeting of the Stamens. A meeting of this magnitude has not happened for centuries. The items I need retrieved are of the outmost importance. You will have no chance of defeating Lannar and his cohorts with out them."

"Understood," said John.

John quickly got off the phone with Andrews. "He said that he would call back with the info. He also said he was organizing a meeting with Stamen members."

"Let's decide how we are going to find the building," suggested Julia.

"I don't think that'll be easy," said Emily, raising her eyebrows.

"It might not be easy, but it has to be done. We know our goal and have no choice," said Julia, with a bit of frustration in her voice.

Julia thought logically. It was the scientist in her that caused that. Emily was also a scientist, but her area of expertise was in biology. Emily believed in free will strongly, for all forms of life.

"I understand the importance of finding the building. But I think that we need to be careful in how we proceed with this," said Emily.

"Fine, let's discuss if we should find the building with the information we need to defeat the Scrutatores, or just hope that it appears to us in a dream... or maybe another ghost will reveal the info," said Julia, displaying the frustration and anger for all to see and hear.

"Julia, that's not what I'm saying. We have to search for the building. But in case you haven't noticed, Chicago is a very large city. We cannot spin our wheels and hope that it will present itself. I say we wait for Andrews to have his meeting and hopefully we'll have a place to at least start looking," said Emily.

John just sat on the couch, not bothering to get involved in their conversation. "Hey, you two need to relax on that."

They both took a moment to relax and decided to wait for the phone to ring. It seemed like hours when the phone finally rang. John got up and walked briskly to it.

"Hello. You find the building?" There was silence on the other end of the phone. Several seconds went by before Andrews started speaking.

"Yes and no, I have the name of a place where you can begin searching." There was another pause John quickly surmised that something had gone wrong.

"What's wrong?"

"There has been a development. If your phone has speaker capability, use it. What I'm about to tell you everyone needs to hear," said Andrews in a very serious tone. "All of the Stamens members won't get here until tomorrow night, your time."

The news was tough to handle. This was a difficult conversation for Andrews. "Since it was confirmed that they are not coming, you just need to relax and find something to do. But I do have name of a person that may be able to help," he said.

"We are conducting an investigation, but remember we do not exist," said John, wondering how he was going to get someone to believe him.

"Listen, this person is part of the Catholic Church. He may be able to help. Remember the Council of the Supernatural once worked closely with the Stamens and the Order. He is a man that can be trusted and is familiar with the past," said Andrews. "Go to St. Michael's Church. The items needed are important to the Stamens, not the Order. Sullivan's Journal mentioned that their place of rest is in Chicago."

"Should one of us come back to help?" Emily asked.

"No! You all have to stay together. There will be a delivery coming to you today. Do not leave until the package is delivered. Then go to St. Michael's Church and speak with the head pastor. We will discuss the incidents here on another day. Good luck and be careful," finished Andrews, and disconnected the phone call.

None of them said a word. Things could only become more difficult and dangerous. As they sat in silence, a knock on the door startled them.

"Well, we need to get our heads on straight. We're going to face more difficult things than a knock on the door," said Emily.

John made his way to the door. He opened it slowly. Standing in front of him was a man dressed in a solid black suit. "Are you John Williams?" Asked the man.

Inside, Emily and Julia heard John talking. "You got to be kidding me?" John exclaimed.

The man had handed John three keys. "The vehicles are property of a Jonathan Andrews, you have been assigned to drive them and use as you see fit."

With that, the man walked away. John thanked the man and closed the door.

"What did he want?" Julia asked.

"He wanted nothing, he made a delivery."

The two ladies looked at each other with a puzzling look. "I don't see a package," said Emily.

John jingled the keys.

"You were delivered keys?" Emily asked with curiosity.

"No, jackass, not just keys--car keys. Andrews arranged for us to have cars, three black Grand Cherokees, fully loaded and then some."

32

ST MICHAEL

John, Emily, and Julia walked outside to examine the vehicles. The cars were parked around John's apartment. Two were parked directly in front of his door. The third car was parked up the street.

They walked up to the two cars parked in front of John's apartment.

"I'm sure that all three of them are fabulous for the environment," said Julia sarcastically, obviously disapproving of the cars. John just glanced at her, not wanting to get into an environmental debate.

"Come on Julia, if we are in a situation that we have to get out of quickly, this is a ride that I would want to be in," said Emily, not worrying about the direction the conversation was heading.

"Figures." Julia responded, and walked back into John's apartment. Julia knew she was outnumbered in this debate.

"I care about the environment too," yelled John, as Julia walked inside. Emily looked over at him shaking her head.

"What? I do care about the environment."

"Look, we may need to get in and out of some predicaments and I, for one, want a durable car to get me out," said Emily.

"I agree with you, too."

Emily started to walk back to the apartment. "You should find the third one," she said to John as she went in.

"Yeah, I guess I should. I will do that, and now I'm talking to myself." John walked a block down, and he found the third vehicle, also black and a Grand Cherokee. John thought to himself: why do they have three vehicles? They could easily use just one. While he was walking back to his apartment, it dawned on him that only two were for them, and the other two for the Order members staying at the Sullivan house. That wasn't a pleasant thought for him.

Inside the apartment Julia was sitting in the lazy boy chair. She was thumbing through material she found in a large brown envelope in one of the cars. Emily was mapping the route to St. Michael's Church. She was reading up on the church from her laptop.

Julia got off the chair and walked over to where Emily was sitting.

"Two of those vehicles are for us, the other two are to be used by the younger Order members," said John, quickly noticing that neither of them was paying attention to him.

"Hey, did you know that St. Michael's Church is one of seven buildings that survived the Chicago Fire?" Emily asked. "Well, only parts of it did. It's been rebuilt since then."

John walked over to where they were. "So one of those cars is for the younger members," he said.

"Yes, one. Now drop it, they are old enough to drive and each have a valid license, so drop it. We have important matters to discuss," said Julia.

"Fine, I'll drop it and I'll do most of the driving since I know Chicago best."

Emily looked up from her laptop. She gave a John a glare that clearly did not approve of his offer to do the bulk of the driving. "I think that with GPS on the car and Google Map any of us would be able to find our way around," said Emily.

"The driving will be between you two, I want no part of it," said Julia.

"I located the church and I think we should headed over ASAP," said Emily.

"Yeah it's eleven, we should get going," said Julia.

"I'll drive," said John.

Julia jumped into the back seat. Emily was in the passenger seat entering the church's address into the GPS. St. Michael's was located in the Old Town neighborhood. It was a great day for a ride. Sun shining brightly, a slight breeze and very little humidity. John had always loved the weather in early June.

It took them only twenty minutes to get there. The quick ride to the church brought John down a little, as he was enjoying the car ride. Traffic cooperated nicely with them. They parked the car in the St. Michael's parking lot, exited the car and headed for the front entrances.

"We need to find Father Ericson," said Julia.

They reached the main doors and walked inside. As they made their way in, the beauty of St. Michael's was overwhelming. As they walked down the main aisle towards the altar, they were mesmerized. Along the walls were small depictions of the Stations of the Cross. The large stained glass windows had pictures of different religious people and events. There were seven large pillars that ran toward the altar on each side of the aisle. Hanging from the ceiling was a series of lights. The ceiling was easily over one hundred feet in height. As they neared the middle of the church, they noticed that the ceiling was painted a light blue and the borders that circled the ceiling were painted white, matching the walls and the pillars. The altar was large and magnificent. Behind the altar was the traditional area where the priests sat during different parts of mass. St. Michael's Church had two large figures of Jesus Christ and what appeared to be a statue of Joseph. To the left of Joseph's statue, about ten feet away, was one of St. Michael. There were many statues of Angels throughout the altar.

"This is an incredible church," said John.

As they stood in front of the altar and looked around, they were unaware that a male figure had made his way toward them.

"Hello," said the priest, as he walked towards them. Startled by his voice, they quickly turned and faced him.

"I believe you are the messengers that Jonathan Andrews informed me were coming." His voice had a deep, pleasing sound to it.

"Yes, we are," Emily replied.

"Andrews called you recently?" John asked, suspiciously.

"Well, yesterday morning."

In a quiet voice, Julia addressed the priest. "Did he tell you about anything else?" The priest was taken aback by the question.

"If you are referring to the murders that took place in Rome, they've been all over the news. But we did talk about them. Excuse my rudeness I didn't even introduce myself. I am Father Ericson."

"I'm John, this Emily and Julia."

Father Ericson had a folder with him. "In here, you will find all of the possible buildings that are associated with the Stamens."

Julia reached out for the folder. Father Ericson handed it to her.

"I have taken the liberty of circling the area where you should start. Unfortunately, it is the downtown area."

John, bad at hiding his emotions, had a disturbed look on his face.

Father Ericson picked up on that. "From my conversation with Andrews, and the developments in Rome, time is no longer a friendly companion. I wrote down all the information you need, and attached it to their pictures."

"Thank you," said Emily. John and Julia echoed the response.

John knew that the priest had acted properly and saved them time. "If I can be of any assistance, please do not hesitate to call or stop by. No time is a bad time."

With that they exchanged goodbyes and John, Emily, and Julia headed for their car.

33

SHOPPING

The sun beamed brightly. Emily returned from her morning jog to find Julia up and dressed.

"This is not normal," said Emily, as she walked in. "This is definitely out of the norm. You are never up early and are always the last one ready to go anywhere. Excited about shopping?"

Julia stood up with her cup of coffee. "Hey, we spent two months in Sicily and not once did we go shopping or sightseeing. We spent eight months or more in London and again nothing. Finally, I'm going to enjoy this incredible city!"

"You're preaching to the choir here. Let me shower and I'll be ready to head out," said Emily.

"I'll go and wake up John," said Julia, excitedly.

Emily was always the first one up and she knew John was not exactly a morning person.

"You might want to hold off on that," said Emily.

"Why? I think we should get going."

"Julia, its seven in the morning. Stores won't open for a couple more hours, so relax and let him wake up on his own. He'll be up soon."

Julia reluctantly agreed and went into the living room to watch the morning shows. Emily went into the bathroom and got herself ready for the day.

Julia sat in the living room for an hour watching 'Morning Joe' on MSNBC. Emily finally came out and joined her. While the show was coming to an end they heard John stumbling into the bathroom. Within twenty minutes he joined them in the living room with his usual Chicago Cubs coffee mug. He stood there in a pair of cargo shorts and a Chicago Cubs T-shirt with sandals.

"Bit of a Cubs fan?" Julia teased.

"Hey, now that you are going to be living here in Chicago you're going to have to pick a baseball team."

"Why would I have to pick a team, aren't there two baseball teams here?" Julia asked.

"Yeah, the Cubs and White Sox."

"I don't understand why I have to pick one. They're both from the same city," said Julia.

"Look, you don't have to do it now, but you eventually will," said John. He reached into his pocket and took out his phone. "Hi, Bridgette. I'm doing well. Emily and Julia are going shopping; I'm going to spend time outside in the area. You guys going to the lake? Okay, be careful and I'll call you when we are heading back here, talk to you later, bye."

"That seems so stupid, I'm done talking about this idiotic topic," said Julia, referring the baseball teams. She headed out the door.

"Can you believe her? She will pick one," said John, as he put his phone back into his pocket. "You realize the stores aren't opening up for some hours."

"Relax. Let's head out," said Emily. "We'll look over the Water Tower before we enter Water Tower Place for some power shopping." Emily headed out to join Julia.

John was the last one out and locked the door. Emily walked over to the car where Julia was waiting. She stood by the car in a yellow spaghetti strapped sundress with brown flip-flops. Emily wore white shorts with a black top, also in black flip-flops.

John was glad to have a day to just relax. As they drove by Water Tower Place they noticed the Water Tower across the street.

"Can you believe that the Water Tower survived the Chicago Fire?" Said John.

Emily and Julia were also looking at the tower. Julia was reminded of a rumor that she heard back at the University where she taught. "There is a legend that's grounded in the Chicago Fire and the architect of that building. Now I know it's true," she said.

"Really, do tell," said Emily.

"Give me a second to try and remember it," said Julia.

"You think about it while I pull into this parking garage," said John.

John pressed the button that dispensed the parking ticket. Next to the parking gate is was a sign with all the fees. "Nice. Parking here will only cost thirty dollars. What a bargain," said John sarcastically, annoyed with the exorbitant fee. He parked the car on the fifth floor. So much for leaving early in order to get a good parking spot, John thought to himself. As he finished parking the car, Emily and Julia quickly exited and started making their way to the elevator.

"No need to wait for me," shouted John. They both looked back, smiling at John's comment.

"Come on old man, walk a little faster," replied Emily.

"I'll give you 'old man'," retorted John.

The ride in the elevator was quick. They had to walk half a city block to reach Michigan Avenue. Once on Michigan Avenue they were in clear view of the Water Tower. Julia had remembered the entire tale.

"You guys want to hear the legend behind the Water Tower?" She asked. Emily and John nodded. They crossed the street and made their way to the tower. As they reached the tower, there was a green bench with nobody sitting on it. They walked over to it and sat down. As she started the story, she stood and walked in front of Emily and John. The Water Tower was now a backdrop to her story. She began the tale.

"As we know, the Water Tower was designed by William Donavan. He was a well-known architect in his time and owned his own construction company. Several of his buildings had survived the Great Chicago Fire of 1871. His construction company had been awarded several building contracts after the Chicago Fire. From those contracts and several designs, William Donavan made his great fortune. However, Donavan had a darker side that he kept from his wife, family and close friends. He had a belief that there was another plane of existence. He believed that he could design a building that would connect other planes of existence to this one. He believed that all the creatures and stories regarding mythology were actually based from another reality that had been seen or experienced. He believed that the connection would allow him or anyone to travel to the other planes and vice versa. The combination of limestone and metal along with ancient artifacts would allow this to happen. His goal was to travel to where his wife and children's souls would go after leaving this plane and spend eternity with them. His son's deaths had both been accidental. His wife could not cope with the untimely deaths of their children so she took her own life after burying their eldest and last child. Donavan had sent anthropologists to travel the world in search of special artifacts that would work with his construction. Of course his goal was never accomplished and he died in 1888, I think. It's just a legend. There was never any proof of this. But we know different, don't we?"

"Yeah, we do know different now," said Emily.

"It's weird hearing a folk legend, knowing that it's true," said John, in a quiet and somber tone.

They sat there looking the building over. The Water Tower was not a particularly large building. Julia walked up to two doors located at the back. To her surprise, the door was open. She called over to John and Emily and they walked inside. The inside of the building was painted yellow with pictures of Chicago over the past century. They came across a green door that was roped off. As they looked around, they were curious as to how a ceremony could be conducted in the building.

"When we get back, we need to examine the blueprints and try to figure out where a ceremony could happen. There is no way it could happen in here...well, in this part of the Tower," said Julia.

"We should get out of here, in case one of the Scrutatores shows up," said John. "I don't want to lose the element of surprise."

"Agreed," said Emily. "Besides, the mall is open now and we need to start shopping." She finished her sentence with much enthusiasm.

They exited the building. Emily and Julia started heading for the shopping mall. John started walking in the opposite direction.

"Where are you walking to?" Emily asked.

"I'm going down to the Tribune and Wrigley Buildings," said John.

"Okay, call us in a couple of hours," said Julia.

John continued to walk south on Michigan Avenue while Emily and Julia walked to Water Tower Place. John took in the sun and admired the buildings in the area. John walked into the Tribune Tower. He loved the small objects from different places around the world. He looked at a piece from the Great Pyramids of Giza. As he took in the different objects, he was reminded of his days as an archeologist. He looked forward to when he could go back. Earlier in the week, he had resigned from the University of Chicago. He did not know when he could go back and didn't want to take a sabbatical. John felt that it was best for the University to move on without him.

John decided to cross the street and check out the Wrigley building. He did not want to go inside. What he loved was the architectural design of the building. He walked along the front portion and made his way to the bridge that crossed over the Chicago River. As he looked out towards the Trump Tower, he had no idea that the people he needed to stop were living in a luxury condominium inside it. I could use some new shoes, he thought to himself. John decided to walk back to the mall. He briefly thought about calling Emily and Julia to see if they were still in the mall. He then quickly realized that could possibly be the dumbest thought he'd had in a long time. As he walked back, he stopped dead in his tracks. He could not believe what he had just come across. The building next to the Tribune Tower just across the street has what looked like three knights carved into its side.

John took out his phone and called Andrews. He was not concerned with the time difference. John walked to the building and saw it was the Intercontinental Hotel. Andrews did a history check and confirmed it was the building they were looking for. John decided not to call Emily and Julia for the moment, and check things out on his own. He noticed that Michael Jordan's restaurant was also in the building. John thought for a minute before entering. He needed to have a plan once he entered the building. After several minutes outside and pacing back and forth he finally decided on a plan of attack.

John walked up to the check-in desk and asked a question about the knights carved into the building. "Excuse me. I'm curious about the knights on the side of the building," he asked the very attractive blonde behind the counter.

"Oh, I know it is interesting. I wish I knew why. Honestly, no one knows," she said.

"Oh, that's a shame," said John.

"Well, there is a tale that this building was built for the Knights Templar of France. But I heard they all died a long time ago."

John resisted the quick history lesson. "Oh yeah, I've heard of them," said John.

"I shouldn't say this, I don't want to keep spreading a preposterous rumor. They say a secret item was left here by the Templar, or for them, that was never picked up...but I don't believe it. There is the old section below this building that is closed to everyone," she said.

"Why? I would think it would be a great attraction," said John.

"You see, the passage down is in the kitchen and the health inspector would not be fond of all the possible traffic."

"I see. Well thanks, that's an interesting story. Is there a bathroom I may use?" John asked.

"Yes, it's around the corner. Have a nice day," she said, as she turned to answer the phone that started ringing.

John walked over to the bathroom. He entered it and looked around to make sure he is was alone. After he confirmed, he placed the tip of his index finger on his chest.

"Invisibilis." Instantly, John became invisible. He carefully walked out of the bathroom. Luck was on his side that no one was in the area to notice the door open and close. John made his way toward the kitchen. This took some time, for he had no idea where the kitchen was. After fifteen minutes of searching he finally reached the kitchen. He waited outside until someone went through the two-way door.

John walked around the kitchen, being careful not to run into someone or something. He walked past all the ovens and storage units. There were at least twenty people in the immensely large kitchen. He made his way to the back portion. He noticed a staircase leading down with a red velvet rope running across the door-less doorway. There was a sign on the rope informing employees that if they were caught trying to go down the stairs they would be immediately unemployed.

John carefully stepped over the rope. He quickly came to realize the stairway was extremely narrow. He carefully walked down. As he reached the bottom of the stairs he realized that the lighting was non-existent.

"Finis Invisibilis." As he finished the phrase, he was no longer invisible. He then said "Lux" and a light emanated from the tip of his finger. The entirety of the basement walls was made of cement blocks. John carefully walked around. As he shined his light on the wall, he noticed a crescent moon on the back wall. John walked back to look at it, and ran his hand along it. He noticed that the blocks on the wall were loose.

He pointed his hand at the wall. "Subvolvo." The block levitated from the wall and was placed gently on the ground. John took a deep breath and reached inside. He felt a small tin box. He removed the tin box and opened it. Inside, he noticed old paper. As he unfolded it, he noticed the same crescent moon. He knew he had the correct documents.

John slid the cement block back into place, then used the invisibility spell to make his way out of the basement through the kitchen and back into the bathroom. Just as he came back to being visible, a man walked out of one of the stalls. John greeted the man, exited the bathroom, and walked out of the hotel.

"Emily. Listen; meet me at the parking garage. No now, not later. I found the building and retrieved the documents. Look, we'll talk later, just get there immediately."

"Bridgette, listen you guys have to get in the car and meet us at the Sullivan house. No, it has to happen now. I found the documents. I'm sending them next day air to Andrews. We have two weeks until the summer solstice and that means we have very little time. Great, we'll meet you there. Bye, sweetie."

John met up with Emily and Julia at the parking garage. He handed the box to Julia. They got into the car and headed to James Sullivan's house.

34

THE PLANNING AT SULLIVAN'S HOUSE

John met up with Emily and Julia at the parking garage. He handed the box to Julia. They entered the car and headed to the FedEx store and then to James Sullivan's house. Emily drove while John sat in the back with Julia and looked through the papers found in the tin box. They desperately tried to read while Emily drove like she was in the Indy 500. She bobbed and weaved around traffic. She even ran through some red lights, swerving around pedestrians crossing the intersection. She entered Lake Shore Drive and within minutes exited at the Fullerton exit and soon brought the car to a stop at the FedEx store.

John glared at Emily, displaying his displeasure at not being able to read the documents due to her reckless, but admittedly effective driving. John exited the car walked into the FedEx store and sent the package off to Andrews. John was back in the car after fifteen minutes.

"Well I hope that Andrews will be able to inform us about what we just sent him," said John as he seated himself in the front passenger seat.

"I believe that this package of some importance to the Stamens," added Julia.

"Why?" John asked, as Emily placed the car in drive and resumed her fast-paced driving.

"It's simple, he asked to have the artifact retrieved. The spell translator is already in place, The Book of Spells also in place, the documents to find each in place, Sullivan's personal journal in place. Each one of the aforementioned essentials aids the Order. We have all we need. I really think the contents of the box is for the Stamens."

"I agree. Remember, they're all meeting at Andrews' castle," said Emily, as she ran a red light.

"Emily, darling...if we don't make it to the Sullivan house, then we won't make it to stop the Scrutatores," said John in an extremely calm manner. Emily slammed the breaks. John and Julia's seat belt restrained them from being flung forward.

"Made it in record time," said Emily, beaming with joy. She turned around and her joyous feeling quickly left.

"Am I still alive?" John gasped.

"I'll tell you in a second, my heart is still somewhere on the floor, again," said Julia.

"Oh, come on, you're here now, let's get in," said Emily and exited the car.

Emily waited for them at the door, shaking her head at the pace they were walking. They went into the Sullivan house and proceeded straight up the stairs to the gathering room. Emily wheeled the white board to the fireplace area. Julia cleared the couches and the chairs from items left on them. John then placed a call to Andrews.

"We are at the Sullivan house waiting for Bridgette and the others, I sent the box next day," said John into his phone.

"I'm going to wrap up the Stamens meeting and charter a flight into Chicago," Andrews responded.

"Stay there just in case things go wrong here. You'll have to reorganize the Order."

"John, I think I can be of some assistance," said Andrews.

"I'm sorry Andrews, but you can't perform any magic and that would put you in great danger. We can at least defend ourselves. Plus, I think that if you're there, if something goes wrong you will be able to reorganize the future Order members and that would be vital to the survival of the human race," said John.

"You've made your point," Andrews conceded, "and I will follow your suggestion. I will inform my fellow Stamens of what is happening and start organizing them. Good luck John, and be careful...all of you."

"Thanks. I'll talk to you soon."

Just as John got off the phone with Andrews, Bridgette and the others came walking in. David, Dwayne, and Rosa went right over to Emily and Julia, who were standing by the white board. Bridgette walked over to her uncle.

"Hey, what's up?" Bridgette asked.

"We need to plan, prepare and be ready in a few days. We have little time."

"Don't worry, we're ready," said Bridgette, and placed a kiss on his cheek and walked over to Emily and Julia.

John paused for a moment. He had been spreading papers on the Ping-Pong table when Bridgette walked up to him. A rush of emotions was running rampant in him. The first and foremost was his love for Bridgette. The second was his concern of getting everyone through this alive. He felt it was his responsibility.

"John are you ready?" Julia asked. John remembered that Emily and Julia were in their mid-twenties, just a little older than the younger ones, and this made him feel worse.

"Yes, I'm ready," said John, as he rolled the Ping-Pong table over. On the table he had placed several documents. The age of the papers was evident. One did not have to be a history major to know it was an old paper. Bridgette and Rosa occupied one couch while Dwayne and David occupied another. Emily and Julia stood by the white board. John remained at the Ping-Pong table.

"Emily and Julia, why don't you two take a seat. I'll take it from here."

Emily and Julia looked at each other and then slowly went to the couches. Emily sat between David and Dwayne and Julia went to Bridgette and Rosa.

"All right. First, I want to let you all know it's okay to feel nervous. The second is, we'll get through this and be successful."

All six of them were listening intently to John. The time had come for him to assert himself as the leader of The Order of Seven.

"The first thing we have to do is cast a massive protective spell on the entire house and the backyard."

"We know of a extensive protective spell," said Julia.

"That is true, thanks to the Book of Spell and the translator. By the way David, James Sullivan is your great, great grandfather. Just a side note."

David felt honored being related to the man that worked at preserving the Order and working toward a battle, even though there was no threat in his time.

John pointed into the air. "Nullam Praesidio." A white light came out of his hand. The light penetrated the ceiling and engulfed the entire house and the backyard.

"Was that the protective spell?" Bridgette asked, curiously.

"It is the protective spell," said John. "All right, now we don't have to worry about the Scrutatores confronting us here."

"Do they know where we are?" Dwayne asked.

"They have the Book of Knowledge. They know where we are," said John. "I'm going to go through our plan. Do not hold any questions ask away. There may be a better way if we discuss it."

They nodded and waited anxiously for John to begin.

"The first thing we have to do once we get to the Water Tower is conjure a time alternate spell. This will allow us to stop the world right where it's at so we can act. Once the spell is removed, the world will have no clue as to what happened and most importantly, humanity won't have felt a thing."

"Cool, but what about the Scrutatores?" David asked.

"Magic of this manner will have no affect on other magic-based people, or anyone wearing any protective clothing," added Julia.

"Okay," John regained everyone's attention. "After that, we will break off into two groups. The first group is Emily, Julia, Bridgette, and myself. The second is Dwayne, David, and Rosa. My group will enter the Water Tower. We will engage the Scrutatores and force them outside onto Michigan Avenue. The second group will be situated outside the Water Tower and the Pumping Station. Our goal is to fight them out in the open. The group outside will also keep an eye on the people outside. You have to make sure that time stands still. If people start moving, cast the spell again. We have no idea what the Scrutatores are going to come at us with. I don't think the spell will falter, but why take a chance. Also, if more Scrutatores show up, you need to engage them in combat. The Scrutatores will not be affected by the time spell."

"Then that will not interfere with their actions in the Water Tower, right?" Emily asked.

"I think, but again I'm not sure. We'll find out at the moment we're in there," said John. "We will get to the Water Tower through the underground passage from the Pumping Station. My guess is that's how they will get there too. I'm sure we'll run into resistance in the Pumping Station."

"When we engage them, what spells should we use?" Rosa asked, wondering if her question was inappropriate.

"We are the Order of Seven. We do not use the death spell. Stick to the stun spell and any of the other spells we practiced. When the time comes, we will discuss the death spell but under no circumstance should you use it. Most of you aren't able to anyway.

"Once inside, one of us must use the 'Delere' spell. This spell is a counter spell that will end any spell being cast. We will leave here at six pm Thursday night."

"This sounds great John," said Emily.

"But?"

"Well your plan is sound and appears to work, but is based on everything going our way. I don't think that it will go smoothly. The Scrutatores are not going to go down without a fight and they have no problem using the death spell," reminded Emily.

John thought for a minute. "You're right. We need to have alternate plans. I should have thought this myself."

"Why? Are you the only Order member? Remember there are six more of us that will also contribute. It's okay, you've had a lot to think out, but we are here and will help in planning," Julia said lovingly to John.

"Yeah, it can't be easy for you working with all new members and we are all much younger than you," chimed in Emily.

"Thanks for the reminder on my elder statesmen position here," said John.

His comment allowed some needed laughter to erupt. Bridgette had held back some concerns but after Emily and Julia spoke up she decided that it was her turn to share her thoughts.

"Well, I think it's safe to say that they will have a larger number than us. I also think that both groups will be under attack the entire time. Let's discuss how both groups should engage the Scrutatores and how both groups should retreat if they have to."

"There will be no retreating," John said, forcefully.

"If we are about to be defeated we will need to regroup and live to fight another day," retorted Bridgette, matching John's tone.

"Bridgette, if we fail, the doorway will be open and who knows what will come through. There may not be another day."

"We can figure out that it will be Seeker," said Emily, sassily.

"Duly noted, Emily," said Julia, imitating Emily's sassy tone.

"Let's talk about the transformation being successful second. The outside group will be battling on their own and remember there are only three of you. David, Dwayne and Rosa, you will have to be strong and accurate with your spells."

On the board were the Pumping Station and the Water Tower. In between the two was Michigan Avenue. Emily joined John at the board.

"I have an idea. Is it okay if I show it?"

"Please do."

Emily uncapped the blue marker. "One of you should be here by the Pumping Station, keeping anyone from entering. One of you should be here on the south side of the Water Tower. This way whoever goes there will have a view of the Pumping Station and the middle of Michigan

Avenue. The one here on Michigan Avenue will have view of the other two and will assist as needed. I suggest that Dwayne you are the one the street, since you run the fastest."

John's display of approval toward Emily's plan solidified the plan for the outside Order members.

"The inside group will follow me," said John. "There will be some resistance, but the main battle will come when we encounter Lannar and his main cohorts. I will engage Lannar and one of the other three will attempt the spell to end any magic being cast inside the Tower. I figure that our best chance of success will be to have three people attempt the spell. My guess is that only one of you will be able to cast it. Lannar's followers will engage us as soon as they spot us. The other objective is to not be discovered. Let's hope for the best."

Julia stood from her seat and walked over to the board. "I think that I have come up with a plan if someone is injured."

Emily went back to her seat.

"Emily and I brewed some healing potions while we where in London. There are five vials of potion for each of you. Do not consume it if you have minor wounds. However, you need to drink it before you are physically unable to perform any spells or actions. The potion will take several minutes to take effect."

"Only five?" David asked.

"If you need more after five you are likely to need last rites," Julia said chillingly. "If a spell appears to be weakening you must recast it. The strength of your spell will be determined by your concentration, understood. There will be a lot happening and concentration will be broken at times, do not get frustrated. Simply recast it. Also, do not question yourself on the spell you cast. Whichever spell you choose at the moment is the one you think will work best. Believe in yourself and your abilities and all will go well."

Everyone including John and Emily nodded their heads. John took the lead role again.

"Now if the group outside is being overrun you will need to regroup if possible and return here. I'll cast a longer protective spell before we leave that will recognize each you and allow entrance. If you cannot regroup, make your way on your own. If escape is not possible, try to enter the Pumping Station. Once inside, cast the fortifying spell on the main entrance and head to the underground passage. I have a map of the inside for each of you. Let's say you defeat all the forces outside, make your way inside, cast the spell and then find us. There will be a problem inside if you finish and we haven't joined you. One of the two scenarios regarding the outside group will take place and follow the contingency plan on the one that presents itself. The inside group, there is no backup plan for us. Once we engage Lannar, we are in there till the end."

John picked up on the emotional state of the young Order members. "Is anyone scared?" John waited for a brief moment then raised his own hand. "There is nothing wrong with being frightened. Hell, I am. There is a great chance of dying. That scares me. Is there anyone else scared like I am?"

Everyone in the room now raised their hand. "Better," said John.

"Bravery comes from fear," he continued. "The fear of failure or death will bring out the courage that is in each of you. I do not fear that any of you will run away from this inevitable battle. I fear that I may lose one of you or become greatly injured. That will summon the courage that will lead me into battle. It will do the same in all of you. We are all embarking on a task greater than any of us have been involved in. Being scared or nervous is normal and expected. In all of us is the courage needed and it will arise when the moment calls for it. Trust yourself and your abilities."

Even though their nervousness was not diminished, each person felt comfort in John's closing words.

"If there are no other questions or concerns, I suggest we get some rest and start gathering our equipment. Oh, before I forget, I also was busy in London. Following the Book of Spells, I constructed protective clothing that will deflect most stun spells; unfortunately it will offer no protection against the death spell. I have placed the clothing in your rooms. I had borrowed clothing that I observed each of you wearing."

"I was wondering what happened to my favorite tee shirt," said David.

They exited the former recreation room and headed off to prepare themselves for the inevitable battle.

35

THE BATTLE

The Order drove to the Water Tower in two cars. John, Emily, Julia, and Bridgette in one car. Dwayne, David, and Rosa in the other car. They parked the cars on a side street next to the Water Tower, where they met. Emily was the first to hear the marching feet behind them. David was about to cast a stun spell in the direction of the fifty men marching behind them, when John grabbed him by his shoulder.

"Wait, we know these men," said John.

As the group neared everyone noticed the men dressed in Templar battle garments. The group stopped directly in front of them.

"I thought we agreed that you would stay in London," John said, as Andrews walked toward him.

"The Knights Templar and The Order of Seven fought together many years ago. We are here to renew our alignment and fight by your side once again!" Andrews sounded extremely noble.

"How are you going to fend off spells that will inevitably be cast at you?"

"I now know you did not look at the package you sent. The contents of the package let us know the location of our forefather's weapons, and battle attire was located. The clothing we wear will deflect spells cast for some time. Eventually, if enough spells are cast, we will lose the protection against magic and will be vulnerable. A chance we will take. Besides you are greatly outnumbered and you greatly need our assistance. What did you think we were meeting for?"

"Well, you're here and all dressed up and there is no time to debate this. You and the other Stamens will engage the Scrutatores that are outside. Try to stay alive my dear friend," John said sincerely.

Andrews simply smiled and nodded his head. Together, everyone walked across the street from the Pumping Station. Once there, the Order said the spell in unison, "Subsistos Vicis!"

Everyone and everything came to a stop. People stopped walking, cars stopped moving, clouds stayed in place. Not a single sound could be heard outside or inside any of the buildings in one of the largest cities in the world.

John and his group walked to the Pumping Station. It felt weird walking past people stopped dead in their tracks. Dwayne walked to the middle of Michigan Avenue between the Water Tower and the Pumping Station. He looked at all the cars around them in amazement. The amazement continued as he examined the inside of the cars. In one car he looked at a baby's drool stop before it landed on his top. In another, a man's finger appeared lodged in his right nostril.

Rosa walked to the Water Tower. She positioned herself at the rear entrance. Around her, pigeons had stopped in flight, and a group of five girls had stopped in mid-laughter.

David walked with the John's group and positioned himself outside the Pumping Station.

Andrews and the other Stamens were standing at the intersection south of the Water Tower.

Rosa raised both her hands and cast a spell. "Invisibilis Spatium Protego." Suddenly the cars and all the people outside around the Water Tower and the Pumping Station were cleared from the battleground. The spell sent them to a safe place from the fighting that was about to begin.

Dwayne was several feet in front of the Stamens. With everyone at their place, Dwayne raised both hands, "Appareo Hostem." Dwayne shouted. The spell forced their enemies to appear, canceling their concealment spell. Standing on the opposite street from Dwayne were one hundred Scrutatores. As the army of Scrutatores appeared, Andrews waved for the Stamens to charge them. Each Stamen had a weapon of choice in hand. Some were using swords while others had maces or battleaxes. Their weapons were drawn and they full-charged at the Scrutatores.

John and the rest of his group entered. As soon as they got inside, Julia was immediately struck by a stun spell and was slammed into the wall. John looked around quickly to locate who cast the spell and then shot one of his own in the man's direction.

"Attono!" Bridgette and Emily each fired one at the two men charging toward them as well. The two men dropped down to the ground.

"David, get in here!" John shouted.

David ran into the building. "Guard Julia," said John. "If anyone tries to attack you...hit them with everything you've got." David looked at John with determination in his eyes. "You have to protect the both of you. Do not hesitate." John motioned for Emily and Bridgette to follow him.

"We're lucky it was just a stun spell," said Emily.

John approached a doorway that opened to a set of stairs leading down. "Make sure you're at the ready at all times. Once we reach the bottom, the room with the passage is off to the right. We enter the room, go to the back and open the hatch that leads to the tunnel."

"No time for fear," said Emily.

John led them down the metal staircase. Once at the bottom, he approached the room and entered it. To their surprise, they did not encounter anyone or any type of protection spell. This made them wary. It might be a trap. John opened the hatch and was the first one down. Emily and Bridgette followed closely behind him.

David decided to carry Julia outside. He carried her over to Dwayne. He had a group of Stamens provide protection. "John said I should use whatever spell necessary to protect her."

"Works for me," said Dwayne.

Rosa was coming around from the back of the Water Tower, when suddenly a group of ten men came charging from the other side of the Water Tower, shooting spells at them.

David quickly raised his hand and cast the shield spell. "Shiels!" A large transparent medieval shield deflected the spells coming at them.

"What do we do?" Dwayne asked, starting to panic a bit.

"Cast some stun spells at them!" David shouted.

"We're outnumbered!" Rosa exclaimed. "Attono Maximum!" She shouted, knocking out seven of them.

"Diffusus Maximum Attono!" Dwayne said, striking the other three in the charging group with a red beam of light that split off from his hand.

The Stamens were fighting the Scrutatores head on. They managed to occupy over fifty of them. A Scrutatore cast a stun spell that struck Andrews head on. He fell backwards onto the ground. The Stamen standing next to him was struck by a death spell. As Andrews lay on his back, he looked at the man next to him. Andrews knew that it was each Stamens decision to fight, however, he felt saddened by the young man's death.

Dwayne had fifteen men charging him. He cast a spell in their direction. "Maximus Aqua Unda!" A giant wave of water started from where Dwayne was. The wave of water was higher than the Water Tower. It came crashing down on them. Dwayne gleamed with pride at the thought and use of the spell. The water moved from the ground and knocked over Scrutatores fighting in the area around the spell. As the men fell, Dwayne then cast a stun spell to keep them down for a while. "Attono!".

Rosa looked up and noticed that the time spell was beginning to give way. She quickly recited the spell, reinforcing the previous spell. As she finished, she noticed Andrews lying on the ground. She quickly ran toward him. Before she reached him, she noticed a Scrutatore casting a spell at him. She quickly covered him with a shield spell. The spell deflected, hitting two Scrutatores and killing them instantly. Rosa cast a spell at the Scrutatore, "Maximum Subvolvo." The spell raised the Scrutatore easily fifty feet in the air. She then waved her hands and flung the Scrutatore off to the right and crashed him into a building. Rosa reached Andrews and cast another protective spell around them and dragged him over to David. "Protect Andrews."

Julia drank another vile of healing potion and was on her feet. She was now ready to join the fight outside. She hugged David and kissed him on his cheek. Julia ran to the last remaining battle between the Scrutatores and the Stamens. The battle was happening on the north side of the Water Tower. As she neared, she saw both Scrutatores and Stamens on the ground. Some from both sides had been killed, and others injured. She witnessed Stamens being killed by death spells and badly injured by massive stun spells. The Stamens were standing their ground. The injuries being inflicted onto the Scrutatores by the Stamens were also severe. Scrutatores being stabbed by swords, limbs severed by battleaxes, even heads. The ones using maces were causing major internal injuries, knocking their opponent to the ground and looking for the next opponent. There were only ten Stamens left in this area. The twenty Scrutatores left were overrunning them. Julia cast a massive stun spell as she ran at the Scrutatores.

"Diffus Maximum Attono!" Half of the Scrutatores fell where they where standing. Four of the remaining Scrutatores were engaged and slain by Stamen warriors. The remaining Scrutatore cast a death spell at Julia. As the spell was about to strike her, a giant shield spell wrapped around her. Julia turned and saw that Dwayne was casting the shield spell. David was standing next to Dwayne. He cast a spell at the last remaining Scrutatore. "Diffus Maximum Attono." The last Scrutatore was knocked off his feet and sent ten feet backwards.

* * *

Back in the Pumping Station, John and the other three walked cautiously through the five hundred foot long tunnel. They reached another metal staircase that led upward. John took the lead again and carefully started to ascend the stairs, the others following closely behind. As they neared the end, they could hear someone speaking in Latin. Lannar was reading from the Book of Knowledge. John reached the top of the stairs. He carefully looked around. He noticed the symbol of the Scrutatores on the ground and in the center of it, the Golden Plate with a set of bones on them. Standing outside the circle he saw Kantra, Wrightwood and Macnar. Facing them was Lannar reading from the Book of Knowledge. Rising from the plate was a dark thick black smoke. John signaled to Emily and Bridgette that he was about to attack. The element of surprise was on their side.

"Attono Maximum!" John shouted. The red light arced toward Lannar. Lannar turned to his side and the spell struck the book, sending it flying to the other end of the room. Macnar quickly retaliated with the death spell, but Emily anticipated the attack and called out a deflection spell. The spells' beams struck each other, the deflection spell sending the death spell back at Macnar. He was struck on his chest and fell to the ground. Lannar waved his hand in the air and a black cloud surrounded him as he disappeared. Kantra and Wrightwood were left to fight the three. Suddenly, Wrightwood performed the same spell as Lannar, and he too disappeared.

"Cowards!" Kantra shrieked, then cast the death spell, aiming it at the staircase where they were standing. It struck the ground before John and caused massive sparks. Bridgette climbed over John and quickly shouted the stun spell toward Kantra. It struck her and she fell to the ground. Trying to recover from the stun spell, she waved her hand in the air, and then disappeared.

John ran over to Emily. "Are you okay?" He asks her.

"Yeah, I'm fine," Emily, replied, weakly.

"You?" John asked, looking at Bridgette.

"I'm fine, and check out what I have," she said proudly, holding the Book of Knowledge.

"We did it," said Emily, with a sigh of relief.

Right after she said that, a voice filled with ominous laughter echoed inside the Water Tower and outside.

"No, you did not stop us. Yes, the plague has been stopped and you have thwarted the entrance of Seeker into this plane. But the doorway has been opened for the arrival of things you cannot even begin to imagine. The time will come, Order of Seven, when the battle will be that much greater. Let's see just how well you can protect the world from us. You may have won this battle, but the war will continue..." Lannar's voice faded.

John, Emily, and Bridgette made their way outside. They were happily relieved to see Julia standing with the others.

"Let's take care of these guys," said John, indicating the stunned men lying on the ground, where the others had bound them. "Let's bury their dead and get ours back to London."

Andrews slowly walked toward John. The Order members and Andrews gathered at the entrance to the Water Tower. They noticed black marks from spells that went astray. Rosa and Julia started casting the same spell at the Water Tower. "Interdum." The black marks vanished and the building returned to its normal look. They knew that they would have to cast the spell on the other buildings that also suffered damage before they left.

"Job well done. Everyone did their part and did it well, even you, Andrews. Did you get to fight?" John said musingly to Andrews.

"Yes, I did until I was struck by a very strong spell. My participation was extremely short lived."

"It was a massive stun spell that knocked you out," said David.

"How do we bring the injured to justice? We aren't known to the world and bringing them to justice would mean we have to explain who we are," said Emily.

"We're not bringing them to justice. I will erase their minds of this and all Scrutatore memories. They will go back to the life they were living before Lannar got to them," said John.

"But that would allow them to be recruited again," Andrews said reproachfully.

"True, but we'll have to take that chance. This was not the final battle, Lannar escaped with two others. The doorway to one of the planes has been opened. He will regroup and form another army," John said, speaking tightly.

"So, you are now a believer of the existence of other planes?" Andrews quibbled.

"Yes. I have changed my view, and I...we will be better prepared for our next encounter with the Scrutatores."

"I'll let you finish up here and meet you back at the castle. Godspeed."

As Andrews was about to walk away, John reached for his shoulder. Andrews turned around John embraced him. "Thanks for showing up. We would not have won this with out the Stamens."

Andrews placed both his hands on John's shoulders. "Always, my friend, we will always be there for the Order, and I'll always be there for you." Both men embraced one last time and Andrews turned and headed toward the other Stamens.

John had Rosa return the people and cars back to their places. Emily, Julia, Dwayne and David started repairing all visible damage. John was about to awaken the now healed.

"Can we use the doorway to enter another plane?" Bridgette asked, clutching the Book of Knowledge.

"I'm sure we could, we'd have to learn how. Why?"

"Our parents are on the third plane," she said, hopefully.

"I know. That's one of our next tasks."

"Next? It should be our immediate one!"

"I'm not saying we won't but we have to protect this realm first. I promise it will be one of our main focuses when we return to London."

"Okay, but just so you know I will bring it up after we're back there."

"I figured as much."

John walked up to Bridgette and embraced her. "Your parents would be so proud of you. Especially your father," he said as he kissed her on the top of her head. The return of the other members ended their embrace. They moved to the intersection south of the Water Tower. As John awakened the healed Scrutatores, the others reversed the time spell and Rosa reversed the invisible spell. The Scrutatores looked around in confusion. Some of them had come from outside of the Chicago land area. The people that were going about their day returned and continued from their last action. The street light next to the Order members changed and traffic resumed. Dwayne joined John and Bridgette, followed by the others.

"I feel great." Said Dwayne as he ran his left hand over his head. John quickly noticed what was on his index finger.

"Can I see your ring?"

"Sure." Dwayne extended his hand to John.

"Oh my God. I cannot believe what I'm looking at. My brother found this ring and brought it up to the lake house. This is the Ring of Seeker. Thankfully no one noticed it on you. Let's get going and head back to London. We have a lot to prepare for."

The End

25525774R00157

Made in the USA
Charleston, SC
06 January 2014